Iron Horse Prize for a First Book of Collected Prose
Katie Cortese, Series Editor

Sing With Me at the Edge of Paradise

STORIES

Joe Baumann

TEXAS TECH UNIVERSITY PRESS

This book is typeset in Adobe Caslon Pro. The paper used in this book meets the minimum requirements of ANSI/NISO Z39.48-1992 (R1997). ∞

Designed by Hannah Gaskamp
Cover design by Hannah Gaskamp; artwork is *The Rebuke of Adam and Eve* by Charles-Joseph Natoire. It was donated into the public domain by the Metropolitan Museum of Art.

Library of Congress Cataloging-in-Publication Data

Names: Baumann, Joe, 1985– author. Title: Sing With Me at the Edge of Paradise: Stories / Joe Baumann. Description: Lubbock, Texas: Texas Tech University Press, [2023] | Summary: "A collection of short stories surrounding queer men of various ages trying to temper their expectations of the world with their lived experience"—Provided by publisher.

Identifiers: LCCN 2022024276 (print) | LCCN 2022024277 (ebook)
ISBN 978-1-68283-160-1 (cloth; alk. paper)
ISBN 978-1-68283-161-8 (ebook)
Subjects: LCGFT: Short stories. Classification:
LCC PS3602.A96276 S56 2022 (print) |
LCC PS3602.A96276 (ebook) | DDC 813/.6—dc23/eng/20220606
LC record available at https://lccn.loc.gov/2022024276
LC ebook record available at https://lccn.loc.gov/2022024277

Printed in the United States of America
23 24 25 26 27 28 29 30 31 / 9 8 7 6 5 4 3 2 1

Texas Tech University Press
Box 41037
Lubbock, Texas 79409-1037 USA
800.832.4042
ttup@ttu.edu
www.ttupress.org

for my parents and sisters

Contents

Sing With Me at the Edge of Paradise

Give Us
Your Pity,
Give Us
Your Love

NO ONE LIKED THE LUFTWAITHS. THEY WERE THE sort of people who used words like "peripatetic" and "anodyne" in casual conversations during sporting events or at bars eating buffalo wings. They wore boat shoes even though they didn't own a boat, and they were seen on several occasions checking out ski goggles despite the fact that they never went to Aspen or Vale or Switzerland. She smelled like depilatory creams, he like hair spray. They installed a wine fridge next to their dishwasher but stocked it with four-dollar bottles from Aldi. Nick Luftwaith drank German beers, pretending that they didn't cost five ninety-nine a six pack. He insisted on pronouncing *hefeweizen* with the proper Aryan vee-sound in the middle to prove he was cultured and world-worthy.

No one liked the frangipani that grew around the sides of their house or the fact that they paid Mexicans to take care of their grass and trim back their hedges and crape myrtles. Everyone agreed that Lina Luftwaith had the voice of a screech owl, so pitchy and raw our stomachs contorted whenever she told a story, and hell was to be paid by anyone who made her laugh. Jokes were verboten at a Luftwaith gathering.

Yet go to their gatherings we did. Because despite all of the things we hated about the Luftwaiths, Lina was a brilliant cook, home-taught, as she never failed to remind us when we huddled around her canape platters and took generous helpings of her niçoise salads. She made delectable beef tartare, which no one, to this day, is quite sure how she convinced any of us to eat, we who were used to medium well sirloins at Applebee's and no-pink burgers at Red Robin. With her culinary prowess Lina Luftwaith could make us momentarily forget how annoying she and her husband were, how much more they belonged in some sleepy New England cubbyhole teaching Sylvia Plath and Plato than nestled in our Midwestern suburb where the rainbow flag they hung from their porch in support of their daughter coming out as a lesbian was almost as great an eyesore as the electric charging station they installed on the side of their garage for their Pininfarina.

So we were in equal measure affronted, shocked, and gratified by what happened with Troy. Troy Luftwaith: captain of the baseball team and a thespian both, the boy who also played a mean Beethoven concerto, the boy who took the girl with Down syndrome to prom, the boy who nailed a full ride to Reed and chose the study of Japanese instead of going to Vanderbilt to play left field. The boy who spent half of the summer after his sophomore year of college in Guatemala, building huts that would become a school for little girls. Troy Luftwaith, the boy who spent the second half of that summer back home in his parents' house, lounging next to their in-ground pool, drinking emerald bottles of Stella Artois on the sly, drinking them with girls, some of those girls still in high school, one of them only fifteen.

We never knew her name; it was kept out of the papers. But what we did know was that, on a weekend when Lina and Nick Luftwaith decided to shuck the Midwest for a trip to Portland, Maine, Troy Luftwaith brought his girls over on a Friday night and something happened. The stories are fuzzed and engorged with half-truths and exaggerations: that there were drugs, not just marijuana but cocaine and LSD and even Quaaludes and heroin, that not only did Troy ply the girls with beer and blow but also cheap tequila and absinthe, which the fifteen-year-old drank straight from the bottle so her mouth was ringed an algae color when she slipped and took a tumble, her ankle buckling against the wet cement border of the pool. Then she toppled into the lukewarm water where nary a single leaf or dead bug floated and Troy, being the macho, perfect man that he was, dove in after her, chucking his precious iPhone from the pocket of his Banana Republic yachting shorts onto the grass as he leapt.

We didn't hear the splashes or the shrieks or the laughter that followed when Troy lifted the girl out of the water and the rest of his bubbly coterie, looking on in a mixture of horror and drunken humor, clapped for him. Some of us may have peered out of our windows or around our privacy fences and scowled at their streamlined bodies and perfect tans, their hairless legs, but whatever they were saying or doing was muffled by the electronica and girly pop pumping from the speakers Nick Luftwaith had wired around and into the pool, as if being able to hear Katy Perry and Kraftwerk while submerged in the deep end was a summer's necessity. Those who could see the goings-on would have rolled our eyes and gone back to our *Reader's Digest*s and *Law & Order* reruns, shaking our heads.

Because they were soaked, Troy led the girl inside, and because none of the others followed them, no one knows for certain what took place. But twenty minutes later the fifteen-year-old came stumbling out onto the patio, a gash ripped open along her forehead. The other girls screamed at the horror-film gore, dashing about like a scattering drove of frightened deer. The fifteen-year-old, blinded by her own gushing bodily fluid, stumbled into the pool again. Troy appeared a moment later, wearing nothing but a towel, which was splattered with a suspiciously wine-stain-looking smear, and once again tossed himself into the water, letting the towel fall in a snake heap near the sliding door.

To his credit, Troy called 911. Soon, the spangly, jingoist red and blue of cop cars and an ambulance surrounded the Luftwaith house. We watched from our porches, arms folded over our chests, as the girl was carted away by a pair of hunky EMTs, her body covered in a white sheet all the way up to her chin. She was shivering and moaning, said those who were closest by. It didn't look like she was breathing, said others. We could hear her screams and accusations, said even more. Troy left soon thereafter, led into the back of a police cruiser by a woman officer nearly a foot shorter than him. He wasn't yet in handcuffs.

The Luftwaiths returned the next day, a steamy Saturday too hot for anyone to spend outside. So we did not see how they slumped through their house, but we imagined the looks on their faces as they took in the destruction of their backyard, where broken glass and dusty drugs smeared the concrete. Troy's towel was gone, gathered up as evidence. Police tape fluttered around the pool, a cruel, parading ribbon whipped by the hot wind. We imagined Lina's howling sorrow, Nick's rude stoicism. We imagined what they said to one another as they drove to the police station, short quibbling insults, or maybe glimmering hopeful presumption that the authorities were wrong, that there was some explanation for what had happened. Troy, their Troy, their perfect Troy with his lovely golden tan and well-defined midsection and inscrutably high GPA, would not do whatever he was accused of doing. He was smart, because the Luftwaiths were smart, and a Luftwaith would not do anything stupid and wrong and illegal.

We did not know until the next day that Troy had killed himself. When he couldn't rig the frayed sheets to the bars in his holding cell (because there were none, the door a steel trap with a portcullis window), he took a more gruesome approach. Deep in the night while his parents were in the upper fingers of the Maine mitten and the night clerk at the county jail was nodding off, Troy smashed his head against the concrete wall, over and over. How he had the strength and wherewithal to keep bashing and bashing after the first crack of his skull we would never know, but the story was all over the news by that Sunday night, and we went to sleep with visions of Troy Luftwaith's brain matter smeared on a concrete floor.

Daughter Tina Luftwaith came home from the Twin Cities, where she ran a co-op that sold vegan muffins and omelets. Her arms were tattooed with rainbow waves and tribal swirls that ate up her shoulders and hid the definition in her forearms, strengthened from hauling crates and slicing bricks of slimy tofu. Someone said that she had announced herself as non-binary, a term that made most of us scratch our heads and the computer dorks among us make terrible jokes about ones and zeroes. We watched her arrival, Tina stoic and silent as her parents came out to greet her, Lina letting loose her horsey sobs while Nick chucked a knuckle against his daughter's arm.

We attended the funeral, sitting near the back, a somber affair in a church whose air conditioning was on the fritz. We sweated through our suits and dresses, thankful for the reception at the Luftwaith house where they uncorked bottles of surprisingly expensive Beaujolais and Semillon. The meat trays were catered from Trader Joe's, the charcuterie bought from Cheese Express. We mulled over the delicatessens, filling our plates, popping cherry tomatoes in our mouths for the loamy, warm burst. The seeds stuck between our teeth, and we left them there.

In the following weeks, we gave ourselves to the Luftwaiths. Nick we plied with double bocks at his favorite tavern; Lina we offered our casseroles, left on the stoop in pans covered in aluminum foil, loaded with sour cream and butter and enough salt to cure them for months. The Luftwaiths drank our drinks and ate our foods, and we watched as their lean, hawkish faces transformed beneath the bubble of their tears. We encouraged them to get out of the house as much as possible, to go to the carnivals that cycled around, bopping from one Catholic church to the next, to attend bingo, to join book clubs. The Luftwaiths listened, as if we'd hypnotized them.

But right around Christmas, the Luftwaiths quit their jobs. Nick abandoned the small tech start-up that had something to do with delivering cat and dog food, where he sat on an exercise ball instead of a desk chair and didn't work on Fridays. Lina, who was a part-time guidance counselor at an expensive private school with turrets and free laptops for all students, used all of her sick time to run out the semester, and she gave up the yoga classes she taught on the weekends at the YWCA. On a snowy day thirty-six hours short of the new year, a moving van appeared on the curb outside the Luftwaith house and three burly men started hauling out boxes and bamboo furniture. They worked with a fierce efficiency, ignoring the stinging cold and the buildup of melting ice on the sidewalk. When the moving truck pulled away, it left grimy streaks in the snow. We stared at the Luftwaith house for hours, wondering when they would follow, but we never saw the white Pininfarina. The rainbow flag, we noticed, had been taken down sometime in the night. The only reminder that they had ever been there was the charging station. We imagined it buzzing like a generator, giving away to the sky whatever tiny bit of Luftwaith energy was still there to be had.

•   •   •   •

The Marlins moved in a month later. We wondered, at first, whether the Luftwaith house would go unsold, cursed by the events of the summer. But then, as January spilled into February and an unexpected warm front left our lawns soupy swirls of mud and dead grass, a U-Haul with a Ford Focus hitched to the back pulled up to the empty house. A trio half-fell from the truck's high cab, a pair of trundling, rotund parents and their equally large daughter, their bouncy shape swallowed up in their Target brand puffy coats. Another car arrived, driven by a pimply boy with braces that glanced sunlight off his teeth. They spent hours unloading, nearly crushing one another with their bureaus and mattresses. Watching them struggle with a futon made us laugh into our steaming coffee mugs.

We hated them immediately. Their name reminded us of stagnant water and the terrible smell of canned tuna. They set out potted plants on their front stoop when March rolled around and then summarily failed to water them, leaving the stalks to wilt to a cruel brown and then a black that made us think of Ebola and leprosy. The Marlins did not invite anyone over, nor did they bother introducing themselves up and down the block. When we brought them tins of popcorn or Russell Stover chocolates, they gave us watery thank-yous and shut the door. They didn't wave when they saw us sitting on our porches or mowing our lawns. We never stood around their pool in our cargo shorts, drinking their beers. For all we knew, they didn't keep alcohol in the house. Their daughter played flute in the marching band, her face flushed the color of pezzottaite as she went for the high notes, the plume on her shako writhing like a dying animal. The boy was a nephew who lived across town in one of those hipster neighborhoods full of bistros and art galleries. We never saw him again.

Someone suggested we egg their house or leave fiery bags of dog scat on their porch, and although we nodded in agreement, no one ever did. One time, in early April, a car smashed into the

willow tree in the Marlins' front yard, but the driver was someone we didn't know, his blood canted in way too much booze.
The tree had to be removed, and it felt like the last excision of
the Luftwaiths, who had strung a tire swing from its strongest
branch. No one ever used it, but it made us think of them and
their horrible, apple-pie charm.

Finally, someone admitted it: we missed the Luftwaiths. We
missed Lina's nubuck shoe collection, we missed Nick's Cuban
cigars that he kept on display—never smoked—in his study. We
yearned for his terrible, esoteric jokes that required a working
knowledge of Derrida in order to understand. We'd have given
anything to hear her horrible stories of the times she drank too
many happy hour margaritas when she was underage, flirting
with the Hispanic waiters at her favorite Mexican restaurant so
they didn't ask her for ID when she and her girlfriends got loaded
and devoured basket after basket of free chips then spent the next
day sweating out Cuervo during step class. We wished we could
go back to the night that Troy Luftwaith took that fifteen-year-
old inside the house, so that one of us—any one—could have
leaned out a window and told him to stop right there, maybe
threaten that the cops were coming. Then, maybe, the girls would
have scattered, and Troy would have frozen in his tracks and sent
the fifteen-year-old flying away. The Luftwaiths would still be
here, and we would still frown at them and whisper behind their
backs, but we would also tinkle with joy at seeing them leaving
their garage on a pair of sleek bikes, Lina looking spectacular
in her Schwinn helmet, Nick quirky and weird under his Bern.
We would laugh to one another that their riding gloves made
them look like wannabe Lance Armstrongs. But we would wait
for them to come huffing back, Nick's left arm cocked down at
a ninety-degree angle to signal the turn into their driveway even
though not a single car was nearby. Those gestures meant something to us, something we could only see in their absence. They

kept us awake at night, they pulled at us as we had rhythmic, simple sex with our husbands and wives. They called to us in our dreams.

Because deep down, just a little bit, we wanted those things for ourselves. We wanted to usher the Luftwaiths into our homes. We wanted them to review our carpeted bathrooms, our pink-wallpapered kitchens, our bland living rooms and unfinished basements. We wanted them to take a long gander, then look us in the eye and tell us what they could do to give us just a little bit of what they had.

Melt With You

THE FIRST TIME HUGH PULLED ME INTO A WALL, WE were at a horrible party in an industrial style loft with twenty-foot ceilings, exposed ductwork, slick concrete flooring, marble counters, and glass tabletops. We'd been invited by a long-lost friend of Hugh's who failed to show up and we knew no one there. Everyone was wearing beanies and decorative scarfs and drinking boxed wine out of thimble-sized cups. As people arrived and the sound of their chatter grew, someone would crank up the stereo, which was playing weird folk music without any lyrics. Then, to hear each other over the increased sound, people would speak louder. I wondered at how thick or thin the building's walls were, and whether a neighbor might pound on the door and complain or simply call the police. I dismissed the latter; this was the St. Louis suburbs.

Hugh and I found a quiet corner down the apartment's single hallway and stationed ourselves near the bathroom. After the third person asked us if we were in line for its use despite the fact that the door was open and it was unoccupied, Hugh sighed.

"Should we leave?" I said.

He shook his head. I knew he missed his friend and longed to see him, and neither of us wanted to admit that we'd been stood up.

So instead of swerving our way through the crowded living room and finding something else to do for the night, Hugh cuffed my bicep and said, "Can I show you something?"

I took a sip of my wine, which was white and warm and tasted like sour grapes. I could practically smell the dirty feet that had mashed them. "Sure."

Without another word Hugh leaned back against the wall and tugged me with him. I expected to simply press against the white paint, which I thought, for no good reason, would be hot. Instead, I felt the sensation of breaking, slowly, through the surface of still water, but I wasn't wet. And before I could let out any noises of surprise, we were inside the apartment's wall.

•   •   •   •

By inside the wall I don't mean that we were crammed between layers of sheetrock or bumping shoulders with studs. We weren't tangled up against electrical wires or plumbing or forced to pluck insulation from our hair or avoid inhaling asbestos into our lungs. I wasn't stepping around carpenters' nails or bumping my elbows into air vents. I could still see Hugh, and I could still see the entire party. We'd simply merged into the wall as though painted there, living murals that could see those gathered around us.

"Won't this freak people out?"

Hugh shook his head. "It's like one of those mirrors in police shows."

"We can see them but they can't see us?"

"Yep."

We slithered along the wall—I felt like I was following the directions in "Walk Like an Egyptian"—and Hugh stopped next to a cluster of young women who all looked nearly identical with their brown hair, button noses, and eyeglasses without prescription lenses. They were talking about some class one of them was in, how the men dominated the conversation.

"But when I said so, they all guffawed. I could practically hear them thinking, *Feminist bitch*."

The rest of the women cackled. They all clunked their tiny plastic cups together and drank the swilly wine.

"How often do you do this?" I said. "Have you done it to me?"

"All the time, but no, never."

"Would I know?"

"I guess not." Hugh was staring past the women. The living room was huge—the apartment itself was at least a thousand square feet—and people were packed in like concert-goers. We made our way around the circumference, listening in on conversations for a few seconds at a time. Periodically, Hugh would hover for a good long while, but I didn't ask what grabbed his attention and what made him want to move on. All of these strangers were talking about their lives, the movies they'd watched, the horrible television they laughed at themselves for binging, their hatred for the president and our state governor. When we passed the only bit of wall décor, a black-and-white skyline of St. Louis, the Arch lit up by a haze of rainfall, the sights and sounds of the party momentarily vanished, as if we had walked into a soundproof room. Hugh took my hand while we stood behind the frame—it was at least four feet wide—and kissed me. His lips felt like pressed flowers, flattened and smooth, but still alive with heat. His free hand touched me at my waist, near my belt buckle. I could tell he wanted to pull at my shirt. But then he broke away and we continued our march. When we neared a pair of sliding doors that led out to a small balcony wrapped in wrought iron bars, I said, "What do we do now?"

"What do you mean?" he said. Then he kept sliding along and vanished into the glass.

"Hugh?" I said. Without him in the wall, I felt trapped, breathless, like I would be crushed.

His left arm reappeared, his fingers splayed like a starfish. I reached out and took them. He gripped me tight and pulled, and then I was in the glass, too. The sounds of the party were distorted like we were underwater. He smiled, pointing toward the balcony. I could see in both directions; outside, a trio was passing around a cigarette packed with weed instead of tobacco. They were nodding, though I wasn't sure at what.

"We can see anything," Hugh said. "Any time."

"Wow," I said.

"I've never shared this with anyone," he said. "Not before you."

•　　•　　•　　•

We went to Hugh's apartment that night. A one-bedroom in a honeycomb complex, it was well decorated with photos of his extended family and his mother and father, who had died when he was a teenager. He had a sister whom I'd never met because she lived in Alaska doing something with fish and wildlife. Hugh had hung a triptych of the two of them next to his front door, above the light switch for the living room. They weren't twins—Hugh was a year and three months older—but they looked nearly identical, with the same shag of dark hair and the same nose that slanted to the left just so like it had been broken and improperly reset. She had his cleft chin and even the same square jaw.

I waited for him while he brushed his teeth, worried that my breath would be fuzzy with bad wine even though I'd slugged from his bottle of iridescent mouthwash after taking a leak. His bedroom was spare, just a bed, nightstand, and bureau where white boxer briefs popped out from the top drawer. On the nightstand, an alarm clock with red numbers clicked the minutes by, a copy of *Infinite Jest* stuck beneath it. A bookmark was shoved into its early pages. Hugh said that he tried to read one page each day.

When he came to the bedroom, he stopped in the doorway and looked at the floor. My clothing was stacked in a neat pile. He smiled at me.

"Wait," I said. "I want to see you do it."

"Do what?"

I pointed toward the wall where no closet door or window broke up the clean white paint. "You know. Melt."

"That's what you think it is? Melting?"

"If not that, then what?"

He cocked his head to the side, his jaw and throat lit by the reading lamp I'd turned on while he was in the bathroom. "I guess I've never thought about what to call it."

"You don't worry about naming things?"

Hugh shook his head. "No."

I thought of his parents and what I knew about their deaths. They'd been killed in a car accident of some kind, but I had no idea who was at fault or how it happened. Hugh had spilled this information shortly after we met, when I was telling him about how my mother and father had decided to adopt a pair of kittens just weeks after my younger sister moved out of the house. They couldn't handle the empty nest, I said, and then Hugh, sipping on a beer—we were sitting in his favorite gastropub, where they brewed their own heavy stouts and served schnitzel on metal trays—told me that his parents had died ten years ago when he was sixteen. He blinked and took another drink, and before I could say anything, he waved a hand in the air like he was pushing bugs away from his face and said, "It's fine. I have lots of aunts."

I sat up in bed, letting Hugh's sheets—soft, high thread count, glossy silk—slip down toward my hips. "Will you? Show me?"

"Okay," he said. "If that's something you'd like."

"Of course."

He stepped to the wall. Hugh had also stripped down to his underwear. His stomach was lined with attractive muscles that I liked to touch. A trail of wispy hairs, invisible in the low light, pointed from his belly button to his crotch. Hugh leaned against the wall, his shoulders pinched back. He stood still for a second, not breathing, and then he vanished. It really did look like he was stepping into the wall, as if it was a layer of porous goo pooling around his arms and his thighs and slurping him up.

When he was gone, I peeled the sheets away and stood. I went to the wall where he'd disappeared and pressed my hands against the paint. It was cool and slightly pebbled. I could feel all the bumps that some lazy laborer hadn't wasted time sanding down to a smooth finish. They were like Braille, and then I wondered if maybe the rippling in the surface was from Hugh, that his shifting through the wood had left the lightest signs behind. I pushed my body up against the wall, the paint cold on my thighs, and waited. I turned my face so my right cheek brushed the wall. As I breathed, I imagined Hugh's fingers skimming my skin, pressing my shoulders and ribs and waist, reaching between my legs and raking my pubic hair and then stroking me. But none of that happened. After a moment, I lifted my face away from the wall to step back, but then his hand emerged, cutting through the wood like it was nothing more than clouds, and his fingers found my mouth, his thumb hooking inside my lips and pulling me back. I crashed toward the wall and met Hugh, his minty breath and his hard, clean teeth, his careful tongue that pushed toward my own. For a moment I felt silly, locking lips with my boyfriend with most of his body behind a wall and most of mine on the other side, but then we were tugging each other in both directions. Soon enough, the wall meant nothing.

•   •   •   •

Hugh and I made a game of his ability. When we'd hang out at one of my friends' apartments, playing *Settlers of Catan* or *Agricola,* or when we'd go to a sports bar with his drinking buddies to watch a Cardinals game, he would slip away, saying he needed to use the restroom. No one would notice the conspicuous length of his absence, and I would watch the walls, squinting past framed posters or shelves full of knickknacks or the many mounted televisions and ubiquitous road signs bars seem to think give them flavor but are really just noisy kitsch. I'd keep an eye out for a flash of finger or an entire hand emerging along the side of a bookshelf or the frame of a liquor license. Then I'd nod and smile and that little bit of Hugh would disappear. Sometimes, I would follow him to the restroom and he would pull me into the wall when we were alone and then leave me there, let me be the one to wander. As long as Hugh had taken me in, I could maneuver just like him, emerging when and where I wanted to. Sometimes I'd poke my nose out, or the toe of my shoe, or let a kneecap burst through the surface right next to a promotional poster for half-off wing night. Hugh would always catch sight of me right away, as if he knew, always and ever, where I was going, like I was fitted with a homing beacon.

"Can you see through walls too?" I said one night after he'd sighted the tip of my pinkie finger right away as it emerged next to a friend's toaster oven.

"No," he said. We were lying snug on my bed, the ceiling fan tilting down mellow air at our faces and chests. "I just know you."

"Sappy," I said.

Hugh's arm was snaked around the back of my neck, his right hand draped over my right shoulder. His body tensed, pulling me closer. We'd been together for over six months, a milestone that had come and gone without either of us saying anything. I had never been one for anniversaries, and when I pointed it out, two weeks after the day's passing, Hugh nodded.

"I know," he said. "I just don't like to make a big deal about these things."

•   •   •   •

Sometimes we merged into the walls of his or my apartment when were the only ones there, just because we could. Seeing the world from that flat plane was like going on a tropical vacation. We would come back out into my living room or his bedroom and melt together, lips and hips first, clothing shed as if being in the walls was a powerful aphrodisiac.

We each received wedding invitations for ceremonies dubiously set on the same early October Saturday. Both nuptials were for dear friends, his college roommate and my best friend from high school. They would be held in opposite parts of St. Louis, one at a church downtown and the other at the Foundry Arts Center in St. Charles. The receptions were just as far apart. Hugh suggested going to one ceremony and one reception.

"But the ceremonies are the boring part. No one goes to a wedding for the ceremony."

"My sister didn't have a reception."

I bit the inside of my cheek. Hugh had said so little about his family. I hadn't known, until then, that she was married. I said so.

"You don't ask."

"I figured you'd tell me if you wanted to."

He shook his head.

"What?"

"Nothing."

"People don't shake their heads over nothing."

Things escalated from there, and when we were shouting at one another, Hugh raised his hands, stood, and backed up toward his living room wall.

"Don't," I said. "That's not fair."

He stared at me but kept moving. Without blinking, he started to merge into the wall.

"Hugh," I said. "Please."

But he kept backing away, and then he was gone.

I spent ten minutes apologizing, speaking without pause. My voice was hoarse by the end. I went into the kitchen, found a drinking glass, and filled it with water. I stared through it toward the wall, as if it would bend the light in such a way that would reveal Hugh's location. Despite the soreness in my throat I kept apologizing. I walked the entire perimeter of the apartment with my left hand trailing along the wall, as if I was slinking through a labyrinth or a hedge maze. I kept hoping that Hugh's hand would reach out for me, that his fingers would touch mine. Or that I would feel the shape of his body, a shoulder turned toward me. But I made a full loop without connecting. I ended up back in the kitchen, staring at the same glass. I filled it again and drank one helping of water and then another, drank until my stomach felt bloated. Now I, too, was angry, but because I couldn't melt into the walls, the only place I had to go was out the door.

•   •   •   •

Hugh came to my apartment unannounced and knocked on the door, waiting on the other side while I glimpsed him through the peephole. Instead of opening it right away, I looked at him for a long time. He eventually raised his own face to the hole, his eyes bulging cartoonishly in the rounded glass, and we stayed that way for a long time. What, I wondered, was to stop him going through an external wall, seeping in whenever and wherever he wanted to?

He stuck out his tongue and made absurd faces, and this made me laugh in spite of myself. When I opened the door he was also laughing, and he drew me into a hug before I could recalibrate my anger.

As he held me, he said, voice muffled by my throat, where his lips were pressed, "I'm sorry. I shouldn't have done that."

"No," I said. "You shouldn't."

He held me at arm's length. "What can I do?"

"I don't know," I said. "Rob a bank. Get me a million bucks."

Hugh chuckled and pulled me in for another hug. He said he was sorry again, his voice muffled again. "We can go to whichever wedding you want. I didn't even really like my roommate."

"Did you ever spy on him?" I said.

"Did I what?"

I gestured for us to sit down. Hugh crowded me against an armrest even though there was plenty of room. He smelled of his Brut cologne, which he'd applied with eye-watering generosity. I wondered if I would be able to smell him if he sunk into the wall behind us.

"Did you ever, you know, watch him?"

"Why would I?"

I shrugged. "Why wouldn't you do any of the things you could do?" I started rattling off a list: steal glances at people as they showered, snatch clothing or expensive jewelry when stores were closed, slip into closets in search of sex toys or leather outfits. Examine medicine cabinets for high-powered pharmaceuticals.

"You've never thought about it? Come on."

Hugh shook his head.

"I think you're lying."

Hugh turned his body away from mine, and although he didn't rush to disappear into the skeleton of my apartment, I could feel something rise between us.

•   •   •   •

I imagined that he first slipped into a wall sometime after his parents died, but when I'd posited this theory he shook his head no.

"I was thirteen. It was Thanksgiving, and my family was fighting."

Politics, of course, a disagreement about affirmative action or student loan forgiveness or something. His father had said something insensitive that set off one of Hugh's aunts, who taught English at a low-performing urban high school. She kept saying her brother had no idea, no idea, no idea what the world was like.

"My dad said, 'Just because you don't like the sound of a hard truth doesn't make it racist, Beth.'"

The meal had already been eaten, the only thing remaining on anyone's plates leftover streaks of potato, wayward turkey skin, crumbs of stuffing. The gravy, in its tureen, was skimmed with a hard layer of fat. Hugh and his sister and cousins had been excused to the living room, where they were playing Super Nintendo, taking turns racing as Mario and his friends around tracks made of rainbows and chocolate mud. Hugh was pressed up against a wall, watching. As the noises in the dining room grew louder, the language coarser, he started shaking and then felt himself slipping away into the house's bones like it was nothing.

"I wasn't afraid," Hugh said. "It was nice there, especially when I stepped behind my father's framed poster of the Empire State Building. It was so quiet."

"Didn't anyone wonder where you were?"

Hugh shook his head. "Us kids were always wandering off on our own at family gatherings. We were easy to forget about."

I shook my head. "I can't imagine ever forgetting you."

•   •   •   •

We went to my friend's wedding after Hugh RSVP'd that he couldn't attend his roommate's. He'd stopped pulling me into walls. For all I knew, he didn't slip into them either, but I was a deep sleeper and never woke in the middle of the night to find his side of the bed empty. I tried not to imagine him lurking in my apartment, staring at me when I was home alone, eating chips while splayed on the couch watching a baseball game or *Wheel of Fortune* or whatever Harry Potter movie was on. Every now and then I'd get a tingly feeling on the back of my neck and say Hugh's name, muting the television and going stiff, but nothing, of course, ever happened.

The wedding was in a stone-walled church, one of those St. Louis houses of worship nestled in a residential neighborhood where parking is a bitch and a half, the streets clogged and one-way, businesses crammed in tight. We parked two blocks away. Inside, the church yawned high and wide, the floors a ticking onyx color, the pew kneelers adorned with red fabric. Everything was heavy and thick. I couldn't focus on the ceremony or the vows; instead, I kept looking at the walls, the original stonework, the bumps and ridges and divots, the caulk and cement and limestone holding everything together, the windows with their stained-glass Stations of the Cross glimmering in red and green and saffron. I tried to imagine what it would look and feel like to merge into those surfaces, to see the world from that rippled view. Hugh and I had only ever slid through plaster and wood, and I wondered, then, if brick and rock would feel different. I wanted to ask him, to suggest that we skip the receiving line and take a quick, curious dip inside, but he sat rigid beside me, his copy of the wedding program curled into a tight periscope in his hands.

At the reception I drank too much beer and made Hugh dance with me. The DJ played "I Wanna Dance with Somebody," "You Shook Me All Night Long," and "Love Shack." During slower numbers, Hugh buoyed me around the other couples that were linked close together. I pointed to one of the ring bearers who'd shucked his shoes and was dancing atop one of the bridesmaids' feet, his little hands wrapped around her waist. Two of the reception hall's walls were floor-to-ceiling windows that looked out onto downtown St. Louis, and as Hugh gripped my fingers and led, I imagined us slipping into the glass and staring at the streetlights and pedestrians floating along the sidewalks. I pictured us sliding through the world totally unseen, drinking in the breathtaking views of skyscrapers and private chalets, our bodies leaking through steel beams and stucco. When Hugh left for the bathroom and a dancing break, he was a long time coming back. I raised an eyebrow at him upon his return and sipped from another hefeweizen. He shook his head and said, "Something about that shrimp appetizer didn't agree with me." I could tell he wanted to leave, so I pulled on my jacket and stood. His palm was sweaty, as was his forehead. He glistened when we passed the dance floor, the neon of the standing disco lights turning his skin alien.

We waited for an elevator in a cool hallway, the noise of the reception dampened like we were underwater. I imagined us behind a thick portrait, the world pushed out. When the elevator dinged and the doors started to open, I gripped his hand and said, "I love you."

"Please," Hugh said. "Not right now." He was pale, his lips chapped. I could tell he was holding something in.

•   •   •   •

Despite all I'd drunk, I had trouble sleeping that night, Hugh groaning with what would become a three-day stretch of food poisoning (I hadn't touched the shrimp, and I received a text from one of my friends saying the shrimp had made lots of other people ill). I stared at the ceiling, watching the fan blades tilt in a lazy, lopsided circle, and told myself that Hugh's reticence came from the squeeze in his stomach, the invasion and inflammation in his intestinal track. When he rushed to the bathroom and camped out there, I rooted through his fridge and found a flat bottle of ginger ale and scoured his pantry for a sleeve of crumbling, stale crackers. I arranged them on a plate. I poured the ureic-looking soda into a glass. I knocked on the bathroom door.

"Hugh," I said.

"Please," he said.

"I brought food."

I heard him retch.

"I don't want you to see me like this," he said. I pushed the door open anyway. He'd shut the toilet lid and was balancing his forehead against the lip.

"People get sick. It's okay."

His head rocked back and forth, his nose brushing the porcelain's curve. I set the crackers and ginger ale on the vanity, careful they didn't tip into the sink, and squatted next to Hugh. My vision cradled and swayed; I was still drunk. I put a hand against Hugh's back and rubbed. His skin was slippery and hot. The muscles rolled under my fingers and Hugh let out a small noise of I couldn't tell what. We sat that way for a long time, until my legs started wobbling and Hugh felt another roil in his guts and shoved the lid of the toilet up, banging it against the water tank. He stared down into the water, then looked at me, his voice cracking with something more than illness.

"Please," he said. "I have to—" He struggled up onto his feet.

"Oh," I said. "Don't forget the crackers. Maybe they'll help."

"Go," he said, his voice stern. I went, standing too fast. When I pulled the bathroom door shut behind me, I had to reach a hand out to steady myself against the wall so I didn't topple over. My vision was filled with color. I took several deep breaths. I wished my fingers would sink into the wood, not so I could spy on Hugh at such an intimate, horrible moment, but just to know that I could if I wanted to. That nothing, not even whatever was rushing through him, could truly keep us apart.

The Water Is Coming, the Water Is Here

GABRIEL WAS DEBATING WHAT TO WRITE ABOUT FOR his ethnography assignment the day he found the flyer on his windshield. *THE WATER IS COMING*, it said in large black letters that slanted in hard, bolded italics. The only other thing on the half-sheet of paper was a link to a website: TWICOMING.COM, in all caps, too.

He looked around the parking lot, still full of cars but empty of students. Most of the other kids at the community college were quick to peel out as soon as they were done with classes, but Gabriel liked to spend time in the library reading something or finishing a few math problems before he left, and even then he tended to take wandering loops around campus before heading to his car. The school was home to two duck ponds with asphalt trails spooling around them like ribbons, and he walked them, avoiding the angry geese that left little green lines of shit along the paths. By the time he got to his car every afternoon, he was often alone, the next block of class time well underway.

Gabriel looked up and down the rows of cars. The flyers weren't plastered onto every vehicle's windshield; they'd been stuffed at random intervals, sometimes three, four cars in a row, then an entire segment skipped, then seemingly every other car. How, Gabriel wondered, had vehicles been chosen? Make and model and color didn't appear to have anything to do with it, nor did level of external cleanliness. Perhaps whoever had placed them somehow knew about Gabriel and Martin's breakup. Maybe, through some mystical, psychic awareness, the flyers were left only to those in the throes of loss.

Gabriel climbed into the car and dropped the flyer onto the passenger seat atop his messenger bag. As he exited the lot, he caught sight of one of the flyers grabbed by a hard, sudden wind, yanked from its haphazard spot pinned beneath a windshield wiper. Gabriel watched it sail up into the sky then rocket down, somersaulting across the blacktop. He was tempted to leap out of his car and go chasing after it, but he watched it vanish behind a line of cars as he let up the brake and accelerated toward home.

•   •   •   •

"What do you think?" Gabriel said.

Denise, holding a spatula slicked with the greasy runoff of ground beef, blinked down at the flyer. "I think it's creepy."

"Creepy could be good, though."

His sister's hair was green today, a fresh dye job. He was surprised that the veterinarian's office where she worked let her keep coloring it new, wild hues; just last week she'd come home looking like a tangerine. Gabriel folded the paper over and explained how he'd been stuck trying to figure out his ethnography paper for English class.

Denise shook her head. They'd been living together since July, when Gabriel couldn't bear being at home anymore, constantly worried that his parents would barge in on him and Martin. He'd told them he liked men when he was sixteen, when they kept hounding him about a Homecoming dance date. They'd gobbled him up in warm hugs, his mother, father, and sister all drowning him in their various deodorized and perfumed smells. He'd shrugged them off and said thank you for their approval and then never talked about it again until he brought Martin home in March of senior year. Martin was a freshman at the community college at the time and Gabriel was dual enrolled, taking his first required college writing classes. They had met when paired for peer review. After Martin had received good advice from Gabriel about reworking his thesis paragraph and earned an A on the project, he asked Gabriel to go out with him, a celebratory dinner, after which he kissed Gabriel as they idled in front of his house.

"Why not write about being gay?" Denise said. When he frowned, she waved the spatula around. "Sorry. I know, you're not gay. Queer. That's what I meant. Why not write about being queer?"

"What would I say?"

Denise blinked at him. "Isn't that the point of the assignment? Figuring out what there is to say?"

Gabriel had no response for that, so he left the kitchen and dropped into his bedroom. Though the smaller of the two, it was the better positioned, aimed toward the complex's pool, where the glimmering water shot waving arms of light into the room when the sun was at the right angle. Gabriel opened up his laptop and typed the website from the flyer into a search bar.

The site was plain, just a chunk of black text on a white background, the letters italicized and in bold.

Now the earth was corrupt in God's sight and was full of violence.
God saw how corrupt the earth had become, for all the people on
earth had corrupted their ways. So God said to Noah, "I am going to
put an end to all people, for the earth is filled with violence because
of them. I am surely going to destroy both them and the earth.

That was it. The page had no links, no contact information, nothing. Gabriel copied the text into a search bar and up popped a
scrolling list of references to Genesis. He rubbed his eyes and
leaned back in his desk chair, then printed the page.

"Find anything for your paper?" Denise said when they sat
down for dinner, tacos in hard shells, pebbles of ground beef ooz-
ing orange grease.

Gabriel showed her the printout.

"What's this?"

"Genesis."

"So they're like a bunch of religious fundies?"

"Seems like."

"So now what?"

Gabriel sighed and rubbed at his eyes. "I don't know."

"When's the paper due?"

"I have to have a rough draft by Tuesday."

"And you're sure it wouldn't be easier to write about queer people?"

Gabriel's stomach was hurting, his throat burning; Denise
always cooked things that were spicy, despite the fact that she
knew he couldn't handle too much kick. He took a swig from his
glass of milk, relishing the cool rush that settled in his torso.

"Well?" Denise said.

"I don't think so," he said, thinking about Martin. "They're way
more trouble than you think."

●   ●   ●   ●

In the morning, Gabriel was woken by a rattle of lightning, strong enough that he could feel the building vibrate when the flash was followed by a loud thunderclap. He looked out at the pool, where the surface rippled and swooshed. Gabriel pulled on his clothes and met his sister in the kitchen, where she was scrambling eggs for breakfast. Her green hair shimmered under the fluorescent light.

He gathered a pair of plates and drinking glasses, filling one with orange juice for her and the other with milk for him. When Denise was finished with the eggs, she brought the pan to the dining room table and scooped out even helpings. They smelled milky, and steam wafted off the tops of the yellow mounds. Gabriel fished out a pair of forks from the mess of the cutlery drawer, pushing a turkey baster out of the way, and handed one to his sister before they sat.

"Your water's here," Denise said.

"Huh?"

She pointed toward their balcony door, scuzzy with rainwater. "Your water. Your cult. Maybe this is it. The grand flood."

"It's not my water," Gabriel said.

He drove through the rain to campus, where everyone was gloomy and damp; his history class was cancelled, so he sat in the library for an hour and tried to work on his algebra homework, but he was distracted by the heavy downpour, which continued. He started to wonder if his sister was right. Just outside the library was a dip in the pebbled concrete that sprawled between buildings, and water rushed into a small pond there before drizzling down a drain. He watched it spatter and collect, and he imagined that water spreading and rising, the drain unable to keep up with the volume. He pictured it seeping through the library doors, sogging into the carpets, slurping up into all the books and shorting out the computers, electrocuting the students still typing away.

After his last class, Gabriel sat in his car for a long time. He felt the wet from his body seep into the seat's fabric upholstery, which would leave behind a doggish smell for days. He listened to the rain pound hard against the glass and paint. For weeks, Gabriel had convinced himself that he wasn't lost and confused following the breakup with Martin. They'd been sitting in Martin's car, the first day of classes concluded, the weather much like today's, the storm lashing so hard that Martin was half-yelling. As Martin spoke, Gabriel had felt whacked by something hard and sharp, right at the sternum; when Martin told him he was sorry, he thought he might be experiencing heart palpitations.

"What did I do?" Gabriel said.

"Nothing," Martin said, his voice soft, nearly inaudible. "You did nothing."

"Should I have done something?"

"No," Martin said. He was gripping the steering wheel tight. They sat silent for a long time before Martin put the car in drive and said he would still take Gabriel home, as if this was some salve that would heal the wounds blooming inside both of them. As he pulled out of the parking lot the storm intensified, small blobs of hail pelting the car. Between the cacophony of noise out-side and the gonging horrors happening in his chest, Gabriel had felt as if it might have been the end of the world.

•   •   •   •

But just like the day of their breakup, it wasn't the end of the world. Just like the day after Martin ripped himself away, Gabriel woke to sunshine and a fug of humidity so engrossing that his back was fuzzed with sweat in the short trip from the apartment to his car. The ground steamed, flowers stretched out long and high. Because Denise worked a 6 a.m. shift on Thursdays, he ate breakfast alone, just a granola bar and a mandarin orange from the heap she kept in a plastic bowl on the kitchen counter. He dragged himself through his morning routine, bleary and exhausted. The storm had kept him up late, thunder and lightning rattling the apartment, the rain so intense he was sure the windows and balcony doors would crack beneath the assault. On the drive to campus he kept an eye out for signs of apocalyptic damage, but aside from some deep ruts of water on the side of the road and a few wind-clipped branches dotting greenery, the world appeared to have survived unscathed.

He blinked through his classes, but instead of taking a loop around campus afterward, he sought out his English teacher, who kept a half hour of office time past the end of Gabriel's last class. The English building, which shared space with foreign languages and journalism, was the college's saddest building in Gabriel's estimation: two stories of gray walls and gray carpets and not a single strip of differently colored paint aside from each classroom's slick white board. Each floor was taken up by a single long hallway, a suite of offices on one side, classrooms on the other. It felt both futuristic and antiquated at the same time. Whenever it rained, the building smelled of must and fungus for a few days, as if it was a large terrarium.

His professor's office was on the second floor, where all of the English faculty were stored away in a suite off the main hall. A second, parallel hallway was hidden behind a heavy door. Gabriel knew his professor had taught at the college for at least four or five years, but you wouldn't know it from the office décor: the single bookcase held only one shelf of books. The others were taken up by cluttered trinkets: random stuffed animals, a gavel, a framed certificate for some teaching award granted by the school's honor society. The professor's desk was pristine and blank except for a computer and neat stack of manila folders. Gabriel recognized these, because he carried one into their classroom every day and extracted from it their drafts and his notes.

He smiled when Gabriel knocked on the open door and, without standing to greet him, gestured for Gabriel to sit in the only chair on the opposite side of the desk. He kept his hands folded in front of him like a pastor, Gabriel his unsteady charge.

"What can I help you with?" His instructor's voice was pleasant and calm, neither deep nor high. The man was, in Gabriel's estimation, the perfect example of the absolute average: neither tall nor short, neither fat nor lean. His face was neither handsome nor ugly. Some days he wore glasses, others he didn't, and they neither helped nor hurt his physical appeal.

As Gabriel sat, he saw the walls' only two adornments. First, his professor's diploma, framed and full of calligraphy and *Doctor of Philosophy* in curlicued letters. Second, a small rainbow flag the size of a miniature, single-serving cereal box, still attached to its chopstick-long pole, skewered to the wall by a thumbtack, like a butterfly on display. Gabriel blinked at it, then looked at his instructor again. He'd never given any indication that his sexuality might be anything other than perfectly straight. But then, Gabriel wondered, what would be the signs other than the kinds of stereotypes he himself rejected?

Finally, Gabriel cleared his throat and said, "I'm really struggling to come up with a subject for my paper. The ethnography."

His professor leaned forward. "Okay, well, I can't just tell you what to write about, because part of the assignment is for you to define a particular group using whatever parameters you set."

"I know."

"But, I guess what I can tell you is that I'd advise you to pick a group that interests you."

"Okay."

"So what interests you, Gabriel?"

Despite anticipating the question, Gabriel had no idea what to say. He'd been posed that question before, by Martin when they went on their first date, by Martin's parents when he met them over dinner at an expensive restaurant where the price of a simple salad made his eyes bulge. He'd always stuttered out something nondescript like sports or movies or music because he didn't really know what he was interested in. During orientation at the college, he'd been sent through a maze of tables where student clubs were assembled with informational handouts and free pencils and buttons, each group yearning for him to scribble his name down on their sign-up sheet. There was a chess club, a board games club, an extreme hiking club, an accounting club, club after club after club, one for music lovers and even reality television watchers and for every sport imaginable, even ones he hadn't heard of and was convinced were jokes. One group was all about drug reform, another about drug prevention. The cacophony made his head spin, and by the time he'd left the room his hands were full of papers and goodies and yet he'd written his name down not once.

So he said, "I'm not really sure."

The professor blinked and leaned back. "Well, what do you do in your free time?"

"Do homework, I guess."

"Does that really count as free time?"

"I guess not."

"So?"

"I don't really know!"

It came out louder and angrier than he'd meant it. Gabriel felt his face flare, and he let out a deep, sorry breath. Then, before he could stop himself, he started crying, loud, wet sobs, ugly sobs, the kind of sobs he didn't feel like he deserved to be letting loose, which only made him cry harder, his tears a blooming deluge wetting his face.

•   •   •   •

Gabriel's face was crusty with dried tears, his vision a bit blurry, when he reached his car, so at first he didn't notice the new flyer. He stopped and stared at it. The same white, the same half-size sheet of paper, bent in the same way by the wind as it clung to the glass beneath the wiper. Gabriel looked around the lot and couldn't decide if it was his imagination or not that the flyers were affixed to even fewer vehicles this time. He plucked it up. *THE WATER IS COMING.* This time, at the bottom of the page in all lowercase letters was a date, time, and address. Tomorrow evening.

Something tingled at the back of Gabriel's neck. He felt an itch in his throat and glanced around, wondering if he was being watched. Then he heard an unexpected crack of thunder and looked up: the sky was all barren blue aside from a single cloud off in the distance, dark like a pimple. He watched its slow tumble across the sky, waiting for it to come, to drop its rain, to soak everything away all by itself.

●   ●   ●   ●

"This just seems like a bad idea," Denise said.

"It's like two miles away. I'm not rushing off to the Amazon or something."

"And you want to go to this meeting of theirs why?"

Gabriel sighed. "Because I want to write about these people for my paper."

"Did you not talk to your professor about what you might do?"

At the mention of the meeting, where he'd broken down and his instructor had come around the desk and laid a hand on Gabriel's shoulder blade and then offered him extra time on the paper, which Gabriel waved away like he was swatting a fly, he felt his stomach cinch up.

"Yeah," Gabriel said, his mouth feeling tinny as he lied, "he told me the cult was a cool angle."

"That seems irresponsible."

Gabriel shook his head. "I didn't, like, tell him I was going to go join them or anything."

"Is that what going to this meeting means? That you're going to join them? Maybe I should go with you."

"Don't you work late tomorrow?" He extracted the new flyer from his pocket and pointed at the time.

Denise sighed and rubbed her face with her hands. Her green hair flashed and shimmered. Gabriel wondered when she would change it again. Soon, probably. She was always changing, slipping into new shapes, new versions of herself, with such simplicity and ease. During high school she'd had a nose ring, but she'd let the hole close up eventually. When Gabriel asked why, she shrugged and said, "It wasn't me anymore." He'd wondered about that, how someone could just know something wasn't a part of them any longer, the way Martin had known it was time to excise Gabriel from his life like he was a cancer or a wart.

"I'll be okay," Gabriel said.

"That's what they all say until things go wrong," Denise said. "Haven't you ever seen, like, a single movie?"

"I don't really watch movies anymore," Gabriel said. Denise shut her eyes and shook her head. Gabriel ate his food, tasting nothing.

•   •   •   •

The next morning, Gabriel was awoken by another downpour, this time the hard clink of hail ripping him out of sleep, where he was in the midst of an intense sex dream. He and Martin tearing at one another's exposed skin, his fingers raking through the hair on Martin's head with one hand and the other snaking along the little fuzzy trail that drizzled from his belly button to his groin. Gabriel's mouth was gluey, his eyes crusty with sleep, and he felt

a momentary discombobulation, expecting to feel the warmth of
Martin next to him. It took him a second to remember that he
was alone.

He didn't have any classes on Fridays, so Gabriel had nothing
to do and nowhere to go. He stood at his bedroom window and
stared out at the mammoth darkness, the trees whipping in the
wind, the surface of the pool's water being violently stirred and
walloped by the hailstones chuffing down. Thunder clattered and
lightning illumined the scene over and over, and with each crash
and flash Gabriel felt something crumble in his chest.

Denise slept in on Fridays too, so he didn't encounter any resistance or interrogation when he slipped out the front door, clutching his keys in his hand and prepared to rush through the deluge
to his car. He was quick to get down the stairs and unlock the
door, but he was still sopping wet when he shut himself in the
driver's seat, his soaked pants leaking into the upholstery. Within
the confines of the car, the pounding was heavier and symphonic.
Even with the headlights on high, he could barely see.

Driving to Martin's house was a mistake, he knew, on many
levels. Gabriel thought, several times, about pulling over. The
rain was thick and opaque; he felt his right wheel clip a curb
more than once because he was drifting, driving with an abandoned blindness. He felt the pull of water as it rambled down the
road, tugging at his car's tires, and Gabriel remembered images
he saw on the nightly news during flash floods. Cars submerged
up to their rooftops, drivers wading through shoulder-high muck
to pull themselves to safety. He always wondered how people
wound up in those situations, how they didn't foresee the danger
they were putting themselves in. But as he pushed on, fingers
gripping the steering wheel too tight, his whole body hunched
forward as if he was driving drunk, he thought he understood.

Martin's car was in the driveway. He also had no classes on
Fridays. Gabriel sat in his car, wheels barely humped onto the

curb. He let the drumming noise deafen any regrets or considerations he might be making. Then he tossed himself out of the car, ran around the front, slid on the slick grass, and tumbled up to the front porch. He was only in the rain for a few seconds but was freshly wet again as he stood in front of the door. The heavy downpour was spraying bursts onto his back and hamstrings when he knocked.

Martin's front door featured a glazed glass ocular window through which Gabriel could see diluted, blurred shapes: the grand staircase leading to the second floor, the drop leaf table with a decorative bowl and a vase of peonies, the archway to the left leading to the living room. He waited and wiped his hands on his jeans, but his skin was still slick and squeaky. For a second, he considered rushing back into the rain, but he clenched his jaw and pressed the doorbell.

He saw movement after a few seconds and made out the familiar shape of Martin's body through the window. Gabriel felt a twinge in his stomach. They hadn't seen or spoken to one another since the breakup, and Gabriel was still trying to think of what he would say when the door opened and there he was, Martin, standing tall and lanky and confused.

"Gabe?" he said. "What are you doing here?"

Before Gabriel could respond, Martin ushered him inside and led him to the kitchen, where he sat Gabriel down in the breakfast nook. Martin disappeared and eventually came back with a white bath towel. He asked if Gabriel wanted something to drink, tea, maybe, and without waiting for his response started boiling water. He didn't sit, wouldn't look at Gabriel or ask him questions. Martin bustled about while Gabriel dripped water onto the bench seat.

It wasn't until Martin brought the two mugs of tea and sat down opposite him that he repeated his initial inquiry. Gabriel still hadn't settled on what to say. The look on Martin's face was full of pity, which made Gabriel queasy. He felt foolish. He steeped his tea and didn't say anything.

Eventually, Martin let out a sigh, as if he was a learned old man about to impart wisdom on Gabriel, his foolhardy charge.

"I'm sorry things went the way they did between us." He wrapped a hand around his mug. Gabriel stared at Martin's knuckles, remembering the way his fingers would clutch Gabriel's jaw, his shoulder, his throat, such kind, warm caresses that sent pleasant chills down his body.

"Why did they?"

Martin sighed again, removed his hand from his coffee mug so he could rub at his eyes. Gabriel imagined his palms must be warm, soothing. He yearned for them to touch his cheeks, his forehead. He wanted Martin's lips to brush his ears and throat.

"Look, Gabe. Just because a relationship doesn't end with wedding bells and lasting forever doesn't mean it wasn't good or successful."

"I don't understand."

"We had a nice time together, didn't we?"

Gabriel nodded, slowly, like he was on the edge of a precipice.

"Then, well, let's just be happy about that, okay?"

"Was there someone else?" The question shot out before Gabriel could stop himself; he hadn't even been planning on asking it, because the idea had never occurred to him that Martin would cheat or stray or dump him for someone better. But all of a sudden it was a clocking realization, a hard hammer blow on his throat, behind his ears. As soon as he asked it, a fresh wave of hard rainfall smacked against the window above the breakfast nook, so loud they both flinched and stared at it; the morning was all tight, gray gloom, as though evening had fallen already. Maybe it had, Gabriel thought: time seemed so dizzy and out of focus.

"There is now, if that's what you mean."

Gabriel swallowed a hard breath. His throat was dry, but he couldn't bring himself to drink the tea.

"Was there when you dumped me?"

Martin looked away, and Gabriel didn't want him to answer. Gabriel didn't want to be there anymore, but he had no idea where he wanted to be instead. He stood and moved to leave, and even though Martin exhorted him to stay, Gabriel went. Whatever little drying he'd accomplished sitting at Martin's kitchen table was immediately undone when he stepped outside and dashed across the grass, his body soaked and heavy again when he threw himself into his car, where he once again listened to the forceful slap of the rain as it fell and swirled and splattered the glass, the roof, the windows, everything.

•   •   •   •

Because he had nowhere else to go, he went to the meeting. He'd memorized the address, which was for a small, squat building that he was sure had at one point been a daycare. Its front was all brown and cream, the roof low and slanted. He could see a few shingles were missing, the tar paper beneath like holes in a punched-out mouth. The parking lot was pebbled and dusty and his was one of only four cars in the lot even though the meeting started in only five minutes. The rain had not abated.

Gabriel wished Martin were here in the car with him; he would drag Gabriel right out and march through the doors and plop himself into the middle of the meeting. Hell, he'd probably run the meeting. He had taken Gabriel to his first keg party, right as senior year was winding down. Gabriel had trailed Martin up the front steps of an unfamiliar, gargantuan house in a nice neighborhood where every home had a decorative balcony held aloft by humongous white columns. Martin had slithered through a crowd of strangers all yelling to one another over the bass line of heavy rap music, leading Gabriel to a kitchen where a keg with a three-pronged tap was being slowly emptied of its Budweiser. Martin filled two cups and gave one to Gabriel, offering him a silent "cheers." They drank and danced and eventually Martin led him to a quiet corner in a dining room, where they crowded next to a hulking oak curio cabinet filled with bone china and made out, Martin's lips slick and hot.

"People can see us," Gabriel had said.

"So what?" Martin said. "Fuck 'em."

But Martin wasn't here. He wouldn't be here again, ever.

Gabriel took a deep breath and slid out of his car. The rain soaked him yet again as he jogged to the building's entrance, the glass dark and reflective. He tried one door handle, but it was locked. So was the other. When Gabriel squinted through the glass he could see nothing but the dark shadows and irresolute shapes of foyer furniture: a table, a wing-backed chair, a vase filled with blooming flowers. No movement or life.

Something inside him roiled. He grabbed both door handles and shook them, so hard he thought the glass might break, but of course it didn't. His hands slipped along the metal. His back was hit over and over by raindrops, like he was turned away from a firing squad.

"It's here," he shrieked. He pounded the glass with his fists. "The water is here!"

He kept yelling. Despite the cars in the lot, no one came. Maybe, he thought, they couldn't hear him over the sound of the storm. Or maybe there was no one. There might never be, or in seconds, maybe someone would come and unlock the door, drag him inside, warm him up, and tell him all the things he needed to hear.

The Louder You Are, the Faster They Ride

UNTIL HIS FAMILY'S TRIP TO SAN ANTONIO WHEN HE was twenty-three, Newell Barnes had never been to a rodeo. He'd never smelled the loamy-sweet scent of manure, never walked over hay-strewn dirt paths leveled flat by thousands of cowboy boots. He'd never seen so many flannel shirts tucked tight into blue jeans or so many shades of gingham. And he'd always thought the image of Texans decked out in Stetsons and Milanos and gigantic belt buckles was a stereotype, like the *yeehaw* and nasal twang of television accents, but when the announcer's voice crowed out the bull riders' accolades or celebrated the speed of the roping teams, he realized it was all, to a certain degree, true.

He also saw more hands glowing blue than he expected; each pair sent a jolt down into his stomach and made Newell glance at the person's face, looking for other outward signs, the kinds that people besides himself might actually be able to see.

The stands at the Tejas Rodeo were packed. So he, his sister Leelo, brother Tommy, and Tommy's fiancée Angie had to stand. At first, they crowded into a corner in front of the bleachers, but midway through the men's steer wrestling a woman in the second row yelled out to them that they were blocking the view as the bulls bolted down the length of the arena. A man reeking of whiskey teetered up the steps behind them and joined the woman. "That's why the sign says no fucking standing," he muttered.

Tommy whipped around, eyes wide. Angie pointed, some twenty feet past them, toward a metal sign affixed to the railing that said, in large red letters, *No Standing*. Three men in Lucchese boots leaned against the rail just past the sign, elbows propped on the metal, hands curled around sweating bottles of Shiner Bock.

"He didn't tell them to move," Tommy said when they'd tumbled down the stairs and back into the concession area. "We must not look the part."

Newell glanced down at himself. He was wearing a pair of black Vans, khakis, and a slate-gray windbreaker for which he was grateful: night in the San Antonio desert had descended and his nose was runny from the chill.

"I'm getting beers," Leelo said. "Who wants?"

"Yes, please," Angie said. She was actually dressed to fit in, as was her modus operandi wherever she went. Newell thought she must be cold in her cut-offs and the flannel whose bottom she'd tied into a pseudo-halter top, the fabric knotted just above her belly button to reveal a buttery swath of smooth, tight skin.

"Sure," Tommy said, shoving his hands in his pockets. Not once had Newell caught the slightest sign of glow in them.

"Check. Newt?" Leelo said, snapping a finger in his direction.

"I'm okay."

"You can live a little," Tommy said.

"I'm driving."

"It's Texas. You're more likely to get pulled over for not having a beer on your person than for drinking one."

"Fine," Newell said. "Whatever."

Tommy extricated a hand from his jeans and slapped Newell's arm. "Yeehaw."

A girl and boy in their late teens cut through their small bubble of bodies and mumbled an "excuse us." When the boy passed them by he put one hand on the girl's hip, guiding her toward the concession stand where they got in line behind Leelo. Newell felt a bite in his cheek: the boy's hand was glowing just so, the tiniest bit of light bleeding out of his fingers. His face was pitted with acne scars, his upper lip brushed with the fledgling line of a mustache. His skin was olive, baked, Newell imagined, by afternoons raising hay or perhaps trotting horses across a clover-filled field. Newell could picture the boy's hands in his gloves, letting out their tiny glowing light, haloing his wrists in teal. He tried to envision the boy and girl kissing, their hands plying toward one another's most intimate skin, the boy seeing the little illumination in his fingers and calluses. What, Newell wondered, did the boy think it meant? Did he accept this about himself, or did he kiss the girl harder, snake his hands toward her breasts or between her legs with greater urgency? Did he take sharper, tighter breaths, trying to will himself to excitement and desire? Or did the vagueness of his glow mean that he did truly desire her but also something else?

Leelo returned with their beers. Tommy raised a toast and let out an obnoxious "Yippee ki-yay!" at the end. Then he took a long glug, his Adam's apple bobbing like a fishing lure. Angie rolled her eyes and Leelo laughed. Newell drank, the liquid cold and harsh against his teeth.

•   •   •   •

Newell was thirteen when his hands started glowing a hot, ice-fire blue. He'd woken on a Tuesday morning from his first pinching dream of another naked man, the Hollywood star from the blockbuster film he and his siblings had watched the night before; there'd been a sex scene, the man's muscled body framed in low light, the rounded edge of his glutes in shadowed relief as they tightened and contracted in faux-thrusting. His lumbar muscles were thick, corded, the backs of his shoulders cratered with sinews that pulsed as he propped himself up above his co-star, whose hands raked at his obliques. Newell woke with a sour stickiness in his underwear, his throat dry, and his hands pulsing the tetra-blue of a fish tank illuminated by a uv light.

He stood in the bathroom for a long time after he showered, staring in the mirror as he styled his hair and wiped a cotton ball doused in salicylic acid across his nose and chin. His fingers flashed hard iris-blue light at him. When he marched down to the breakfast table he kept them in his pockets as long as he could, until his mother wondered why he wasn't eating his cereal. He sighed, finally, Tommy and Leelo glancing at him, and plopped his hands on the table in display.

No one said a word. No one noticed a thing. His father, folding over his morning newspaper, said he was going to drop Newell off first this morning because he had a meeting near Tommy and Leelo's high school and didn't want to backtrack.

"Your mom will pick you up after football, okay?" he said, thwapping the paper against the tabletop.

"Okay," Newell said, eyes buggy. He stared down at his hands, their glow pulsing against the wood surface, creating the slightest reflection against his cereal bowl.

"You okay, Champ?" his dad said. "Not feeling a fever or anything?"

"There has been something going around," his mother said, plopping down in the last empty seat with a cup of coffee and buttered sourdough toast.

"I—no," he said, picking up his spoon. They really couldn't see it at all. Newell glanced at his family's hands: all normal, peach. His brother's fingernails were thicker than Newell's, cut to the quick. Leelo had recently painted hers the hard white of eggshell; his mother's were chipped green on the right hand and magenta on the left. His father's hands were regular dad hands, large and square, the knuckles chapped and dry.

Even though both Leelo and Tommy were old enough to drive and had their licenses, they all rode together to school, Tommy up front with their father, Leelo in the back with Newell. The whole way there he felt a bite in his stomach and kept staring at his glowing, blue hands. The green veins on the back were louder, more prominent, the deoxygenated blood pulsing across his ligaments and bones. He splayed his fingers long against the black surface of his Jordache backpack, the nearest zipper stained cerulean by the plush of color.

Newell had seen the faint swipes of glow on other students' hands—a few boys, a handful of girls—but had always thought he was just druggy-tired or seeing some trick of the light. But now, as he slow-lurched toward his classroom after being dumped at the school's mouth by his father, he wondered. He stared at the boys and girls he'd gone to school with ever since first grade, their hands dangling at their sides or clutching the straps of their bags or buried in their pockets. He passed Phyllis Nightling, captain of the cheerleading squad; the backs of her hands pulsed with a faint, icicle blue, like she was numb. Carlton Schumacher, who won the spelling bee every year, was blasting out so much delphinium blue that his hands looked like strobe lights as he waltzed down the hall. The palms of the science teacher, Mrs. Nordebeck, radiated the color of cool glass when she held up a beaker, the liquid inside the same aquamarine as her fingertips.

He didn't remember much of that day. His heart was busy fluttering and pounding, his head swimming and achy. Classes flew by; lunch was a whirl of sandwiches and sweaty meats, crinkling paper bags, trays booming against the inner lips of trashcans. The parking lot where recess was held was full of flashing bodies. Newell spent his time trying to focus on the blips of periwinkle he saw when hands palmed basketballs or battered the tetherball on its high pole.

That night, his father asked, at dinner, how each of the kids' days went. Leelo said fine; she'd had a history test she thought she aced. Tommy also said fine, murmuring something about the upcoming PSATs. So Newell did the same, eking out a small, "It was okay," while looking at his hands. They pulsed as he held up a forkful of spaghetti, which, thanks to his glowing skin, looked like it had been boiled in blueberries.

•   •   •   •

They took their beers back to the arena, where the women's barrel races were about to begin. A tractor-trailer dragged what looked like a humongous concrete comb behind it, tilling up the soil. Below the bleachers was an open ring of standing room at eye level with the arena floor. Spectators sat in folding chairs or leaned against the metal barrier separating the crowd from the cowpokes. Tommy found empty space along the edge of a raised flower bed, enough for all of them to balance there and see over the folks pressed right up against the action.

"Give her a big hand, folks," the announcer said in his thick drawl after introducing the first racer. "The louder you are, the faster they ride."

The rider came shooting out of the open gate, her horse already at a heavy canter. The cowgirl's hands screeched out a hard teal where they gripped the reins, matching her checked shirt. Newell watched her long braid whipping as she guided her horse into a tight turn right near where they stood; he could see the horse's legs straining, the muscles contracting as it wheeled around the white water barrel, body nearly perpendicular to the ground at one point. When the horse straightened out and shot toward the barrel on the other side of the arena, the woman riding seemed suspended in the air, her ankles the only point of contact with the horse's body. After horse and cowgirl made the second and third barrel turns and shot back toward the starting line, the crowd started clapping and hooting.

"Fifteen-eight-one-nine!" the announcer crowed. "What a run that was! Don't see under-sixteens too often here. Give it up for Lexa Santana, ladies and gents!"

Newell clapped, his hands flashing with each smack of applause. Tommy let out another obnoxious *yeehaw*, and a woman in front of them glanced back, but instead of frowning she smiled and tipped her beer bottle in Tommy's direction.

• • • •

In high school, girls dragged Newell onto the dance floor at Homecoming and Coronation, his hands brightening their corsages and making the backs of their silken dresses transparent in a way only he could see. He received several invitations to the Sadie Hawkins dance each spring, and he excelled as a wide receiver on the football team, which made the state semifinals three times. Every year during their final home game he was lavished with praise and homemade signs written in the cheerleaders' swirly script. When he went off to college on an academic scholarship rather than an athletic one, girls, and some boys, swooned over his bare shoulders and triceps when he went to toga parties. He didn't drink much beer because he liked having abs, and people glanced his way when he stood at the squat rack at the fitness center. Where his brother's hair had started thinning after he turned twenty-one, little bite-size chunks receding on either side of his widow's peak, Newell's golden hair stayed thick. Women would latch themselves onto him at house parties, flirtatiously assigning him drinks during card games. They would paw at his hands when he made shots in beer pong; their hands gobbled up the blue light in his fingertips. A few times, he did let these women take him to bed; one of them peeled away his virginity when he was a sophomore. Their bodies slid together in her dorm room which smelled of canister air freshener, lemony and acidic. The next morning, she ran her fingernail down his arm, threading her normal fingers between his illuminated ones. She, like the rest of the world, couldn't see the glow. They dated for a few weeks, then floated apart; he didn't really know that things were over until he saw her on the arm of a stranger on a Saturday night at a party neither had told the other they'd be at.

And despite being able to see the hands of men, knifing through afternoon sunshine, buzzing with blue light in office buildings, in line at the grocery store, singing out sharp bursts as their fingers rapped against the slick surfaces of bars, he could never bring himself to make a move. Not when men with hands so blue they looked detached from the body of a Smurf were standing near him, shoulder to shoulder in a packed pub or introduced to him by a mutual friend, shaking hands so that their shared glows touched with electric overlap. And none of these men with sapphire-hued knuckles ever pressed themselves upon Newell, probably thanks to his straight-leg jeans and his shyness, his unkempt hair and his deep voice. So he spent years looking on from afar, wondering what it would be like to touch another man's hard skin, to feel another strong chest against his own, to know the roundness of deltoid or the drizzle of stomach hair. At night, the glow kept him up unless he tucked his hands under his pillows or kept them beneath his blankets, where he would roll them over his skin, pressing against his hips, his thighs, between his glutes, imagining they were someone else's, phosphorus and excited and glorifying.

•   •   •   •

During the last event, bronc riding, Newell noticed that one of the three rodeo clowns had glowing hands, a faint lapis lazuli glaze. The clown, his face obscured by a wide-brimmed red sombrero and dripping white triangles painted on his cheeks, came rambling around the arena before the first rider was released from the pen, horse huffing and jostling. Only two of the cowboys managed to stay atop their broncos for the full eight seconds required to earn a score; the last, with the crowd clapping and hooting in a frenzy as the bronc sprayed bullets of soil into the air, raised his off-hand high above his head. His fist blazed like a topaz Olympic torch.

When the competition was over, the crowd reconstituted itself beneath a huge white canopy whose sides were protected from the chill wind by translucent tarps. Groups sat at picnic tables and couples strutted around the dance floor to a live band. Tommy and Angie sang along, and Leelo swayed her hips.

"So weird," Leelo said, crashing her hip against Newell's. "It's like a high school dance with drunk adults."

"And we seem to have found ourselves in the kids' section," Tommy said.

They were thronged on all sides by teenagers, the boys in checked shirts, the girls in their Daisy Dukes, legs creamy and long and wrapped in leather boots. Some of them were dancing in awkward, syncopated rhythm. Then there were the adults, including a trio of twenty-something guys dancing in rabid, epileptic motion in the middle of the dance floor, arms raised over their heads, each of them clutching a sweating bottle of Budweiser. None of their hands glowed. Others, in their forties, fifties, even sixties, swayed to the music, which shifted to a slow number.

A flash in the corner of the dance floor close to the stage caught Newell's attention: a man in a black hat that looked carved out of fine crushed felt stood by himself, drinking a Lone Star. His hands bloomed a neon blue, calling out their light when he adjusted the brim of his hat. He stared at the dancers, bobbing his head to the rhythm of the drums.

"Let's dance," Angie said, prying at Tommy's arm. Newell looked away from the man in the corner and watched his brother and Angie disappear into the crowd, Angie leaning her head back and laughing, Tommy mouthing the words of the song. Leelo tugged on Newell's arm, and before he could object, he was plunged into the herd of couples two-stepping. He let his sister lead. She dipped left then right, knees bending, body swaying. At first, they were stationary, but then Leelo shifted her weight and started dragging them along with the ellipsis of couples circling the floor. Some dancers' palms, flat against the backs of their partners, glowed; it was as though he was on the edge of a field of Chinese lanterns that turned off and on as bodies turned toward him and then away. He glanced at the man in the corner as he and Leelo passed close. His glow was the brightest, a rich tanzanite that seemed to call to Newell.

"Lots of girls you could ask to dance," Leelo said, raising her voice as they swayed past an amp.

Newell nodded.

Her grip on his hand tightened; the color seemed to ooze from his skin into hers. Leelo leaned in close, pirouetting on her tiptoes then falling against him as she finished a spin.

"Lots of boys, too," she said. She winked and whisked him across the dance floor. Newell's hands felt numb; everything did. Newell had never said a word to any of his family members about his attractions; why bother, he thought, if he'd never done anything about them himself? He wasn't worried about what his family would say or think. They were the kind of people who still came together for a family vacation even though the kids were all in their twenties, after all.

Leelo guided them back to where they'd started and let him go. Despite the air's chill, her forehead was beaded with sweat. Tommy and Angie were still among the throng; Newell could see the high rise of his brother's shoulders in the middle of a swarm of gently gyrating bodies. When Leelo asked if he wanted one more beer before they left, he nodded and watched her thread her way to the line at the concession stand and wondered how much of him she could really see.

•   •   •   •

The restrooms were on the edge of the rodeo grounds, tucked near the entrance in a low building with rotting slats of wood shielding the fluorescent-bathed interiors from prying eyes. Few people were around as Newell entered; the night had reached that hazy spot where no one new was arriving and anyone still around was staying for a while. The bathroom was empty and shockingly clean: hardly any paper towels had made it to the floor or been left on the sink, and the urinals were free of the usual drunken splatter. Newell's footfalls were loud as he left. His siblings were already on their way to the car.

Something caught Newell's attention as he turned past the side of the building: a hard, strong light, a powerful blue like the richest azurite, echoing from the back. Newell's breathing slowed. He kept walking parallel to the building, following the dirt path leading toward the exit, so as to give himself a wide berth but so he could keep the glow in his periphery. When the path toward the entrance turned he was approaching, from some thirty feet away, the back of the bathrooms. He stopped and took out his phone and pretended to be taking a call, keeping his voice an indistinct, low whisper.

He reminded himself that he alone could see the light, that whoever was giving this off was probably, to the rest of the world, bathed in the convenient rich fudge of Texas night; the back of the building was otherwise hard and black thanks to the angle of the roof and the shadow created by the grounds' sodium lights. But Newell wasn't the rest of the world. He could see.

It was the rodeo clown; Newell recognized his shorts, his clay-caked Carhartt boots, the shredded ends of his button-down shirt. He was kissing the loner from the edge of the dance floor.

Newell felt a jolt that ran from his navel to his throat. His crotch tingled. The loner was pressed up against the back of the building, his hat tilted high to reveal thick waves of black hair. His jaw was relaxed but sharp, his mouth open to receive the clown's tongue. Their glowing hands were pressed against one another's hips, giving off more light than Newell had ever seen. Their entire bodies were revealed to him: the press of their knees against one another, the flex of their forearms as their fingers prodded, the pucker in their cheeks as they kissed.

Newell gave up pretending to be on his phone and simply stared. His knees felt weak. Saliva built up in his throat, which was dry from too much beer. He felt a cough trickling up and did his best to tamp it down. Before it could erupt from his mouth he turned and started walking away, but a hack burst out before he'd made it more than fifteen feet. Newell didn't stop, didn't look back, but he could feel the encompassing light looming behind him like an explosion, a rapid sunrise.

Somewhere up ahead was his family's rental car; he could hear Tommy singing lyrics to the last song he and Angie had danced to. Then his brother's voice faded out and Newell could hear only his own footsteps scratching on the dusty path. But soon they were joined by something else: a voice whispering, "We see you."

The back of Newell's neck tingled. Desert breeze cut at his wind-breaker, and he walked faster.

"We see you!" the voices said. They weren't harsh or angry, instead beckoning, loving and creamy. Still, Newell ran. His legs twitched and darted, faster, faster, ducking around pickup trucks and suvs. The voices kept calling, growing louder and louder. The entire night was turning to a shimmering turquoise. It may have been nothing more than the halide lights illuminating the field where cars were parked, but it may have been the men, calling out for him to join them. Or it may have been the incandescence of Newell's hands, growing and growing, ready to touch something they had never before felt.

Shearing

THE BOYS WERE WAITING WHEN HOLLIS UNLOCKED the door to the barber shop, milling in a cluster by the planter box. Two of the shortest ones sat on the concrete lip, their legs kicking at the brick. As soon as he clicked the lock open, they hopped down and all six came marching in, looking like they'd been pulled from a boarding school, dressed in the same off-the-rack suits, charcoal gray and not quite the right size for any of them. Their jackets were all unbuttoned, revealing identical white Oxford shirts. The four eldest wore ties the shiny red of ripe pomegranate, the two tiny ones matching clip-on bow ties.

"We need haircuts," the eldest said.

Hollis smiled. "You've come to the right place."

The boy, sixteen, maybe seventeen, didn't quite look like the others: he was tan, his skin golden and glowing where the others were pale; though not sickly, they clearly spent their afternoons inside while this boy was either out on a soccer field or playing tennis or swimming. His hair was shaggy and long, unkempt along the ears and back of his neck, the brown strewn with sun blond. They were all clearly brothers, with matching cheekbones and aquiline noses. Even two of the younger ones, who were pudgier than the rest, had the same narrow faces and long necks. Hollis could see the resemblance in their jaws and lips, which were thin on top but plump on the bottom, as if they'd all been injected with a hit of collagen. The red-pink glistened under the barber-shop's fuzzy white lights, matching the sheen of their loafers.

Hollis plucked up the black chair cloth and made a show of snapping it clean, even though it had no hairs on it; he took a lint roller to it every evening when he shut the door behind his last customer just as he'd been taught by his father. The shop had two swiveling, pneumatic seats, but Hollis had long done away with hiring a second barber; he couldn't really afford to pay anyone well enough after his dad's retirement, and benefits were off the table. He'd once tried hiring a hairdresser to attract female cus-tomers, but that had been a nonstarter. Most of his business came from regulars who were willing to wait until he was available, which left whoever he'd brought on spending half their time sit-ting in the seat themselves, flipping through *People* magazine or the *St. Louis Post-Dispatch* or watching daytime court dramas on the television in the corner. It made Hollis feel bad, seeing that, so when the last one had quit—a woman who found a better gig at an upscale salon across town where a shampoo went for twice what Hollis asked—he hadn't replaced her. Now, that seat was filled with paperback books that he read during dead hours in the middle of the week.

"Go on, Robbie," the leader of the pack said, gesturing toward the tiniest of the boys, whose hair was the color of bleached straw. His body was itty-bitty, his shoes too large, and they clomped as he stepped forward. Though his eyes were wet and his face scrunched with the effort of keeping tears at bay, the boy didn't issue any complaints as he climbed into the chair.

"So what'll it be?" Hollis said, both to Robbie and the older boy.

"He just needs a clean-up."

Hollis nodded. The little boy's waxy hair was still short enough that from far away no one would think he needed a trim. But up close, Hollis could see how uneven his hair lay against the sides and back of his head, as if a previous stylist had been drunk or working with one eye shut. He knew that, if he combed the boy's bangs straight down, they would hang like broken piano keys.

Hollis placed a paper collar between the cloth and the boy's shirt. He'd removed his jacket at his older brother's urging, on whose arm it hung like a waiter's towel. The bowtie he clutched in his tiny hands, buried under the chair cloth. While the boy arranged himself in the seat, Hollis debated whether to read him. He hadn't touched someone's head like that in a long time, because it was no longer worth what it cost. But here were six boys he'd never seen before, sitting in an awkward, buzzing silence. The only sound was the hiss of the chair as it raised the crown of Robbie's head toward Hollis's face.

Before he sprayed the boy's hair, he reached out and gently touched Robbie's skull. The hair was soft as qiviut, but Hollis hardly had time to notice. He didn't have to root around in the boy's head at all to uncover the reason they were there; it was floating right at the surface, screaming to be heard. It took all of the concentration Hollis could muster not to gasp.

●   ●   ●   ●

Hollis waited until after he and Dave slept together for the first time to tell him what he could do. They were lying in Dave's bed, the top sheet clinging to their waists. The room glowed from the sodium light affixed to the corner of Dave's apartment building, the fizzy color bleeding through the Venetian blinds. Hollis felt as if he was glowing, too, his heart still thudding from the vigor of their bodies. He was taking in deep gulps of air even though they'd been lying still, shoulders touching, for several minutes. Dave's fingers pressed into his side and he said, "You alive?"

"More than," Hollis said. And then he added, "I want to tell you something." When Dave leaned up on one arm, Hollis cleared his throat. "Actually, do something."

Dave smiled. His teeth were bright white even in the dark. "Didn't we just do something?"

"Something else."

"Oh?" A finger stroked at Hollis's sternum.

"Something weird. Something you won't believe if I say I can do it but don't actually do it. I'm not explaining well."

Dave lay down again. "You know, usually people are nervous before they have sex with someone for the first time, not after." He spread his arms and legs wide, kicking off the sheet. "Do what you wish."

"I just need you to think about something you haven't told me. Something important."

"Okay."

"You're thinking about it?"

"Does it have to be a deep, dark secret?"

Hollis blinked. "Only if you want to share it with me."

"By thinking about it? Can you read my mind?"

"Just wait."

He placed his hands on Dave's head like a priest offering a benediction. Dave had walked into his shop on a lazy Tuesday two months prior, Hollis half fallen into a light sleep during the doldrum hours before kids were out of school and after his few older clients came in before lunch. His father had just stopped working during the week, a signal that he thought Hollis was ready to manage the shop on his own. When Dave sat in the chair, Hollis hadn't read him, but he knew he'd done a good job with the cut; Dave nodded and whistled at himself when Hollis was done trimming Dave's mess of shag into a sharp high and tight. He'd come back three weeks later for a touch-up and asked if Hollis wanted to get a drink that evening after he closed shop. Hollis, feeling his throat go tight, had nodded. For once, he'd skipped the lint roller, instead spending a long time staring at himself in the mirror.

Dave started giggling, so Hollis shushed him and told him to think. The secret came into Hollis's head immediately, but he liked the feel of Dave's thick hair, tangly and damp, beneath his fingers. He could feel the bumps and humps of his skull, the first beady touch of what would later become a benign sebaceous cyst Dave would have removed in a year, not long before they broke up. A scar, too, that Dave hadn't explained, a keloid line hovering above his left ear.

"Your dad left you and your mom for six months," Hollis said. He lifted his hands away from Dave's head. "He came back, but you never forgave him."

Dave sat up, triceps bulging under his body's weight. "How'd you do that?"

Hollis flexed his fingers into claws, then relaxed them. "If I touch your head, I can read your mind."

"But you've touched my head before."

"I don't do it automatically. And I don't really like to."

"Why?"

"Because of what I have to give up."

•   •   •   •

The boys went in age order. The eldest called out their names—Richie, Ronny, Ryan—and then leaned against the window next to the door, arms crossed as he held the sportscoat of whichever brother was in the chair. After the first one, Hollis didn't read them; he didn't need to. He wanted, desperately, to say something consoling, but he couldn't. How would he explain how he knew what he knew?

When it was the time for the second-to-last boy—Roy—to take his turn, he and his brother fought. Roy, clearly, didn't want to get his hair cut. He had a mop and kept shaking his head so it shimmered and danced. He complained that it was his hair, no one else's, and that he should be able to grow it out if that's what he wanted.

"This isn't about you," his brother hissed, grabbing Roy around the bicep. Roy's cheeks had retained their baby fat but also bore the chisel of oncoming adulthood. He was right on the edge. Surely, Hollis thought, the events of today would push him over.

The boys, Hollis knew from reading Robbie, were headed to a funeral. For both of their parents.

Robbie hadn't given up much else, which didn't surprise Hollis. He was too young to be processing their deaths in a linear, conscious way, as if anyone was ever old enough to put such pain into clear, understood order; hell, the quick way his own father had died—pancreatic cancer—was still an inexplicable jumble to Hollis months, years, later. Robbie, like Hollis, wasn't thinking about what had happened to his parents or what he felt about their deaths or what it really meant for his mom and dad not to be alive anymore. He couldn't articulate a narrative that would provide clues, context, details.

Roy slumped low in the chair, the pneumatics wincing at his thrown weight. When Hollis drew the chair cloth over him, Roy didn't move to sit up straight. He stared at his brother, holding his jacket, which Roy had tossed like a newspaper he was finished reading so that his brother had to scramble to catch it before it hit the floor. Roy's tie was the messiest, loose like a noose around his neck.

Hollis cleared his throat and cinched the cloth tight, which was a challenge with the kid sitting at such an angle, body propped on his right elbow. He took his time, careful with the paper collar. Hollis plucked up a comb and his spray bottle and stared at the back of Roy's head, where a complicated cowlick spat out hair in all directions. He looked toward the eldest brother. The entire shop was silent. The younger boys were watching. He wondered if, usually, these silent feuds would have been settled by their parents.

Hollis waited. He was glad his hands were full. Otherwise, as the tension mounted, he may have simply put his fingers to the boy's head, asked in his silent, probing way what he wanted. Be a peacekeeper, no matter what he would give away to do it.

• • • •

"It's not that I forget, exactly," he explained to Dave, who was now willowing his fingers through Hollis's hair. "It's more like things go fuzzy."

"Fuzzy."

"Do you have any memories where you know a thing happened, but the details are light?"

Dave's hand stopped. "Yeah, I guess."

"That's what happens. I know that whatever I can only kind of remember is something I used to be able to remember clearly."

"And you don't get to choose what fades?"

Hollis shook his head. "Like just now, when I read your mind. There's a Thanksgiving where my parents had a horrible fight that I still remember, but I can't remember who said what. I think my mother threw a wine glass, but it might have been the pumpkin pie. I can't quite visualize what she was wearing."

Their bodies had cooled. Hollis needed to pee. He swung his legs out of the bed and Dave said, "Have you done it to me before?"

He was splayed out, his body on full display. Hollis felt like he knew it with a jarring, pulsing intimacy. The biceps, the craters of stomach muscle, the little hairs where Dave's glutes rose like tiny hills.

"No."

Dave wasn't looking at him but at the popcorn ceiling where the fan tilted in lazy circles. "Would I even know?"

"I guess not."

"So you don't need permission."

"No, I don't. But I would always ask."

Dave's fingers went to his mouth as though to suck on an invisible cigarette. He said nothing. Hollis slipped out of the bedroom and into the bathroom, where the overhead light was spongy and hard and glowed like the urine he dumped into the toilet bowl. After flushing, he washed his hands for a long time, letting his fingers sit under the water until they started to prune. He thought about turning up the heat, scalding the tips and his palms, as though he might burn his ability away.

•   •   •   •

The standoff ended when Roy sighed, sat up straight, and waved his arms, saying, "Just do whatever. Make it short." He glared at his brother. "That good enough for you?"

"No mohawks."

"Of course not." Roy turned to Hollis. Up close, Hollis could see he was wearing some kind of eyeliner. "Make me classy, a good American boy. You know." He pointed toward his forehead. "The spikes and all that."

Hollis nodded and got to work. The other boys, he could see, were growing restless, the shortest ones kicking their legs like they were on a swing set. The eldest of those four kept wiping his hand against the back of his neck, as if phantom hairs were still piled against his skin. One of the little ones asked the oldest if he could get some candy from the gum dispenser in the corner. When he was denied by a shake of the head, Hollis, setting down his scissors to grab the electric razor, opened the cash drawer and plucked out a quarter.

"Here," he said, holding it out. "Let him get some. The Mike and Ikes are fresher than they look."

The boys leaned forward in their seats, necks stiff with desire. The oldest brother sighed and stood up straight. "They're not supposed to have sweets."

"Oh, give it a rest, Royal," Roy said. "Who's going to know?"

Hollis froze. All of the boys froze, even the younger ones with their swinging legs.

All eyes went to Royal, who was clenching his jaw; Hollis could see the bones grinding. He felt a pressure in his chest. Part of why he loved cutting hair was that he found peace in it, a simplicity and ease that most other professions couldn't offer. Who got into fights in barbershops? They were where people went for renewal and expulsion: not only could they transform themselves, they could jettison their concerns, blathering and exhorting while the barber snipped and combed and shaved and offered affirmative nods and laughter. Over the years, Hollis had also used his ability to pull a small strand from a customer's head to get them going on whatever matter weighed heaviest on their mind. Despite the price he paid with his own memory, this almost always led to an exorbitant tip and a body that would be back in his seat a month later.

Royal pinched the bridge of his nose and shut his eyes. "Fine," he said. "Whatever. I don't care."

The little boys sprang up, jostling to be the one to get the quarter from Hollis, who gave it to Robbie, his brothers staring at him with hard-edged jealousy.

"Share, now," Hollis said, pointing to the turn-crank machine. He watched them skitter to the far end of the shop, where Robbie dropped the coin into the machine while his brothers stood in edgy anticipation. Hollis turned toward Royal, who was frowning. "I think they'll be okay," he said.

Royal blinked. "Almost done?"

Hollis looked down at Roy. He just needed to finish off the nape of his neck and clean up the sideburns and said so.

"Good," Royal said. "We're kind of on a tight schedule."

Here was his chance. Just say, "Oh?" and let Royal pour out what was clearly bottled up. But instead, Hollis nodded and went back to work.

•   •   •   •

When he'd come back to bed, Dave was still staring at the ceiling.

"I think that maybe you should share something with me."

"Like what?"

"I don't know. A deep, dark secret of your own."

Hollis looked at his hands, still beating from the hot water. "I already told you."

"No," Dave said, rolling onto his side. "You showed me an ability. That's not the same as telling a secret."

"But I've never shared it with anyone else."

"Not even your mom or dad?"

Hollis shook his head.

Dave blinked at him.

"Okay," Hollis said. He took a breath, felt his stomach contort. "You're the first man I've ever had sex with."

"Really?" Dave said, his voice flipping up an octave.

Hollis nodded.

"But you were so good at it."

"Beginner's luck, I guess."

"Huh."

"Is that a bad 'huh' or a good 'huh'?"

"Neither. Just processing."

For several weeks, Dave had slipped into the barbershop while Hollis worked, watching and waiting for him to close up, helping out by sweeping away cut locks and spraying the mirrors with Windex. Then they would find a restaurant or bar and, after their meal, part ways. Until the night Dave cuffed Hollis by the arm and kissed him. Hollis had been desperate until then to read Dave, to figure out what he wanted, but he'd resisted, imagining he would lose the first moment he saw him, when Dave walked through the door, ringed by the miraculous timing of a beam of sunshine slicing in behind him, his hazel eyes wide, his handsome throat long, tendrils of unkempt hair glowing.

Hollis looked at Dave's face in profile, the pointed chin, the slightly squashed nose that he knew had been broken in a messy basketball incident when Dave was fifteen. He found himself walking through all the things he knew about Dave and his body, the scar in his palm from accidentally smashing a glass under his weight when he worked as a busboy in a greasy spoon, the mystery line above his ear. The knots of muscle in his legs from playing water polo and tennis. The smart words that he breathed out thanks to his four years of biology and philosophy classes, neither of which he used now as a financial advisor.

He pressed his hand to Dave's chest and felt the slender beat of his heart there. Dave laid his hand over Hollis's.

"Can you read my mind here, too?"

"No," Hollis said. He tapped a finger in tune to Dave's pulse. "But I don't need to. I can feel plenty."

• • • •

As soon as Hollis swiped the chair cloth away from Roy he was up and out of the seat, mumbling something about waiting outside. He pulled a phone from his pocket and snatched his jacket from his brother, who shuffled aside to let Roy pass. Hollis watched him flop onto the planter box's edge. Royal sighed, squeezed the bridge of his nose, and approached the chair. He paused and pulled off his jacket. When he looked around, finding nowhere to hang it—the one thing Hollis had never invested in was a good coatrack—Hollis held out his hand for it and draped it with care over the books crowding the second chair.

"And for you?" he said after he whapped out the cloth, spilling Roy's hair onto the floor where it mixed up with the sheared bangs and curls of his brothers.

"Cut it all off."

"All of it?"

Royal nodded, running his hand through his hair.

"Yes," he said. "A buzz. Close. A two? That's short, right?"

"It is. Are you sure?"

"I'm sure. Please."

"I'll have to trim it down first," Hollis said. "Just so the clippers don't clog. It'll take a bit."

"That's fine. Please do it."

There was something in Royal's breaking voice, his desperation for Hollis to clip away his long, bouncing hair, that made Hollis purl into his mind when he pressed his thumbs beneath his ears to position his head. It felt like skimming through a book, looking for a page with large print or a picture. Human brains were a flurry of rushing, inchoate sounds, swishing noises that often didn't make much sense unless they were thinking something clearly and immediate.

Royal was thinking about the funeral, which was at 11 a.m. Still an hour and a half away. Beneath that sat an image of his parents, dead on a mortuary slab. Hollis discovered that Royal was the one to make the official identification, a shock to Hollis because, surely, the boy was too young. But there it was: he'd had to look at his mother and father's bruised bodies, the gashes to their foreheads and chests where they'd been clobbered by their car imploding during the accident that took their lives. Hollis felt a wave of sickness and had to let go. He managed, just barely, to remain standing up straight. As he cut Royal's hair, Hollis worked hard to keep his hand steady, his lines clean, even if it didn't really matter: it would all get shorn off eventually. But something about cutting in clear, even strokes felt important.

Suddenly, he couldn't remember how he had lost Dave. He remembered an argument, half a dozen years ago, the sound of Dave's voice crisp as a fresh sheet, but he couldn't put any words to the noise. He could remember the months of distrust, Dave at first joking that Hollis was reading his mind and then believing it, never accepting the truth of Hollis's denials.

He kept Royal facing the mirror and took his time, as if, at some point, as long strings of hair fell to the floor or gathered in his lap, Royal would change his mind about the buzz cut. But the boy remained silent. Behind him, his younger brothers watched their brother's hair disappear. Royal himself seemed to have zoned out, letting Hollis tilt his head left, right, back, forward. When Hollis had his hands on the side of Royal's neck, fingers pressed along the tender meeting of jaw and throat, he pulled more: the moment that Royal had answered his phone, late on the previous Monday. He was lying on a bed in a small, attic-shaped bedroom in shorts and a sleeveless t-shirt, watching television. No, a movie—a movie on television. The image was bright and hard, something Royal had obviously replayed in his mind several times. He was, as far as he knew, the only one still up, his brothers long in bed, their parents out for a date night, Royal in charge of keeping the peace and getting his younger siblings' teeth brushed and beds occupied at a reasonable hour. And then the phone call from the unknown number.

As Hollis finished, he realized he couldn't remember the moment he first read his father. He knew he'd just given his dad a haircut, his first real attempt after his father had spent weeks explaining, demonstrating, talking through technique. Hollis stood behind him, both of them facing the mirror, his father reaching up to feel the back of his head. Hollis, desperate for his dad's approval, had put his hands on the crown of his father's skull without thinking anything except that he wanted to know what was going on in there, and then he knew.

But now he didn't.

He pulled the hair cloth away carefully, as it was dense with spilled locks. His hands were starting to tremble. With a snap of his wrist he sent all that lost sun-blond onto the floor like hundreds of little snakes writhing at his feet. Royal stood immediately and rooted around in his pocket.

"It's fifteen per cut, right?"

Hollis wanted to refuse the money, but he said, "That's right."

Royal produced a small wad of bills that Hollis could see were fresh. He looked from the money to Royal, who, with his bristling corona of short hair, looked like a new person: both older and younger at once. Perhaps that was the point.

"Here," Royal said. "Keep the change."

Hollis took the money, but then saw that it was a pair of hundreds. He swiveled back toward Royal, who was barking orders for his brothers to get up and go while he grabbed his jacket. Their eyes met and the boy raised an eyebrow. His forehead was longer and more prominent than it had been with the flop of surfer hair, the look in his eyes hard and glassy, almost a challenge.

Hollis's mouth was dry. Even though he wanted to say thank you, words wouldn't leave his lips. He watched the boys march out the door, Royal at the back of the pack. Roy, who was still waiting outside, lurched up and nodded at his brother, a sighing bit of truce.

There was a moment at the end, when they were the only two left in the shop, that Hollis thought Royal might say something. He glanced back, but instead of speaking, he stared at Hollis and offered him nothing but a single nod of the head. As if he could read Hollis's mind. As if he knew that they had both changed. That they'd grown both weightier and lighter. That each of them had gotten rid of something important.

We All Yearn for Defenestration

MY BOYFRIEND AND I WERE THIS CLOSE TO FINALLY having sex. We were both in our boxer briefs, and I could feel how hard he was through the fabric. He was lying on his bed, and I was lying on him. While I kissed him at the tender spot under his jaw where blood beat from his brain to his heart and back, he did this thing with his hands where he pressed his fingers into my spine and then drew them out in an arc beneath my scapulae, like he was giving me a deep tissue massage. He let out a sharp groan when my fingers poked into his underwear and felt at the thicket of his pubic hair. His breathing was shallow and hard and throaty. But then he lifted his hands and said, "I need to tell you a thing."

I blinked at him. The lights were off, but the glow from a streetlamp outside his house bled through the blinds. He'd inherited an absurdly chic Craftsman bungalow from his parents, all sharp gables and sloped roofing with huge double-hanging windows in the front sitting room. My boyfriend was just as chic, and the most handsome man I'd ever seen nearly naked: his hair was sandy and thick and always tangled when he met me early in the morning to go jogging. He had pale jade eyes, like most of the color had been scrubbed away by an eraser, and his jaw ended in a pointed, cleft chin. I was convinced, all the time, that I'd seen his face in glossy magazine spreads, but this made him laugh and remind me that he was an English teacher. That's what he called himself—not college professor, but English teacher—which made me want him more.

"A thing?" I said. I propped myself up by my hands, hovering over him.

"If we're going to do this, I kind of need you to do something first. Or during."

"Like what?" I leered at him, trying to make my voice sexy.

"Throw me out the bedroom window."

Some noise sputtered out of me, a horrific combination of a cough, a cry, a laugh.

"Don't worry," he said. "It's not a long fall, and you don't need to push me hard. Just a little nudge. The bushes are thick and soft."

"Is this like a fetish?"

He thought about this, as if the idea hadn't occurred to him. "If that makes it easier to imagine doing it, then yes."

I crawled off him and gestured toward the window. "I guess. Okay."

"Don't worry," he said again, even though I like to think I wasn't acting worried. I wasn't asking questions, even though I probably should have been. "I already took the screen out."

He launched himself off the bed and padded to the window. His lower back was, in my estimation, his best feature, a scooping slide of muscle that cleft into strong butt cheeks. I could tell he used that one machine at the gym where you're on your knees and you push one foot back into a stirrup; he had well-formed upper glutes. I watched him open the window, sending in a spume of chilly night air. He leaned over and pressed his hands to the sill and canted his head out. I didn't move. I liked looking at the lines of his arms and the backs of his shoulders.

"Ready when you are," he said.

"I'm just taking in the view."

"Sooner is better than later."

"Don't you want it to be a surprise? Like, you shouldn't know when I'm going to push you out, right?"

"It's more about the falling than the shoving."

"Will I need to go downstairs and let you in?"

"Well, I'm not hiding a spare key in my underwear."

"All right, all right," I said. "Here goes."

I stepped behind him and put my hands on his back. His skin was still hot from being sandwiched between me and the bedspread.

"You sure we can't fool around more first?"

"The sooner you push me, the sooner we fool around a lot."

"I'm not sure I can do this," I said. "What if you land wrong and you die and I go to jail?"

"I won't die. It's like twelve feet."

"Or what if you're paralyzed and have to use a wheelchair and we never do have sex after all?"

"We never will have sex if you don't push me."

"I really like the way your skin feels," I said, running my hands up to his neck. "And I'm not just saying that."

He peeled one hand from the windowsill and reached around to take mine. "That's sweet. Now will you just push me?"

"I'm not sure if I can. I really, really want to have sex with you, but I don't know if I can do this."

"The two go together. That's how it has to be."

"Couldn't I just push you onto the bed? If you close your eyes, you might not know the difference."

"I'm telling you," he said, sighing, "it's fine. Just do it."

So I did.

I didn't push him very hard, but he wasn't expecting it. I pressed my palms against him as if I was shoving a weight sled that wasn't very heavy. He let out a little noise—I couldn't tell if it was shock, surprise, or pleasure—and out he went. My boyfriend must have helped himself along, because there was no way I gave the push enough gumption to actually send him toppling out the window, but he must have sensed my reticence and realized he was getting the best he could. Down he went, into the darkness. I heard a swoosh, then he called my name.

He was splayed on his back in the sprinter boxwood below, staring up at me. His arms flashed pale in the moonlight.

"Are you dead?" I said.

"No," he said. "Content." He pulled his hands in and fiddled with the elastic band of his underwear. "That was fantastic."

"We haven't done anything yet."

"Open the front door and we will."

I scrambled out of the room, my feet pounding on the hardwood. I nearly tripped and tumbled down the stairs. When I yanked the front door open, my boyfriend was already stepping out of his underwear. Our mouths crashed together and we stumbled, a mess of saliva and hands, back up to his bedroom.

•   •   •   •

"Hang on," he said two nights later. We were at my apartment, and my mouth was on his navel. I was about to unbuckle his belt.

"What?" I said. "What's wrong?"

"You know."

"I do not know," I said, dropping my hands to my sides. I leaned back on my knees. My boyfriend's head lolled back and forth on my pillow.

"We've been over this," he said. "You know what I need."

"Again?" I said. "I thought that was a one-time deal."

He shook his head. "It's an ongoing thing."

"But we're on the third floor. There's no comfy brush to break your fall."

He sighed. "Why don't we just cuddle, then?" He slapped at the space beside him and made a cubby out of his arm. "Come here."

"You really can't manage without falling out a window? How do you jerk off?"

"I need to be thrown, pushed. And I guess I just don't."

I tumbled onto the bed, my head pressed against his shoulder. My boyfriend smelled like vanilla rum; we'd been at a bar, but he'd been drinking beer. His odor was always a mystery, like, apparently, many other things I thought I knew about him but didn't.

"So we just, like, lie here? You don't want to mess around?"

"I do want to. But I'll disappoint you."

I rubbed my eyes with the palms of my hands. "I can't believe this. I can't believe that you can't have sex otherwise."

He kissed me on the cheek, a chaste gesture one saves for a plump aunt. My boyfriend's breath was warm and minty; he chewed lots of gum and had unpacked a spare toothbrush in my bathroom.

"I'm curious," he said.

"Oh?" I wriggled a hand into his underwear, which he promptly extracted. I frowned.

"You've never asked why I need to be thrown out a window."

"Oh. I just assumed it had to do with some kind of traumatic experience when you were younger. Maybe you were abused or something. Or you had homophobic parents who threw you out in a fit of rage when you told them you liked boys."

He laughed. I loved my boyfriend's laugh, the real one. He had several fakes, breathy chuckles that came out as little puffed pockets of air with almost no noise. His real laugh was a sharp bark, a sound he half-swallowed as it came out, as if he was physically incapable of letting the entire thing go. I knew it was real because it sounded too obviously fake to be fake.

"No," he said.

"So then why?"

He shrugged. "I don't actually know."

"Have you tried having sex without first being thrown out a window? Like, ever?"

"The first time I had sex, yeah."

"Tell me how that went." My hand wandered back toward his underwear. When he let me slip one fingertip into the elastic, I added another, and then another, my fingers dipping in all the way to the second knuckle. He had a faraway look on his face, so I just let my hand sit there against the lower curve of his hipbone and the tender edge of his thigh, blipping out nonsense Morse code. If he felt it, or read some message I didn't even know I was delivering, he didn't let on.

He sighed. "Not well. But that might have been because I wasn't attracted to her."

I sat up. "Your first time was with a girl?"

"Wasn't yours?"

"Well, yeah."

"So then?"

"You've just never told me yours was too."

"You hadn't asked."

I swallowed a hard, empty breath. "I guess I hadn't. I'm sorry. I should ask you more things."

"That's okay. I should just tell you."

I pressed all of my fingers into his leg. My boyfriend's skin was shockingly smooth; he claimed that he just didn't have much body hair, which was okay with me. He was slick and feathery, and this appealed to me, aesthetically. His clean-shaven face always reminded me of a Gucci model or a Christian Dior cologne advert. I pulled my hand from his underwear and stroked his chin.

"Maybe I should try it."

"Try what?" he said.

I fluttered my hand toward my window.

My boyfriend sat up and blinked at me. "Are you serious?"

"Maybe not here. Maybe at your place. Maybe from the first floor. Just a little tip backward to see how it feels."

He smiled. He kissed me, hard, his tongue thick and warm in my mouth, glossing my teeth. That was all we did that night, but I fell asleep with my head on his chest, where I could hear everything inside him moving fast.

• • • •

My least favorite question was, "How did you two meet?" I found origin stories boring, and so when my boyfriend, talking about his writing, said the same, I nearly jumped his bones. We were in a coffeeshop, so I didn't, but I said, "Me too!" so loudly the baristas stopped their work pouring lattes and blinked at me. I blinked back and sipped my chai tea before swiveling back to my boyfriend. He wasn't really my boyfriend yet, as we had only gone on a handful of dates and hadn't committed to one another in any way, made no offers of fealty or monogamy, but I was already thinking of him in this way. I was thinking lots of things about him, like how much I wanted to undress him, the fact that his fitted polo shirt was the perfect size on him, revealing his musculature but not in that squeezed-in-a-sausage-casing kind of way. I was sure I'd never seen another person wearing such a perfect green shirt before.

"I try to never write flashbacks," he said.

"Could I read something of yours?" I said.

He turned sheepish; I could tell because his lips curled up on the left side, a tell I'd come to know meant I'd said something that made him uncomfortable. "I could send you a link. They're not published anywhere prestigious."

"But you have a book."

"A short book. It didn't get many reviews."

"I haven't written any books," I said.

"It's not as hard as you think."

"But to write a good book, I bet."

"Definitely harder than you think."

I laughed. He smiled. I sipped my tea and said, "I bet yours is a good book."

•   •   •   •

"Are you sure about this?" my boyfriend said. He set his hands on my bare shoulders.

"Oh yes," I said. "Yes I am." I could hear the lie in my voice and my boyfriend, who told lies for a living (I read his students' papers sometimes when they lay scattered about and regularly questioned his grading scale), could surely hear it. I looked out the window into the dark; I could smell the evergreen trees that lined his house, and I could see the vague blob of the sprinter boxwood below the window; because we were on the first floor, I could reach out and touch the bush if I wanted, but I didn't. My boyfriend had removed the window screen, and it leaned against the wall next to us.

This, I told myself, was nothing. It was hardly a hop. But I had trouble jumping into pools, my brain always wracked by images of cracked skulls and broken ankles. I took a deep breath before prying my fingers off the windowsill and waggling them into the night like a swimmer letting loose any last nerves.

"Okay," I said. "Do it."

"You're positive."

"Yes," I said.

My boyfriend pushed me, hardly a nudge. His fingers were little flashes of heat-pressure.

I didn't move except to rock forward the tiniest bit.

"Harder," I said. I took a deep breath. "I think I might need you to actually launch me out."

"Then duck your head," he said. "I don't want to give you a concussion."

"That's sweet," I said, turning to look at him. We were both in only our underwear, and his body was, somehow, even leaner than it had been just days ago. I wanted to lick him somewhere, anywhere, but I knew that would lead nowhere until this window business was taken care of. I turned back to the window and cantilevered myself out so my head and chest were hanging out over the bush.

And then he shoved me, hard.

My knees scraped the windowsill; I wasn't prepared to hop out, tuck my legs up toward my chest, as my boyfriend would later advise I should have done while he applied hydrogen peroxide to my abraded skin. I toppled forward, yelping, and my hands pressed into the boxwood, the tender flesh of my palms scraping against the scratchy, plasticine buds before my entire body crushed against it. My face scraped against its slanted surface, and I slid down it onto the ground, the bush raking my chest. My knees clopped into the grass.

"Oh jeez," my boyfriend said.

I twisted around, my mouth tinny, and looked up at him without acknowledging the pain throbbing through my entire body.

"I'm fine," I said.

But I was more than that, though I didn't say so. The fall had been short, hardly a blip, a single breath's worth of distance, but something had slid out of me as I toppled onto the boxwood, a little heave of weightlessness crowding in and pushing my fear, my worry, away. I lay on the ground, listening to my boyfriend say he would come out to me. I took in deep inhales of the dewy night air and yearned to fall again, for a longer period, from a higher height. I suddenly understood what my boyfriend wanted.

I heard the front door open, then the slap of my boyfriend's feet as he trundled across the front porch. I saw him vault with immense grace over the porch's side rail. He landed in a crouch, his underwear bunching toward his hips, and then he trotted over to me. When he reached out to help me up, I tugged at his outstretched hand and pulled him down on top of me. The grass was dewy and chilled on my back, but my boyfriend's body was warm like a heated blanket. I held him close, hands wrapped around his back. I pressed my ankles against his calves.

"What are you doing?" he said.

I kissed him and pressed my pelvis toward his.

He whispered my name, his voice breaking. He leaned back, propping himself up with his hands. A cool rush of air slid in between us, and my skin prickled. I reached a hand up and fiddled at his crotch. He let out a hard, dry chuckle and shook his head, but I felt his body press toward mine. His cheeks were flushed, and when his face met mine I could feel their heat. He kissed me hard and ground his hips against me. I felt my breath go flat and shallow, and my legs loosened their vise on his. With my fingers I pried down his underwear. I kissed him hard and said, "Let's do that again."

•　　•　　•　　•

To my surprise, my boyfriend decided that as long as one of us went out the window, everything was fine. We took turns, stripping down to our underwear, one of us leaning out over the bushes below while the other gave a gentle nudge. I learned how to pirouette as I fell, turning back to see my boyfriend just before my body crunched into the hedge. He would stare down at me and I would look up at him, licking my lips and sticking my hand into the band of my underwear. I could see the glossy want in his eyes, and he would scramble down to me. When it was his turn I stayed in the house longer, gazing down at his body piled on the boxwood, stretched out like a hide pulled over a tanner's workbench. His hips did this thing where they cut his body downward at an impossible angle, a sharp line dividing the muscles of his waist and his thighs. On one occasion I snapped a photo of him with my phone and set it as my background before I chased him outside.

The falls left us bruised and scraped; I was always more beat up than him because I still hadn't quite gotten the hang of the graceful landings that he had somehow perfected. Watching his descents was like sitting up close to a diver springing from a platform, but instead of a splash at the end came a rustling thump, my boyfriend's body splayed and stretched on the bushes below, which in its miraculous, helpful way retained its shape and spring despite the pounding of flesh it took every night. And it was every night: I was rarely home anymore, spending all of my evenings with my boyfriend, curling up next to him in the aftermath of sex, letting his alarm rouse us in the morning. Because I worked later in the day than him—he was teaching a class at eight in the morning, claiming that the best students were the early risers—I would lie in his bed and watch him stilt through his morning routine. I'd listen to him whistle as he showered and then shaved, I'd watch him dress and tie his shoes. Then I'd finally get up and retrieve my own clothing from the night before and we would eat bowls of grain cereal in his kitchen, leaning against the sink, and drink a cup of coffee before I went home to shower and also head to campus, where I worked in the library at the reference desk.

"You know," he said, one night as I was settling into my spot at the sill, "you haven't been home in a while."

"I go home every day," I said, leaning out the window. Instead of the pushing weight of his palms, however, I felt the tug of his fingers, yanking on my hips to drag me back inside.

"That's not what I mean," he said. "And I think you know it."

I blinked at my boyfriend. His hair had gotten long, messy, and it washed across his forehead in a thick rake. The look was good on him, though I was constantly brushing his hair from his face, as it crowded at his eyes.

I sat down on the windowsill and let the outside air trickle up and down my spine. My arms buoyed between my legs. I pressed my heels into his carpet. "So what are you suggesting?"

"Live here," he said. "Move in with me."

"Hmm," I said.

"You don't like that idea?"

"I just need to think about it. Come here." I held out my hands. As I'd expected, my boyfriend took them, no questions asked. He was nodding and smiling, a minute version of the Cheshire Cat's grin, as if he knew he'd already won. And he had. We both knew it. We both knew I'd say yes and not renew my lease, and that I would start hauling my things over to his house. I'd get rid of my bed and my couch because his were much nicer, but we'd keep my cast iron skillet and drinking glasses for the same reason. I'd bring the throw rug from my bedroom and we'd settle it in his guest room, which was covered in chilly laminate hardwood. Even though my feet were square on the ground, I felt like I was dropping from a great height.

•   •   •   •

My apartment lease was not up for three months, so I began the migration of my things slowly despite my boyfriend's suggestion that we just get it over with fast. I hated packing, I told him, but the truth was that when I looked at my things in all of their ideal places—I'd lived there for three years, and things were finally settled in their appropriate nooks and cabinets and stationed on the proper side tables and shelves—I had difficulty wrenching them from where they belonged. I started with some clothes, a drawer's worth, mostly because my boyfriend made such a big deal about clearing out space for them in the interim before we hauled my actual bureau to his house, though he also made a shebang about rearranging his bedroom furniture to accommodate my things.

He found me at the reference desk one day, a month into my slow sojourn over (my apartment was now absent most of my wineglasses and my winter clothes, as well as the Gaugin and Monet prints that had decorated my walls; we'd also flubbed our way through transporting my recliner, which was my favorite place to sit, and stuck it in my boyfriend's living room; he insisted it matched his couch, though any fool could see that was a stretch of the imagination). My boyfriend hadn't really visited me since we'd gotten together except for when he brought a class to the library, so his appearance surprised me. He hovered off to the side of the desk while I helped a kid who was bewildered by a research assignment for his anthropology class, pointing out books and articles he might want and imploring him to write down call numbers and titles. When we were finished, I blinked at my boyfriend.

"Hi," he said.

"What's up?"

"I have an idea," he said.

"Okay. Shoot."

"It's a surprise."

"So why are you telling me about it?"

He smiled, crooked and sheepish, a sign that he didn't have a good answer for that. "Just to give you something to look forward to," he said, then waved and walked away. I frowned and watched him leave the library and turn toward the English building, which was across a long expanse of pebbled walkway. I'd have kept staring at him, but a student, struggling to find a book for a psychology project, stepped into my line of view. I smiled at her and asked her to sit down, thwacking the tabletop between us. It took only a few seconds for me to give her the call number for what she needed, but by the time she was gone, so was my boyfriend.

•　　　•　　　•　　　•

"This seems like a bad idea," I said.

We were standing in my now-empty bedroom, which my boyfriend had insisted we clear out. All my clothing had been yanked from its hangers and extricated from its drawers, tossed into laundry baskets he had brought over with him. He'd taken the lead, because when we'd walked into my bedroom I froze and stared at my things, still in the places where they belonged. He muscled by and pulled open my underwear drawer.

"You could decide if there's anything you don't want."

"How would I know if I don't want something?" I said. My mouth felt numb.

"If you haven't worn it in six months, that's probably a good sign."

He straightened my boxers and paired my socks, then arranged my button-down shirts on the bed.

"Is this the surprise?" I said. "It's not a very good one."

"No, this is the precursor to the surprise." When he finished with my clothes, he tossed me his car keys and ordered me to take my clothing over to his place. "Give me twenty minutes," he said.

"To do what?"

"That's the surprise."

I rolled my eyes and picked up the last basketful of clothing, a lump of winter sweaters of which I'd chosen three to give away, partly because the sleeves were too short, and left the apartment. At my boyfriend's house, I set the basket on the living room floor, but instead of unloading them, I wandered. I hadn't ever been in his house—now our house—alone before. I opened all the kitchen cabinets and stared at the pantry's highest and lowest shelves. I traipsed down into the basement, searching for any secret hideaways or evidence that he was a murderous psychopath (all I discovered was the washer and dryer, the water heater, and a box of Christmas decorations amongst a bevy of spiderwebs and furnace filters). In the guest bathroom I scanned the contents of the cabinet below the sink. In his bathroom, the only medicines were off-brand Tylenol and two tubes of Icy Hot. His closet contained no skeletons. My pulse throbbed in my wrists and temples, and I couldn't decide if I was relieved or disappointed.

As I drove back to my apartment, I wondered if my boyfriend had been busy doing the same thing, which didn't make a lot of sense because most of what I owned was already tucked into his house. I pictured my boyfriend's own disappointment to find nothing of interest in my bedroom closet or behind my bathroom mirror (the antidepressants I no longer took regularly but still had a storehouse of I'd already relocated to a safe spot in his master bath's vanity). Did we already know everything deep and dark about one another? What layers were there to still pull back on each other's skin? I imagined a life of no new surprises and felt a clammy sweat break out on my forehead and palms.

I took longer than I should have getting back to my apartment building. Thirty-five minutes had passed, because I sat in my car outside my boyfriend's house staring at its facade, imagining myself decrepit, sitting like a crone in a chair on the front porch, my boyfriend, somehow still youthful and spry, spooning mushy food into my mouth. Or perhaps I was the mobile one, he a babbling mess thanks to a stroke or dementia. It took me five minutes to shake the images from my brain like pesky water trapped in my ear after a swim.

When I pulled up, I didn't at first see what my boyfriend had done; the sun was going down, and everything was turning shadowy and blurred. But I could see a lump of material around the side of the building, so when I got out I walked around the side instead of through the front door.

My mattress and box springs were stacked in the grass.

"I had an idea," I heard my boyfriend yell. He was leaning out my bedroom window. Even though darkness was falling, I could see the glow of his white teeth when he smiled, a wide, proud-of-himself grin.

"You said that before," I said. "You're not thinking what I think you're thinking, are you? It's too far."

"Just come up here," he said, then disappeared inside. A corona of light eked out the window, and I could see a tizzy of bugs bapping around, most of them surely diving into the apartment to take up residence along the baseboards and die.

My apartment door was cracked open, and I pushed it with a closed fist. My heart was thrumming, my mouth watery. My living room still held a few vestiges of my life there, and I took a moment to savor their presence: my end tables, my couch, the television whose new place in the house we hadn't agreed on yet (my boyfriend didn't keep a TV in his bedroom and neither did I—but there wasn't much of a better spot for it in his place).

He called out from my bedroom, so I went. My feet thudded hard on the wood floor. I found him leaning against the wall next to the window. In the time it had taken me to get upstairs, he'd kicked off his shoes and peeled away his socks, leaving them all in a small heap that looked huge in the now-emptied room. I felt stripped and scrubbed.

"I'm not pushing you out the window," I said. "It's just too far."

"Come here," he said, standing up straight and opening his arms in anticipation of, I guess, a hug. I went and let him embrace me. He was tinged with sweat. My boyfriend's perspiration was always citric and sweet, an odor I found appealing rather than distressing or noxious. I took it in, breathing against his neck, his hair tickling my nose.

"I thought we could go out together," he said.

"Are you crazy?"

He let go of me. "Probably. But that's what the mattress is for."

"We could break each other's bones," I said. "We could break the mattress."

"I'll pay for a new one."

"I like that one."

"But you won't be sleeping on it anymore."

I felt a hot tingle in the back of my throat. My boyfriend blinked and smiled at me, his face blossoming with dimples. I wanted to tell him that this was the problem, that everything of mine was being turned away in favor of the things that were his. I could already feel the bruises and scrapes I would suffer from the fall.

My boyfriend nudged at my hips, catching the beltloops of my pants with his fingers and pulling me close. "Come on," he said. "I'll make it worth it."

His breath was hot, his face slick still with the exertion of hauling the mattress down the stairs himself. Without saying a thing, I let him position us in front of the window, which was lower to the ground than the one in his bedroom; we had to crouch awkwardly, knees pinching with heat and discomfort, to be about to lean out. I wanted to ask him what he'd done with the screen that usually kept moths and mosquitos out, but my throat was itchy, dry.

"Ready?" he said, moving his hands to my hips and then my shoulders.

I nodded, even though I wasn't. I glanced around my bedroom, stripped bare. The walls, I noticed, were each painted a slightly different shade of white: eggshell, milk, mother of pearl. How had I never seen this before?

My boyfriend gave my body a tug, and he started to tip out the window. My stomach lurched. I closed my eyes and tried to prepare myself, to convince myself that this would be our best fall yet, that the feeling of suspension and flight would be prolonged. That when we landed, we would be in some new, fantastic place, fastened together at the deepest parts of ourselves. We would never be truly separate. But my body was rigid, my legs resistant. His hands were cupped in mine, our fingers a hard basket of bones. He leaned back, fast, and let himself tumble from the window. He expected me to fall with him, but instead I let out a hard yelp. I didn't let go, though. I held on, and he hung in the air, his fingers gripping mine. I could see the hard flash of his eyes, the wonder and worry as he swayed. My back stretched and pulled as I held on. He said something, but I wasn't listening. I was too busy trying to decide whether to let go or to let myself be dragged out the window. Either way, I thought, I was headed for a crash, a terrible, horrible fall.

Where We Go After

WHEN THEY BEGAN TO VANISH, THE FIRST HOUSES disappeared from the East Coast. A trio: one in Boxborough, another in Portland, Maine, and a third in rural Vermont. Aerial shots of the properties showed barren holes, as if small asteroids had smacked into the earth. Reporters flocked to all three properties, and soon there were close-ups of the craters, where the foundations had been yanked out like teeth pulled from their sockets. The mailboxes were still there, one of them with its flag standing up. The driveways led to nowhere, garages blinkered out of existence. One of the families wasn't home when it happened, on a day trip to Montpelier, but the other two vanished along with their house and cars and possessions. The question: where had they gone? Their cell phones, when called, went straight to voicemail. Water pipes and electricity had been sucked out, pulled like stray hairs tweezed from between eyebrows.

The first thing I thought of, watching coverage on CNN, was my twin sister Sylvia, how she disappeared from her bedroom one Friday night when we were seventeen. How, ten years later, no one had any idea what had happened.

The next day brought another burst of vanishings, these in Montana and Wyoming, farmhouses and a pair of row houses in Laramie that had just been built. The day after that, the Midwest was hit, Nebraska and Wisconsin and Minnesota reporting houses there one day and gone the next. Louisiana made headlines when a landmark plantation home snapped out of existence.

My boyfriend Michael sat in our living room, staring at the television, body cantilevered forward. He held his head in his hands, fingers splayed up his cheeks, stretching his lips into a grim smile. Every few seconds he took a loud breath and leaned back, only to lurch forward again. Michael was tall, a former volleyball player and now a coach—high school girls—and yet his body was compacted and tiny as he watched the news, as if parts of him had been pulled out. The day before the houses started vanishing, he'd proposed to me. We'd been at a bar earlier in the evening, drinking our favorite Schlafly wheat beer, playing shuffleboard with our friends. He asked when we arrived home after one in the morning and I laughed, thinking he was joking. He went to bed angry, even though I tried to apologize. I slept on the couch, chilly in my boxer briefs and a t-shirt although it was autumn and we had turned on the heat. We had not yet talked about it again, and now he was distracted by the houses.

The disappearances set off a flurry of essays, editorials, and poems about what homes meant to people, how places took on their own complexions, became characters in people's lives. In other words, nothing new, except that they now had an edge of fear. Wondering what it would be like to have one's childhood home simply disappear.

Michael insisted that we visit the places we'd lived.

"Who knows," he said, "if we'll ever see them again?"

Even though we'd been together for years and now lived in our own Craftsman bungalow, I had not told him about my sister. He had not met my parents, who had fallen into their own stupor after she vanished. They only lived forty minutes away on the other side of St. Louis, in the western hinterlands of O'Fallon, Missouri, but I never visited. They rarely called, and Michael didn't ask.

He picked up his car keys and jangled them in his hand.

"You mean now?"

He looked toward the television. "Why risk it?"

I followed his gaze to the TV. A featurette on one of the families that had disappeared from the Northeast. "How do you think they put that together so fast?"

"When people want something that badly, they can do it that quickly," he said. I said nothing. I thought of Sylvia, how whenever I got sick, she got sick too. I cleared my throat. All I could do was nod, grab my jacket, and follow Michael outside.

•   •   •   •

Until we were thirteen, Sylvia and I shared a bedroom in the tiny ranch house that was all my parents could afford on their teachers' salaries. When we were six, our parents bought a pair of wooden bunkbeds with thick, wide slats. I was scared to sleep on the top bunk because of the height, but I was also afraid of the bottom bunk, convinced that Sylvia's weight would break the frame and send her crashing down, mattress and all, crushing me to death. Sylvia heard me crying the first night and came down, pressing her hands against my back. We slept in that same bed for six months, until I woke up one morning no longer afraid; I had no idea where my fear had gone, replaced by a lake-still calm. She then took the top bunk, and I would spend many nights listening to the wood groan as she tossed and turned.

Where Sylvia was tall, I was short. We were both spindly, a feature she would retain until the day she vanished, but when we were sophomores, not only did I shoot up six inches seemingly overnight, I discovered the school gym, with its barbells and machines. I spent afternoons amidst the football players and track stars, pumping out Zottman curls and hack squats, and my body bloomed. Sylvia and I looked no more like brother and sister than she and her boyfriend, whom she met as a freshman. He was a junior, but he was nerdy and aloof, a hipster before hipsters were hipsters, and my parents found him nonthreatening.

When our father landed a principal position at a new school, we were able to move into a bigger house, where Sylvia and I each had our own bedroom across the hall from one another. I kept the bunk beds in the hope that, maybe, sometimes, she would knock on my door and want to lie down up there and talk to me. But every night I was left alone, my sister ensconced in her new space, which she filled with framed photos of Zhu Cheng's panda poop sculptures and Dalí prints. She slept on a low platform bed with black sheets, and she painted her nails dark red and bright orange, claiming that clashing color combinations were now in. Her lips were always chapped because she chewed them, not because she was nervous but, I thought, because she suffered a deep hunger for something that no one in our family, even me, could give her.

•　　•　　•　　•

We started at Michael's first apartment, a studio in a building whose lobby was damp and smelled like burnt cheese. Paint was peeling off the walls in layers, like onionskin. Each apartment had two doors: the normal interior door, painted white, and a saloon-style thing that reminded me of the doors on department store fitting rooms. These ended at neck-height, leaving a two-foot gap at the top. I glanced at Michael as he stopped in front of his old apartment, number 214. He shrugged.

"There was a whole thing about creating a breezeway. The air conditioning sucked."

The second-floor hallway was, in fact, cool, thanks to the windows open on either far end. Fall was in the air, and I could smell the wet that hung in the leaves starting to go brown.

Michael knocked.

"Is this weird?" I said.

"No."

"But it will seem weird to the person who lives here."

"Maybe. They'll understand, though."

I took Michael's hand and looked at him. I wished he would smile; his was brilliant and white. He had perfect teeth and dimples and he was able to wink in this suggestive way that was flattering and filling rather than sleazy.

The door opened. He let go of my hand.

"Hi," he said.

The girl was tall, platinum blonde. This was a college town, a dinker with only three or four stoplights and a university for waifs and geeks interested in studying ecocriticism and nematodes and Jack Kerouac and Latin American pottery. We'd driven three hours to get here. My legs still ached.

The girl's body was shielded by the saloon door. Her head was large. She had a horse-shaped face with a long, prominent jaw and I could see her teeth grinding as she stared at us.

"I used to live here," Michael said, using the suave voice he saved for strangers. "We're visiting and were just wondering if I could show him the place real fast."

The girl blinked twice, then reached a hand up to rub gunk from her left eyeball.

"You what?" she said. Her voice was throaty like a smoker's.

"We don't even really need to come inside," I said. "Just poke our heads in. I'm told that the kitchen and bathroom aren't really worth bragging about."

Neither of us explained why we were doing this, though the girl must have been able to tell. The vanishings had been all over the news, on Twitter, the blogosphere.

We all stared at one another in silence for a long moment before the girl fiddled with the latch holding the saloon door shut. Without a word she held it open, and I took it, letting Michael slide in first. I had already decided I wouldn't go past the entry-way. I hadn't told Michael I really didn't want to go to his old apartment, even though I knew this place was important to him. At nineteen, probably the same age as the girl living here now, he had finally lost his virginity in this tiny, dense room with cracked crown molding and carpet thin as a putting green, muddy brown and itchy. Well, not exactly his virginity, which he'd sacrificed—his word—to a cheerleader in high school after his first keg party. No, this was the place he'd brought his first boyfriend.

"Wow," Michael said, looking around. "Your furniture is arranged exactly like mine was."

A desk was wedged against the wall to the immediate left of the door. A hulking desktop computer was surrounded by notebooks and science tomes. A lumpy couch, shredded along the sides by a cat, was pressed against the next wall. Directly beneath the window AC unit was a daybed covered in sheets and shams the color of Pepto-Bismol. A bouquet of heliotropes sat atop a tube-backed television facing the couch and a small coffee table, their scent so assertive that my eyes started to water. While Michael scanned the room, the girl stood in its center, arms crossed.

"You don't think a whole building would disappear, do you?" she said, her voice a combination of fear and annoyance, the kind of frustrated conviction of someone who knows danger is near but is trying to assure themselves that it could never actually encroach on their life directly.

"Houses have gone," Michael said, voice whimsical and distant. "Why not an apartment building?"

"But," I said, "nothing this big has disappeared."

"I know that," the girl said. She frowned and cocked her hip to the left. "None of Missouri's border states have even had anything happen."

"It's not a virus," Michael said. Then his gaze settled on the girl. He was standing in front of me, so I couldn't see it, but I could hear the smile. "Thanks for letting us do this. It means a lot." Then he turned to me. "Ready to go?"

I nodded. I tried to thank the girl, but she turned her back on us. We left in silence, as if she, and we, had vanished.

•　　　•　　　•　　　•

Sylvia disappeared on a Friday night in early November. The air was coiled with that wet, snow-is-coming taste. I'd started going with my friends to our high school football games, standing on the metal bleachers and stomping my feet, joining in chants and cheers, most of which were just noise for the sake of making it. We stood in front of the pep band, who played "Eye of the Tiger" and "The Final Countdown" and, inexplicably, the theme from *The Phantom of the Opera*. We liked to change the lyrics sometimes, transforming "We Will Rock You" to "We Will Fuck You" and "25 or 6 to 4" to "You Will Never Score a Goal" only because "touchdown" didn't fit the beat. As soon as dinner with our parents was over, Sylvia had shut herself in her bedroom, as had become routine for her. We shared a car and, like most weekends, I didn't have to negotiate its use. We kept the keys on a small mahogany side table outside her door in a ceramic bowl, and there they were, ready for me to scoop them up and drive to the game. When I grabbed them, I listened briefly at my sister's door, where light pulsed out from the bottom. I could hear weird, twangy music, something stretchy and psychedelic. I imagined her sitting on the floor in some sutric pose, humming and aligning her chakras. As she got into strange art, she'd become meditative.

I would be asked many times for weeks and weeks if I'd noticed anything wrong with my sister recently. I would try, when answering, not to laugh and say that everything seemed wrong with Sylvia ever since we moved into our new house and she had her own room. We'd been so close, so similar, for so long, and suddenly she'd set herself adrift onto a different plane of existence. Our twinness had become meaningless; all those stories about tight-knit connections between such siblings seemed to have withered away. Where we'd once known exactly what the other was thinking and feeling, we were now like strangers.

When I got home from the game, my cheeks weather-beaten and my body chilly, my parents were already in bed (I'd gone out to a party for a while, but, as I told every police officer I spoke to later, I hadn't had any of the shitty keg beer on offer and I'd slipped home by midnight). The light under my sister's door was still on, but the music had stopped. I thought about knocking and saying hi, but I hadn't done that sort of thing in months, and she'd have just called me a weirdo and not let me in. So I went to bed, unaware that in the morning our family would fall to pieces.

•   •   •   •

We slipped out of the apartment in silence, Michael letting the saloon door slap against the frame. The noise echoed down the empty hall.

When we reached the car, a ten-year-old Ford Focus with manual locks and windows, I said, "Was that true? What you said about the furniture?"

Michael's car smelled good thanks to the apple pie vent clips he bought in bulk. He took a deep breath, and I imagined the warm smell flooding up his nose. "As far as I can remember. Mostly."

"Mostly?"

"It seemed like the right kind of thing to say. To put her at ease. Two strangers, two strange men, wanting to come inside her apartment?"

"This was your idea, not mine."

Michael's phone, sitting on the center console, dinged. He picked it up and swiped. "Holy shit."

"What?"

"The top floor of a dorm at UT-Austin vanished. Like two hundred students are gone."

I felt a sudden heat in my throat and said nothing. Michael shook his head and set the phone down, offering no more details. He put the car in reverse. The lot was tiny and shared space with the post office. He checked the rearview mirror, then hit the gas, swiveling the car with a recklessness one usually saves for video games. But he was a good driver. The wheel listened to him, and the car turned in the exact sharp arc he aimed for.

•   •   •   •

It took a long time for my parents to realize something was wrong. Sylvia had a tendency to sleep in on the weekends, not emerging from her room until the time was well into the double-digits despite my mother's desire for us to all sit down to breakfast together on those days when we weren't dashing about, me and Sylvia vying for space in the hall bathroom to brush our teeth and comb our hair, making sure we had all of our homework in our bags while our father cinched his tie for the third or fourth time (he was terrible at the knots, his sausage-like fingers fumbling with the fabric and never getting them to look tight and clean like you saw in Sears inserts in the newspaper). Our mother spent ten minutes drinking a cup of coffee and reviewing her lesson plans for the morning. They left the house before us once we were old enough to drive ourselves, and I always saw the yearning in my mother's face as she said goodbye. So on Saturdays and Sundays she made gargantuan breakfasts of bacon and eggs and waffles with hot butter, the smells yanking me from my adolescent sleep.

On the day we realized Sylvia was missing, I was bloated with maple syrup and cinnamon rolls—an unexpected late-fall treat that my mother presented while actually humming, her red apron slashed with frosting—when she asked me to check on my sister. Ten o'clock had come and gone, and we were blasting toward lunch territory. Usually, she had padded down by now, looking like a wreck with tangled hair and a too-large t-shirt hanging off her narrow shoulders. I went upstairs and knocked on her door but heard nothing inside. I called her name several times, expecting a groan and a verbal dismissal, but nothing came.

I would long regret going back downstairs and jokingly saying "I think she might be dead" before telling my parents Sylvia wasn't answering. At first, they were annoyed, my father already settled in his recliner to watch Gameday before whatever college football game he had no reason to care about came on. My mother was still finishing the dishes from our breakfast bounty and slapped her hands together in annoyance. It was, I would later note, the final moment of domestic bliss I would ever see in our house.

When neither my mother nor father could convince Sylvia to come out, my father went to the garage and found the keys. One of the odd features of our house was that every door—including the pantry and linen closets—had external keyholes on the knobs and a matching set of keys that he'd found on the work bench left behind in the garage. They were a smattering of tarnished silver, but the labels were legible enough. He came back, me and my mother waiting in the hallway, she begging my sister to open the door, the edge of panic creeping into her voice. I felt queasy, and was barely surprised when my father, knocking one more time, fitted the key into the lock, pushed the door open, and found an open window and an empty bed.

•   •   •   •

Michael made a quick drive-by of the fraternity house where I'd lived for two years. I didn't need to go inside. I could still picture the hardwood floors, the composite photographs hung in the entry-way, the staircases leading up to each second-story wing. When I met Michael, a year after we graduated from the same college with our bachelor's and master's degrees—mine both in English, his undergrad major a dual in history and sports management, his MA in teaching—we realized, after regaling each other with stories of our college selves, that we had been in the same places—bars, party houses, my and several other frat houses—at the same times but unaware of each other's existence. He turned onto the proper street, hidden in a rundown grid of homes several blocks from campus where lower middle-class families lived in ranches with sloping front stoops and peeling paint. Suddenly those ramshackle houses gave way to an avenue with a grass median and two-stories that ballooned wide and deep, cheap vinyl siding replaced with school-house brick and two- and three-car garages. Poplars and cherry trees turned the road into a small oasis of whimsy, and crowning the area was the fraternity house. Michael came to a stop at the edge of the property and we both looked at the house, where the fraternity's letters, two-foot-tall brass monsters, hung above the front porch and shone in the mealy sunlight.

"You sure you don't want to go inside?" I shook my head. I had not been back in years, and everyone inside would be a stranger.

"No," I said. "It's good just knowing it's there." I didn't tell him that I didn't want to revisit the past. That, unlike him, I was okay with any images I held of what had come before fading into dark memory, swirling into uncertainty and shadow. Where he wanted to refresh, I wanted to dampen.

Michael nodded. I thought, in that moment, that I might tell him about Sylvia. How I'd tried, several times, to reconnect with her before she disappeared. That if I hadn't tried to impress her by taking honors English as a junior, the only advanced subject I signed up for in high school on the chance we might be placed in the same class, I might not have picked that major and might not have gotten the job at the community college that led to the end-of-school party where Michael and I met, he a friend of the department chair hosting the bash that brought his college pals, his drinking buddies (including Michael), and his co-workers together in a blur of spiked punch and blistered hot dogs.

I might tell him that yes, I would marry him. I had no reason not to. But I simply couldn't say the words. Then Michael glanced at his phone, even though it hadn't made any noise. Nothing new had disappeared. I was surprised. Things seemed to be going away fast.

•   •   •   •

In the months after Sylvia vanished, I felt like one of the samples we looked at under microscopes in biology, a tiny cellular blob smashed between panes of glass. Everything about my family's life became fair game, detectives rooting through our past and making inquiries into the tiniest red flag. Because we were twins, they seemed certain that Sylvia must have told me something, no matter how much I insisted that we'd drifted apart. They ransacked her bedroom, found nothing that would lead them to any conclusions or suspects, and so my parents became their primary target; the boyfriend Sylvia had nabbed during our freshman year had long been out of the picture, the one piece of the puzzle I was able to provide.

Our classmates were interviewed, and I learned that my sister had this entire other life that no one, at least in our family, knew about. She smoked cigarettes and sometimes sold weed and mushrooms, raking in cash from the desperate stoners. One girl, whom I knew Sylvia had long hated, claimed my sister had driven across the city to Planned Parenthood when she was sixteen to get an abortion.

My father fell into a depressed shell and was put on paid leave, then unpaid leave, then was fired when he could no longer do his job. We sold the house, my parents unable to pay the mortgage and heating bill and continue to make car payments on only my mother's meager salary. The day we had to pack up Sylvia's room, my mother could do nothing but cry, and my father was frozen like a gargoyle on a buttress, so it was left to me to decide what of my sister's we would take with us and what we would leave behind. We were downsizing to a small, two-bedroom apartment, and so I tossed most things into garbage bags, sorted by what was trash and what would be donated. I could think of nothing worth taking with us except for her bed, which I would sleep on. We'd sold the bunk beds on Craigslist.

As we left, my mother cried out, "But she won't know where to go." I thought of many things to say but uttered none of them. I knew that my mother was wrong: Sylvia knew where to go, where she wanted to go, to be. What my mother couldn't see was that it wasn't with us.

• • • •

Michael's list of places to see included his first home in Upstate New York, where he'd lived until he was seven and his father was relocated to Missouri for work.

"But it's okay if we can't make that drive," he'd said with a shrug, though I could hear the wish in his voice.

My list was much shorter. I left off the apartment my parents had stationed us in when my father lost his job, because all I could remember about it was damp walls, cramped bedrooms, and rough carpet. I didn't need to revisit that awful blurry end of my childhood, the closet-sized bedroom where I'd spent the rest of high school, counting down the days until I left for college. If I could have chosen, it would have been the first place I would see dissolve to nothing.

We agreed that, after the drive up to our college stomping grounds, we would swing through St. Louis to each of our childhood homes. As we drove the three hours back from the gray boor that is northern Missouri, Michael outlined our plans. It would be dark by the time we returned home, so we would have to hope that the houses would be around the next day.

"I think the odds are good they'll still be here," I said.

"I'm sure that's what everyone thinks. I'm sure that's what those families who are gone thought. I bet those students in Texas thought they were safe."

"Okay," I said. "Jeez."

I had several chances to tell him about Sylvia. In the past, when we'd talked about our families, I'd said little; I told Michael that I had a strained relationship with my parents, and he was kind enough to leave it alone. During the holidays, we went to his mother and father's house along with his two older brothers and a younger sister, all of whom had spouses and bounties of children that threw themselves across the furniture and scattered toys on the floor. We wore itchy sweaters and drank boozy eggnog. Michael wore a cologne that smelled like pine trees. He settled himself next to me wherever I found a place to sit, and his closeness made me feel warm and loose and like I had lost nothing at all.

The car filled with many silences, the only accompanying sound the thump of the tires and the low whisper of the radio when Michael turned it on as we neared Columbia and could listen to something other than Christian talk shows or country. Michael would hum along to songs he recognized, and when they were over, quiet would descend again. I watched middle

Missouri scroll by, all gun shops and strip malls with questionable buffet-style restaurants. We slid past Fulton, Kingdom City, Warrenton. The miles to St. Louis ticked down, and still I couldn't bring myself to say anything. I kept looking at my hands, imagining a band on my ring finger, and I pantomimed worrying it around my knuckle several times. Michael caught me doing it once, and I actually sat on my hands. I saw him swallow, his Adam's apple waving up and down.

Something hard and cold crawled into my chest as we reached our neighborhood. Michael had glanced at his phone every few miles, waiting and looking for notifications from his news apps of new disappearances. I couldn't tell if he was relieved or disappointed every time he checked. As we came closer to our street, I became convinced that our house, everything we had together, would be gone. By the time we made the final turn, I was sweating and shaky. If Michael noticed, he didn't say anything.

But of course our house was still there. The porch was clean-swept thanks to Michael's daily sojourn with a broom; I had stained and sealed it over the summer, and he had, without a word, taken up the rest of its upkeep.

Michael pulled into the driveway, and I let out a long breath. He glanced at me but didn't ask what was wrong. When he cut the ignition, he popped open his door and was about to pull himself out when I grabbed his arm and said, "Wait." He leaned back in his seat and stared at me. I didn't know what I wanted to say. I had no idea what I should tell him. I glanced at the house, imagining a crater there, what it would mean if everything inside was empty space.

"Yeah?" he said.

My mouth opened and closed. I said nothing. Neither did Michael. Instead we stared at our house, relishing that this, at least and for now, was still here.

There Won't Be Questions

IT STARTS WHEN NIGEL COMES BURSTING INTO Harry's bedroom, where he is finishing precalculus homework. Nigel's face is all fragility and bones, eyes clustered by puffy skin.

"What?" Harry says, shutting his textbook. He stands and Nigel falls against him, letting out staccato sobs that bump against Harry's sternum. Harry leads them both down onto his bed, Nigel unceremoniously crushing Harry's notebook.

"It's Snob," Nigel says. "He's missing."

Snob is the Kunekune pig that Nigel's parents got for him when they took a vacation to Olympia, Washington. Nigel didn't go because it was an anniversary gift from his father to his mother. He stayed at Harry's for fourteen days, a two-week binge of video games, floating in Harry's above-ground pool, eating shaved turkey right out of the plastic deli bag. When Nigel's parents came home with Snob, a little white piglet with splotches of black all over its body, he fell in love. At first Harry had been jealous, because Nigel started spending all of his free time at home, watching the pig toddle among the two dairy cows, three horses, and half-dozen goats on his farm. He sent Harry pictures of Snob curled on the couch, huddled beneath a cow's udder, with his snout pressed into Nigel's armpit.

"What happened?" Harry says.

Nigel shakes his head, his voice gooey. Snot is dribbling down his philtrum, slick and greasy. "He's vanished. I've looked everywhere."

Harry sighs and feels his pulse in his throat. He lets go of Nigel, who slumps but doesn't fall, and goes to his closet. Nigel doesn't ask what he's doing, even though Harry hasn't ever shared what he's about to show him. They've kept, to Harry's knowledge, no other secrets. One night last summer, they told each other their life stories, promising to share every detail they could remember. They lay on Harry's bed, heads cocked toward one another but not touching, so close Harry could smell Nigel's Suave shampoo tinged with cherry blossoms.

But Harry broke the rules. He left out one thing.

He pulls a shoebox, ratty brownish gray, the corners studded with small holes, from a high shelf. He holds it with his palms flat on its sides and sits. Nigel blinks, slurps up some nosy gunk, and says, "What's that?"

Instead of answering his question, Harry says, "Do you have a photo of Snob?"

Nigel nods and pulls his phone from his pocket. He pokes at the screen and then shows it to Harry: a close-up of the pig mid-skitter, dashing across the kitchen, snout raised and glistening in the light. Harry, saying nothing, stares at it, taking in the contours and swatches of black on white.

"Okay," he says.

"What are you doing?" Nigel says.

Harry doesn't answer. He shuts his eyes and sways side to side, not because this is some requisite part of the process but because what he's doing makes him woozy, like he might need to throw up. He feels little prickles along his arms, pleasant dots of itchy touch like when Nigel runs his fingers along Harry's skin.

A heaviness enters the shoebox. Harry opens his eyes. Purple and yellow bursts of light dot his vision.

"Okay."

"Okay what?"

He opens the shoebox, and there sits Snob.

Nigel lets out a funky sound, a screech of joy and release. He snorts as the pig snorts, plucking Snob out of the box with both hands like he's scooping them through sand. Harry gets a whiff of Snob's porcine smell: hay and loam, not so different from Nigel when he's come over after finishing farm chores.

The pig lets out little chuffs of noise as it sniffs at Nigel's forearms and chest. After he's spent a good minute nuzzling Snob, Nigel looks at Harry, eyes shimmering with tears, and says, "How did you do that?"

Harry is still holding the box, its lid open. He runs his thumbs along each of its edges and shuts it. "I don't really know."

"It's like magic."

"Maybe."

Nigel plops the pig down on the carpet and they both watch him waddle around, nose buried in the shag. Harry returns the shoebox to his closet and sits down next to Nigel, who throws himself atop Harry, arms around throat, hips pressing stomach, mouth against jaw. Nigel's breathing is heavy and hitchy like the first time they kissed, when the room was soaked in sweaty nerves. This is how Nigel shows his gratitude; when deeply affected, words leave him, and all he has is the rug of his body to drape in thanks. Harry accepts his silence, and uses his own hands to wrap Nigel up, too, digging into the crags of his upper back where muscle and bone jostle for position, built hard and thick thanks to days of raising hay and hauling firewood and digging post holes.

"Maybe I should take Snob home," Nigel says finally.

Harry detaches himself and nods.

"This is wild. Is it really Snob?"

Harry looks down at the pig. He wishes he could say with certainty that it is, in fact, Snob. That his shoebox has transported the pig from wherever he was to where he is now. But Harry says nothing, simply staring down at Snob until Nigel seems to forget the question, gathers up the pig, and, with a gleeful noise, darts out of Harry's room, not bothering to worry if Harry is following.

●　　　●　　　●　　　●

The other thing Harry doesn't share is the pain.

After Nigel leaves, Harry has to lie down, the anguish in his stomach is so knotting. He knows it will pass, because it has happened before. The first time he brought something back was when he accidentally let Koosh-koosh, the gray kitten his parents adopted right after his mother's nineteen-year-old cat died, slip away when Harry stupidly took the animal out onto the back deck to play. Harry, age ten, had underestimated how fast a blue-eyed ball of gray fluff could be, and when he wasn't paying attention Koosh-koosh caught sight of something in the grass beyond the porch and leapt off. Harry howled and gave chase, but the cat had vanished.

He hid in his room for hours, feeling so sick that he could barely stand. His mother had just bought him new shoes, the empty box sitting atop his dresser, and in a moment of religiosity that jolted from out of nowhere, he found himself saying a silent prayer, hands curled around the box as he tried to breathe. He pictured the cat, its one saggy ear, its tuft of white pubic hair. And then, suddenly, there was a scratching in the box, and Koosh-koosh emerged when Harry opened it.

There followed a sudden bludgeon of pain, as if a pair of steely hands was working its way along his intestinal tract, squeezing and pressing and stirring. He lay on his bed for an hour, gasping in tiny breaths of air until the pain dissipated as quickly as it had come on. Koosh-koosh scratched at his bed skirt and meowed for food.

Now, after retrieving Snob, Harry has to spend an hour with knives in his gut. A small price, he tells himself. His parents do not ask about these pains because Harry has kept them a secret, never sharing the burden that he bears for the sake of the saving he is capable of.

A day later, Nigel is back. He greets Harry with a deep, long kiss, his hands pulling their bodies together. Nigel smells faintly of sweat, a cloying scent that mixes with something oceanic smeared under his arms, covering up the sweet-sour smell of hay and manure that follows him in whispered puffs no matter how much he scrubs at his skin. His body is light and glowing and when he takes Harry's hand and leads the way into Harry's bedroom, Harry thinks: *this is it.* All they've done is kiss, so much kissing that often his lips feel bruised, plumped from the pressure and suck. He's ready for more, but Nigel always pulls away before things can press further. Harry knows this shouldn't upset him—everyone at their own pace—but he's tired of being left yearning and tight.

When they reach Harry's bedroom, Nigel asks him to get out the shoebox.

"Look," he says, pulling a flyer from his pocket. It's a *Lost Pet* sign, ripped from some telephone pole or bulletin board. The picture is of a parakeet, its plumage long and rainforest green, the beak a curved yellow scythe.

Harry takes the flyer and smooths it along his thigh.

"There's a reward," Nigel says, licking his lips and curling his hands together, as if he's slathering on lotion. "So I thought you could, you know." He makes a wriggling motion with his fingers. "Do whatever you did for Snob."

Something plugs Harry's throat. He can already feel the pain surging in his stomach. Even though he doesn't want to do this, he knows that he will.

"How will we explain finding it?"

Nigel shrugs. "People who've lost things don't care how they get them back." He takes the flyer. "There won't be questions, you know? Just happiness."

Harry feels Nigel's eyes on him, probing and wanting and anticipating, so he pulls the box from the closet and sits. He puts his hands on the sides of the box and braces himself for the queasy pain. He tilts his head toward the flyer, and Nigel holds it up like he's a model gesturing toward a car on a game show. While Harry looks it over, he feels the world tilting and turning. Sweat pearls on the back of his neck. He tastes tin and tree bark, then the slightest shift in the atmosphere. He removes his hands from the box.

"It's in there?"

"Be careful," Harry says. The bird is noiseless as he opens the box. It's lying on its side, one big black eye staring up, unblinking.

"It's perfect," Nigel says. He rubs Harry's back, an absent-minded circle.

"What now?"

"Do you have a spare box? We can take it to the owners."

Harry mumbles something about checking the basement, where his parents keep every box they've ever acquired. Nigel rushes out of the room. Harry doesn't follow, not just because of the bird but because the pain is already arriving, a knot of nausea in his gut. The bird rustles its feathers, lets out a small huff of noise. Harry blinks at it and says, "You and me both."

●   ●   ●   ●

Nigel keeps an eye out at the grocery stores and intersections, where people staple their worried signs to utility poles. He brings

Harry a fresh flyer every few weeks because, according to Nigel, they would draw suspicion if they were finding people's pets every day.

"We don't want to be accused of something," Nigel says after Harry hands him a guinea pig. Harry nods and lies down after Nigel leaves, throwing his arm over his eyes. The pain causes his hips to growl and his temples to throb.

He brings back lizards and kittens and chihuahuas. He finds gerbils and hermit crabs and two African parrots. Nigel shows him a flyer seeking a lost husky, and Harry shakes his head.

"Too big."

"How do you know? Have you ever tried?"

Harry opens the empty shoebox. "How would a husky fit in here?"

"Are you sure it has to be that box?"

"It's only ever been this."

Nigel blinks. "Maybe it's not the box. Maybe it's you."

Harry says nothing, but he thinks of all the toys and possessions that have vanished in the past: his favorite G.I. Joe figurine that disappeared during the move from his first home to this one, Harry inconsolable no matter how many offers of replacement his parents made; homework assignments he finished but then couldn't find in his backpack when he arrived in math or science class, as if his folders and the zippered compartments were Venus flytraps that digested worksheets; the ink pen he bought at Cape Canaveral when he was eight, his first solo purchase, egregiously overpriced for a plastic writing utensil shaped like a rocket. It disappeared under a desk or behind a bookshelf and no matter how much he willed or wished, it had never come back.

"I don't think it's me," he says.

"Well, why don't we find out?"

Harry exhales.

They traipse into the basement, an unfinished square of cement and cobwebs and bare lightbulbs. The only furniture is a single moth-eaten couch and a dust-covered coffee table. Boxes are stuffed with old, untouched books, Christmas ornaments, wooden tennis racquets, and croquet wickets. Nigel walks a lap around the room, touching box after box until he finds one that is nearly empty. Harry watches as he dumps out the contents—a pair of old blankets, once white and now yellowed like smokers' teeth—and sets it on the table. He sits on the couch, beckoning for Harry to join him.

"The husky," Nigel says when Harry is seated. He holds out the flyer.

Harry takes a deep breath. The basement smells like forgotten things, decaying wood, a hint of tepid, standing swamp water. Nigel is leaning forward, the flyer droopy.

"The box isn't shut," Harry says.

"So?"

"I feel like it needs to be closed."

Rather than close it, Nigel envelops Harry in a hug. "Don't be scared of this," he says.

Harry isn't sure that what he's feeling is fear. The sensation in his stomach is like when he rides roller coasters, his heart thumping hard as the car reaches the first, highest peak and he can see what feels like the entire world, the horizon line curved and blurry, followed by the sensation of the drop, the bunching of his organs as they float upward, defying gravity for just a second before flying down, down, down toward the asphalt and generators and shiny water in ubiquitous decorative lagoons.

"I'm fine," he says. He's not sure where on the coaster he is.

Nigel takes the box's two top flaps in his hands and presses them closed.

"Do you think it's okay that I'm touching it, too?"

"I guess there's only one way to find out." Harry places his hands on the sides of the box.

After the third or fourth animal—a hedgehog, which trembled and balled itself up in Nigel's hands—Nigel asked what Harry thought about in order to bring the animals back. For a long time he didn't answer, because he didn't, and still doesn't, have words to describe what happens in his head. Is it meditation, focus? Prayer? Visualization, maybe? The animals appear so quickly that, in reality, he's pretty sure he hardly has to think at all, so long as he's been imagining the animal in the moments just before.

The pain hits Harry suddenly and fast, twin drill bits boring into his midsection. He's not expecting it: this is worse, hotter and wider and sooner than ever before. His hands fall off the box and a noise wrenches itself from his throat. All he can see is white, his eyes blurring with tears.

"Harry?" Nigel says, then says it again, confusion transformed to fear. But Harry says nothing because his jaw is locked like a steel trap. He falls back onto the sofa and rolls onto his side, the liquid pain dribbling up into his chest, flaring out like fire spreading across a lake of tarry oil. He groans, and his head falls into Nigel's lap.

Nigel places his hands on Harry's cheeks. "What's happening, Harry?" But Harry can't answer. He starts crying.

Neither of them pays attention to the baying and scuffling coming from the box.

•   •   •   •

"Why didn't you tell me?"

"I thought it would sound like an excuse not to do it."

"That's absurd. You should have told me."

Harry says nothing. He inhales, pulling in the smell of his own unwashed hair trapped in the fabric of his pillowcase. He hasn't moved for twenty minutes, the effort of getting upstairs leaving him sapped and shredded. The pain is still shooting up and down his body, and he can't bring himself to tell Nigel that the way he's massaging Harry's temples and scalp isn't helping any.

The dog, posted on the floor, lets out a small whine and shakes its head.

"How do I make it better?" Nigel says. His voice is close to Harry's head; he's climbed up onto the bed, straddling Harry. Through the pain, Harry feels a wave of brief pleasure, more at Nigel's nearness than anything else.

"Kiss me," Harry mumbles.

"What's that?"

"Kiss me," he says louder.

"Your face is kind of hard to reach."

Harry flops a hand toward the back of his neck. Nigel gets the message, because Harry feels his lips brush against the base of his skull, which sends tingling waves down his body, fighting against the electric hurt in his nerves. The drilling is reduced to an ache, ripples in the surface of water upset by a stone.

"Does that help?" Nigel says. Harry nods.

Nigel's lips fiddle with Harry's ear, and he moans, lifts his hips up and then back down. Nigel's hands are pressing directly against his skin on either side of his spine. His palms are warm like a pair of irons getting ready to push the wrinkles out of fabric. His tongue is doing something to the tender spot at the juncture of Harry's neck and jaw.

Harry turns over, the pain going blinding for a moment before settling back down.

"Feeling better?" Nigel says.

"You're helping."

Nigel, whose hands hover at Harry's waist, lets out a stuttering breath. Nigel's face is twisted in something like concentration. Harry takes Nigel's wrists in his hands and feels the blood beat through the delicate veins wrapped around his fragile, birdlike radii and ulnae, the scaphoid and lunate bones little precious marbles rolling beneath the skin.

Rubbing at each of Nigel's palms, Harry says, "We don't have to do anything you're not ready for." His heart feels like a steel bowl being jarred and clanged.

He sees Nigel swallow, hard, shake his head, and lean away, tossing himself down next to Harry on the bed, left leg arcing over Harry's body like a tiny comet before thumping down on the bedspread. The dog whinnies like a tiny horse.

Nigel rubs his eyes. "I just don't know what I'm doing."

"I don't think anyone does."

"I'm sorry."

"Don't be."

Nigel gets up, and, at Harry's direction, finds an old leash in the garage and manages to hook it around the dog's neck. He asks if Harry wants to come with him to claim the reward, but Harry begs off, citing his still-fiery back and stomach. When he hears the front door shut, Harry forces himself out of his bed so he can watch. The dog leaps up into Nigel's back seat and Nigel goes around the front of the car without a glance toward Harry's window. Harry watches the car disappear, carrying exhaust and heat in its wake.

•   •   •   •

Nigel doesn't bring any more flyers for a while. He comes to Harry's house and they watch television, or they play video games, flaying one another, dousing the screen in pixelated blood and flashy gunfire. Although Harry's stomach hasn't hurt for a while, the rest of him blazes with an ache, a longing that feels like hard tendrils blasting through his fingers, elbows, knees, groin.

Then, one night, they drive to their favorite fast-food joint, where the chicken comes in red plastic baskets, the French fries shimmering with oil, sides of coleslaw brimming with oozy mayonnaise that Harry trades to Nigel for half of his Texas toast. Nigel's car smells like soil and grass, a field of clover, his farm life inescapable. It reminds Harry of summer and the outdoors. While they wait in line, Nigel reaches into the pocket of his jean jacket—he wasn't sure about it, but Harry likes it, says it makes his eyes shine—and extracts a folded piece of paper.

"What's this?" Harry says, even though he knows.

Or, he thinks he does. Nigel unfolds it, nosing the car forward with one hand as a car at the front of the line completes its order.

It isn't a pet. No missing cockatoo or poodle or calico kitten. A girl stares forward, eyes vacant, hair disheveled, cheeks puffy, maybe bruises or drugs or something. It's hard for Harry to tell because the picture is black and white and fuzzy. The word MISSING leaps out at him like a scream.

"Nigel," he says.

"One last time," Nigel says. He hands the paper to Harry, who smooths it along his thighs. "I know how it hurts you. But look at the reward."

The money is a lot. More than Harry can imagine, even though he knows there are people with that much.

"We could do anything," Nigel says, looking out through the windshield.

Harry can see the restaurant's interior past Nigel. The lights are bright; he can practically hear their fluorescent buzz. The leatherette booths are packed with teenagers and families dunking strips of greasy breaded chicken into paper cups full of ketchup and honey mustard. He watches a kid, maybe nine or ten, refilling a cup at the soda machine. Harry can hear the whir, the flow, the whoosh. It takes him a moment, until his angle of vision is cut off as Nigel pulls forward, to recognize the beat of his own heart.

"We can't do this, Nigel."

"Why not?"

"How would we explain?"

"I've told you. People don't expect answers. They won't ask."

"But pets can't talk. People can."

Nigel's jaw clenches; Harry can see the shifting bones in the reflected silver of the headlights. Everything is illuminated just enough and nearly not enough. Harry looks at Nigel's hands gripping the wheel at ten and two, the skin on his knuckles stretched over the bones like hard plastic. Harry yearns to reach out and touch those calcified nubs, but he sits on his hands, his ischium bones grinding against his fingers. The night is cool enough, but the windows are up, and the interior is sour. Harry feels sweat break out on the back of his neck, little angry beads. He wishes he had the shoebox so he could conjure something up. He's not sure what. Maybe a bird. Maybe a kitten. Another copy of Snob.

They reach the front of the line. Nigel lowers the window and a voice comes crackling from the drive-thru speaker.

"We need a second," Nigel says. He looks at Harry, who doesn't say anything. He paws his fingers at the edges of the flyer, then starts folding it. Without a word, he hands it back to Nigel, who slips it into his pocket. Nigel orders a couple of meals, which fill the car with the smell of peanut oil and hot potatoes when they receive them a few minutes later. He hands the bag to Harry, who lets the ambient warmth pulsing through the Styrofoam coat his legs, press past his skin and into his muscles and bones. He shuts his eyes.

When they reach Harry's house, they sit for a long moment. Finally, Nigel says, "Sorry. I shouldn't have asked."

"It's okay."

"It was a stupid idea."

"Not necessarily."

Nigel shakes his head. "I just thought, you know. The money. There are so many things we could do."

"Yeah."

"Places to go."

"Uh-huh."

"We could be anything. Anyone. Do anything."

"Do anyone," Harry says, smiling, but Nigel doesn't laugh.

Another long silence lingers. A car drives by, tires whuffing across the cracks in the concrete. The interior is washed in the white of headlights and then tumbled by red as the car slows at the stop sign at the end of Harry's street.

Nigel releases a long breath. "I don't think I'm hungry."

"Me neither," Harry says, praying that his gut doesn't rumble, doesn't give away just how starved he is.

•　　　•　　　•　　　•

Harry lumps around his house, dragging his feet from his bed to the living room sofa. His body feels like it's skewered through with splinters. Nigel doesn't come over for weeks. Yearning burrows through Harry's bones. He tries sending a text or two, short, simple feelers: *Hey* and *What are you doing tonight?* They go unanswered. Harry rolls through the conversation in Nigel's car over and over, trying to imagine what he could have said differently. He could have—should have—told Nigel that it was okay, it was fine. That they could stay as they were. Or go back, way back to before that Christmas break when he and Nigel managed to sneak a bottle of peppermint schnapps from the supply that his parents kept in the back of the pantry for spiking hot cocoa and drank the whole thing. Harry's bedroom went spinning, his sheets and mattress extra-pliant as they stared at the ceiling and giggled, Nigel's breath like a pine forest, the skin at his neck releasing the rich savor of a barn loft. How they'd glanced at each other like they were in a romantic comedy and the next day Harry wouldn't be sure which of them had initiated the kiss, a slow, careful experiment. They'd spent the night curled up next to each other, fully clothed, because they both passed out before they could so much as pull off their shoes. In the morning, Harry, his entire body feeling slicked by a hard shellac, woke with the memory of the kiss fresh on his tingly lips. He watched as Nigel slowly came to life, their heads still close together. The first thing Nigel did was smile, then frown and moan about his headache. He rushed to the bathroom but made no noise, coming back five minutes later. Nigel hovered over Harry and, despite both suffering odious morning breath, kissed him again: light, breezy, gentle.

And that had been that.

Despite the tightness that has settled in his chest, Harry's parents don't seem to notice anything awry; they make happy quips about the impending school year—senior year!—and applications for college and dates for prom and all those jocular, glorious things that should excite him. But all Harry can hear is squawking, is mewling, is the shuffle of claws and talons. One afternoon he walks through his neighborhood and yanks down every lost animal flyer he can find. His fingers are sliced with papercuts and splinters, little ouchies that he welcomes. He brings the flyers home and leaves them on his dresser in a messy heap while he soaks his weathered hands under the tap, letting the bubbly stream of water ice into all the nicks and divots. He douses his palms with hydrogen peroxide and takes in a stilted breath when it stings his fingertips. His teeth hum, his vision whitens.

He pictures the girl, how wide and lost her eyes were. He imagines bringing her back, transforming her into the most radiant version of herself he could make. He would bring brightness. Joy. He pictures her family gathered around her, hugging and happy in reunion.

And then he knows what he'll do.

Harry's feet slip-slide down the basement stairs. He finds the large box sitting on the table, its sides crinkled with moisture and humidity. He peers inside and takes a deep breath. Then he shuts the box, keeping it closed by folding the flaps under one another. A small, squarish hole sits in the box's center, but he doesn't think that matters.

He puts his hands on the box and pictures Nigel.

Nigel in the good pair of skinny jeans that show off the dimpling growth of his thighs. Nigel with his hair freshly cut, when it looks best, out of the way of his ears and not blocking his eyes. Nigel's arms, sun-blotched and darkened from working on the farm. Nigel holding Snob—no, Nigel holding Harry, his fingers long and elegant and exploratory.

Nigel who wants Harry. Nigel desperate to touch and tug and kiss and hold and lick and tumble and dive and sigh. Harry imagines the two of them on his bed, clothes shed, stomachs flashing with grids of musculature and vein. He pictures sprouts of body hair drizzling from navels and groins. He pictures the glint of hipbones and obliques, pointed striation aiming dead-center.

Harry keeps his eyes closed for a long time. His hands pulse on the box. He feels a knot of pain, one that blooms with gusto, curving outward like a flaming spider web burning against his skin. His fingers tingle with the last memory he has of touching Nigel, of gripping his wrists, feeling the knobby bones. As the pain flares to new heights, Harry squeezes his eyes shut and concentrates on Nigel's hands, his face, his breath. Harry is seized by new hurt, and he feels like he's about to topple over and crush the box with his weight. He gulps in air and tries to steady his hands, which are shaking against the box's sides.

And then, a sudden quiet. He lets go of the box, but he doesn't open it. The basement has a single high window, cut to reveal the stumps of grass in the side yard. Through the thick glass he can hear the tweeting noises of birds, the shake and rattle of a hefty afternoon breeze. And then those, too, disappear. Everything seems to disappear, including the basement's subterranean smell. As Harry stares at the box, his nostrils flood with a new smell: vegetal rot, potatoes and cabbage that have oozed in the sun. Harry coughs. His eyes water. The pain is pooling in his toes, burning behind his eyes. The box releases a noise: the scrabble of fingers, something clawing to escape. The heat in his skin transforms into a slick sheet of ice. What is inside? He remembers what Nigel said about questions and answers and explanations and knows, as his body goes clammy, that he has called forth something that he cannot put back, that he has chased something lost that no amount of seeking will ever find. That he will owe this Nigel answers, because as soon as he pulls open the box, questions will spill out, endless and insensate.

How I Know You're Here

WHEN RILEY'S DAD HITS HIM, HE FLEES HIS HOUSE and comes to mine. I pull a roll of wax paper from the pantry and tear off a strip while he removes his shirt. The spot where his father's fist has bitten into his chest is a bright orange splash the color of Tang. I can still see whispers of the salt-and-pepper mark from the last time, a circle of disappearing snowmelt that crosses over his belly button: the edge of a roll of duct tape Riley's dad threw at him like he was tossing a fastball from a pitcher's mound. And around his arm, a nearly invisible ring of faded forest green from the time two weeks ago his dad cuffed him too hard when Riley tried to slip away while being screamed at for accidentally burning a frozen pizza.

I document this evidence, these marks that capture Riley's hurts like brushes of psychedelic paint, kaleidoscopic scars that I alone see. I push the wax paper against his skin, the orange standing out against the ruddiness of Riley's chest so I can trace the bright splotch with a grease pencil. Riley's breathing is slow and careful, and the expansion of his lungs doesn't disturb my ability to trace. I prop up the paper with my left hand and can feel his body heat in my fingers. Sometimes it feels like my lips are going to burn when we kiss. But I never wince or pull away.

We sit cross-legged while I color in the splatter, which looks like the burst from a water balloon, four plum-shaped spots more intense in color than the rest: his dad's knuckles. I unfurl my pastel set and we both look down, scanning for the right shade, and point at the same tangerine at the same time. This makes him laugh, a dry, angry noise. My room smells of my mother's perfume, heavy with carnations and something sandy, a hint of balsa. Riley inhales and leans back into a prone position while I fill in the color on the wax paper. His jeans slip low, his hip bones a bowl around the tight muscles of his midsection. My mouth feels watery. I want to touch him, but I need to finish this first.

When I'm done, I hold the drawing out to him. He takes it with both hands, one at either edge, fingers pinching it like clothespins holding up a sweater. His face is blurred by the orange mess, but I can see the purse of his lips. He never offers a word of approval or disdain. After staring at it for a minute he sets the drawing on my nightstand and then leaps upon me, his weight heavy and welcome. If providing him reminders of the hurts he suffers is the price I must pay to feel his body atop mine, it is an expense I will shell out forever.

●　　●　　●　　●

Other times, when Riley's father is sober or has gone off on a bender, I go to his house. I wear some junky t-shirt I've bought at Goodwill and let him cut it off me. He likes this, he says: the noise of the swishy scissors, the chirr of separating fabric, the appearance of my skin like an unexpected gift. The lower jaw of the scissors grazes my stomach, my solar plexus, my sternum, the sharp points whisking near my Adam's apple. Riley straddles me, his knees suctioned around my hips, one hand punched into his sheets near my right arm pit, the other pushing the scissors. When he's done he lets the fabric hang there and looks at me. I look back at him, and we don't share any words until his fingers tickle at my belly button and I can't help but wriggle and laugh.

"What's the matter, Ben?" he says when he drops the scissors on the floor so he can poke at me with both hands. When I snort and grab for his fingers, he tries to pin me. We roll and roll, and I'm dizzy fast. His hair smells of Pert shampoo, and it's thick when I run my hand through it. His crooked nose is straight, up close.

When we're breathing hard, we stop. I peel off the t-shirt and he pins it to the sheet of corkboard he's mounted above his bed. If his father hasn't been around for a while, hasn't had occasion to charge into Riley's room and rip down all the evidence of things he refuses to see, the shirt joins several others, fabrics destroyed at Riley's hand. They give him something to take control over. That's why I let him cut them. That's why I let him win when we roll around and try to exert the force inside our muscles upon one another. I know he's jealous that my parents don't care, that sometimes when Riley comes over for dinner I'm willing to fish-hook my fingers around his beneath the table without a worry that they'll catch sight and say something. They saw us, once, when we were walking home from school. I'd let my fingers get caught up in his and when we turned the corner onto my street there they were, unpacking groceries, my father's arms snuggling a trio of paper bags. I could see the highest fringes of cilantro sticking out, obscuring half of his face. Riley tried to yank his hand away, but I held it tight, and he looked at me and I tried to smile. My father waved and asked for some help, scanning us with squinted eyes. His gaze landed on our braided hands, and he said that if we moved fast enough he'd let us gorge on the gallon of ice cream he'd bought.

"They're almost too nice," Riley said once.

"Too nice?" We were in his bedroom. He was tacking up a fresh shirt. Riley had opened his window, and gusty spring air was flowing inside. My skin prickled.

"Like cakes that are too sweet or have too much icing."

I didn't argue, because I knew this was something Riley needed to say, even if it wasn't something he really felt. When he was done tacking up the shirt, he didn't mention it again. Instead he gave me a thorough stare and said, "Well?" and then started taking off his clothes.

• • • •

My mother thinks I don't know that she sits in my bedroom when I'm not home. She doesn't rummage; I would know that, too. I spent my childhood taking meticulous care of my things, hiding magazines I pilfered, clearing my internet search history on the family computer, stacking t-shirts over my journals in a precise order, invisible pecks of paper stuck in the stacks so I'd know if they were disturbed. I lined my shoes up against my closet door in particular pointed patterns that my mother would never be able to replicate exactly if she shoved them out of the way to search. They were never once out of place.

I can picture her while I'm at school, her Chanel perfume filling my room. Her hands glide across my Egyptian cotton sheets, smoothing down the bumps I leave when I make my bed in the morning. She leans back and smells my pillow—smells Riley, smells me—and holds my scent in her lungs. She stares at my popcorn ceiling, where glow-in-the-dark stars I tacked up there when I was twelve still illuminate the dark at the end of each day. At first, I wanted to form real constellations, but I gave up after I kept forgetting what the Big Dipper needed to look like. Riley, one night, said he liked them better in scattered, random formation.

"The way they're organized in real life is just dumb luck anyway," he said. His arm was over my shoulder, thumb padding at the back of my head near my left ear. He was like a blanket, heavy and quilted. "Some stars are lucky to fit together, others are unlucky enough to be alone." He took a deep breath. "Your pillow smells like your mom."

"I know."

I expected him to say I was lucky, but he said nothing else. Soon enough, he was asleep.

•   •   •   •

I sit on chilly bleachers, the cold seeping through my khakis. The wind is whippy but the sun is bright, bathing the soccer players in a glow that has absorbed into their skinny arms and strong legs. It's not hard for me to pick out Riley not only because he has the ball so often but because an aquamarine stripe runs up his right thigh from where his father slapped at him with his belt just two days ago, beaming across the field like a nightlight pushing through darkness.

The stands are full; the team is undefeated with only three games before district playoffs. Riley is the leading scorer. In real life, he walks slowly, canting forward like he's balanced on stilts. His gait is forgetful, plodding, and he turns in small circles regularly, as if he's completely lost track of where he's going or what he wants. But on the pitch, he's like a gazelle on a savannah driving away from some predator ready to suck the meat off his ribs. His feet blur, the blue emanating like a glowstick twirling at a rave. When he possesses the ball, he maneuvers it down the field like an extension of his body. He has scored at least once in every game; somewhere in the crowd are scouts from Stanford, UNC, Southern Methodist, all waiting for him to announce where he'll go when we graduate.

He scores, and the crowd around me erupts. The bleachers shake, the rattle echoing in my teeth. I stand and clap too, looking for Riley, who is caught in the center of a scrum of teammates who are grabbing at his jersey, tousling his sweaty hair. Through the forest of legs, I can see small blips of his blue stripe, as though I'm looking at a neon sign flickering on and off. When the players reset, I keep staring at him, wondering if he'll look my way. But this is the soccer field, the world where Riley forgets everything outside the painted white lines, me included.

•　　•　　•　　•

His mother sends birthday cards to my house because she knows Riley's dad will tear them open and pluck out any cash or checks. She also doesn't want him to know where she is. Riley sees her once in a while. He tells me she apologizes for not being there, but she can't afford to take care of him. When he says that his father isn't in any condition to do it either, she bites her lip, sometimes so hard she starts to bleed, and Riley feels queasy.

"I shouldn't be made to feel guilty for that," he says.

"No," I say. "You shouldn't."

He comes to our house for Thanksgiving, and as a surprise his mom appears, ringing the doorbell right before we sit down to eat. The way my mother says, "I wonder who that could be," tells me she's arranged this. Riley squeezes my hand beneath the table, hard, his foot pressing down on mine so my arch aches.

"It's fine," I tell him. His eyes are wide as ping pong balls. His face is flushed white.

His mother bounds in, a grocery store pie in a cardboard box in her hands. She smells of motor oil and cigarettes, and her eyes are puffy, her hair greasy. Riley rises like he's made of lead and accepts her buoyant hug, the pie clattering against their chests before she laughs and passes it to me. She squares him in front of her, her hands on Riley's shoulders. Her smile is genuine, revealing yellowed teeth. I want to ask her hard, sharp questions, like: *Why are you here now? Where have you been? When will you take care of him?* But I do not. No one does. My parents and I hover in awkward orbit around them.

"Happy Thanksgiving, sweetie," she says, pulling him close again. I know she'll be gone in hours. Riley, stiff, peers at the wall past her. I watch his hands clench behind her back, fingers contracting, relaxing, contracting, like a pair of hearts struggling to beat.

•   •   •   •

When Riley isn't around, I draw him. I draw the both of us, but on separate pieces of paper, so his hand is reaching out of the frame of his picture toward mine, and my fingers are barely pressed into the borders of his portraits. I'm no good at faces, so we both look square, and our proportions are off, our arms and legs rigid and unrealistic. I fail to capture the oval girth of his eyes, the straightness of his teeth, the cleft of his chin. My own gangly arms and legs are blown up and cartoonish, but Riley laughs at them with kindness anyway, telling me he loves them.

"They help me remember I'm still here," he says when I try to take one away from him after he lets out a particularly barking laugh.

"What does that mean?"

"Hard to explain," he says, and then kisses me goodbye before disappearing out of my house. He's comfortable leaving on his own, waving to my parents as he traipses through the living room and out into the dark. I watch his shape from my window, memorizing the way he moves.

Three weeks before Christmas, with clumpy snow pattering on the windows, he pounds on the door at eleven at night. My parents are already in bed, and they flutter to the foyer in matching bathrobes.

Riley's nose is bloody.

"Oh goodness," my mother says, and I know this red is not the kind only I can see.

Something spikes in my chest, and when I look down I half expect to see my own blood cascading out of a hole in my torso, but instead all I see is the t-shirt Riley picked out for me at Goodwill last week, the one he asked me to sleep in for seven nights without washing it. The gray material is fuzzy, and it itches a bit at the armpits where it's too tight.

"He came back," Riley says, his voice gummy. I can see a flash of red outlining his teeth, and I wonder if any of them are missing.

"We need to call someone," my father says, his voice thick and strong. Riley stumbles into the house, his head pressing against my chest as his knees wobble, and I feel the heat of his bleeding nose connect to the shirt, turning a coin-sized spot sticky and warm. I don't pull back but instead pull in, pull him in, bring his body close to mine and let whatever wants to move between us travel without resistance.

•   •   •   •

Riley is gone. I feel like Band-Aids have been torn from all over my skin. Two days after the police come for his father Riley doesn't show up at school. I go to his house and he does not answer; the lights are out that night when I come back, even the front stoop's glass-encased bulb that is always turned on. I climb the trellis around back and peer through the dark into his bedroom. The corkboard is still there, but it bears no t-shirts. I can't see much else. I can't pull open his bureau's drawers or rifle through his closet. I can't find Riley's secrets.

The soccer coach has a conniption. The state championship is only days away and no one will tell him what has become of Riley.

I feel like a chewed-up mass of food that has spent hours clogging someone's throat. My parents keep their eyes on me for too many seconds at a time, and when I ask if they know something, they shake their heads. I feel as if everyone is telling me lies.

Three days after Christmas, which I spend curled up on the couch ignoring the shower of presents my parents have slid under the tree for me, a thick envelope arrives. There is no return address, but I recognize the handwriting from helping Riley with rough drafts of his English papers. I tear it open with an indelicate fury and accidentally rip the drawings inside. Riley has sent me two, one of each of us, and I recognize them as the last pair I sketched: he is slumped in a chair, legs splayed out like a pair of check-marks, his shoulders uneven because I am terrible at perspective and symmetry. He is staring down at his lap, where I've tried to knot his hands together but have made it look like his arms end in a contorted Christmas bow. In my self-portrait I am standing straight up, my eyes slanted to my left; I'm looking at him, but askew, as though I don't want anyone in the world to know where my gaze naturally flows.

He has changed them. Riley's body is striped with all sorts of colors, splashes that angle across his hips, blotches that cover his eyes and mouth. His stomach is a black ball, his elbows serrated pink. He is both fluorescent and opaque.

Riley has colored me in, too: brass, gold. I glow all over. Light shines from me. Light I do not feel anywhere on my real body. His touch on my skin has already faded to a lukewarm memory.

•   •   •   •

He kissed me first. We were both freshly sixteen. My parents threw a party for me, and kids crammed into my basement, spinning the handles on the foosball table, chatting next to the pool table whose felt was skimmed with dust; the chalk for the cues had turned to blue onyx. My friends drank watery Kool-Aid, some of which was spiked with vodka someone slipped in via a flask, and the room started to smell like a doctor's office from so much exhaled booze breath. They swallowed down pizza by the slice and wiped their mouths with their forearms. My parents said *No gifts*, and none were offered. The kids with real parties to attend, with kegs and Jell-O shots and rap music and making out, filtered away, and then so did the rest, until it was just me and Riley. My parents went to bed.

We sat on the living room sofa. His neck was ringed a cartoonish saffron, and I reached out and touched it. He winced and admitted that his father had roped him with a tie.

"God," I said.

"I'm okay," he said. "He didn't yank it tight. Also, I have a gift for you."

"No gifts," I said in imitation of my father, who had bestowed upon me a set of acrylic paints before the party while my mother brought an easel in from the garage.

"Don't worry," Riley said. "This one didn't cost anything."

He told me to close my eyes. I was rigid. I was shaky. Even though I hadn't drunk any of the spiked punch, the world felt woozy when I did as he told me. His hands alighted on my shoulders and I let out a small noise of approval.

"Shush," he said. His mouth was near. Then he put his lips on mine, for only a second or two, but everything became fire. I pictured a licking blue passing from him to me. When I opened my eyes, he was staring at me, smiling.

"Why'd you do that?" I said.

"Because I wanted to. And you wanted me to."

I nodded.

"Do you want to stay?" I said.

"Yes."

Later, when were locked in my bedroom and the only light came from the plastic stars on my ceiling and my reading lamp, whose nose I would bevel down so the glow spread like a serving platter against my nightstand, we would kiss again. I would taste the sugary birthday cake Riley had swallowed down in large bites, and I would smell the mint of his breath from the gum he always chewed after eating. His fingers would tickle down my ribs as if he was playing an instrument. He would lay them against my skin, his iron-warm hands skirted up beneath my shirt. And when he pulled back and asked if this was okay, I would nod and other things would happen: fingers through hair, tongues against throats. I would stutter and hitch, and so would he, and we would laugh, breathless and anxious, wondering where we should search and what we should find. We would barely sleep.

But as we unfurled ourselves from the couch, I took the lead as we walked to the stairs. I paused at the first step. Riley stood behind me. I stopped again halfway up, but I didn't turn around. I lifted my hand from the banister and extended it backward, then waited until Riley took it, his fiery fingers squeezed into mine so I knew he was still there.

Close the Door on This Laughing Heart

AKERS AND I WERE SITTING IN HIS TRUCK BED, DRINKing beers and jacking off, when the laughter started. He was playing porn on his new iPhone—a pair of ripped frat guys and a girl who, according to the video's title, was a stripper, going at it—that delivered crisp, cinematic-quality sound. It, paired with the classic rock huffing out of his speakers, gave me hope that he couldn't hear the giggling, a high, girlish noise a flock of fifth graders might emit. The sun was setting, and katydids were starting to deliver their evening song in ululating waves, honey-colored light spilling over the field, a hidden valley of stalks off Highway N.

Our bodies were hunched forward, our jeans around our ankles. We'd both worn long pants, even though the weather was hot: the middle of June, high school graduation weeks behind us. Akers and I were both going to the same liberal arts college in the fall, which had surprised me when I'd found out, not because I thought I was too smart for him but the opposite: it seemed like he was punching down, not giving his academic prowess enough credit. Akers was on the honor roll every semester, his name right before mine—Anderson—in slanty, thick letters. He didn't play any school sports, but he boxed at a gym nestled in a strip mall between a pawn shop and a music store that was a known front for drugs, mostly pot and ecstasy but periodically harder stuff that some of our classmates managed to get their hands on, sniffing and shooting up behind the dumpsters outside the gymnasium.

Our hanging out had been Akers' idea, floated my way when there were only two weeks of school left.

"We're the only two going there," he said, standing next to my locker as he made his proposal, approaching it like a presentation he was giving to the board of a business. "It'll be good to know someone in advance."

"Okay," I said, sliding my backpack onto my shoulder. "What do you want to do?"

He'd taken me out to the spot we were now. That first time, all we did was sit on the rusted tailgate and drink from a twelve-pack of beer his older brother, who still lived at home and worked at an auto parts store, had bought for him. I had drunk only a few times, and only cheap light beers that tasted like nothing, and the nickel-heavy sting of Akers' Steel Reserve made me cringe and nearly cough. But I held it together while he asked me questions, as though we were interviewing one another. We'd stayed out there until night fell and we were assaulted by super mosquitos and had to scramble into the cab of the truck. When Akers dropped me off at my house, he asked if I wanted to hang out again. I said yes, sure.

"I'm close," Akers said. We'd taken off our shirts and I watched his left arm twitch, the upper half of his pec flexing as he stroked himself. Beads of sweat percolated on his back where his spine curved up toward his brain like a thin stalk shorn of its leaves. As he let out a low moan he leaned his head back, the arrowhead of his Adam's apple pointing toward the setting sun. He lay down, abs stretching, and he came, a long white rope that shot up the center of his body. The laughter increased in volume, and I said, "Me too. Holy shit," and then started murmuring to try to cover the sound. Akers was still stroking himself as his erection wilted, his hand filmy with seminal fluid. Instead of lying down as I felt tightness in my groin, I pushed my hips forward and ejaculated on the grass.

Akers closed out the porn and I felt a cold fear that now, without the panting and slapping and screeching—all from the girl, while her two beefcakes fellated one another and grimaced when they took each other in their mouths—he would surely hear the Gregorian chant of laughter. But instead, he caught the opening chords of "Don't Stop Believin'," his favorite song, and started strumming his fingers on the beat-up truck bed liner, the clang of his thumbs and index fingers smothering the chuckling noise. Then, as he wiped himself off with a rag and tucked himself back into his underwear, he started singing, off-key. His face was all dimples and glaring white teeth. Thankfully, Akers sang loud, without fear or shame, because as I felt the thump of my heart expand, so did the giggling noise. Whether I wanted to be or not, I was definitely in love with him.

• • • •

Akers had told me that he wasn't into guys, he was pretty sure. He said this the third time we hung out. We were sitting at a picnic table behind the frozen custard stand where I worked the summer after my junior year but quit when one of my friends got me a better job bussing tables at a local restaurant where the servers had to tip us out two percent of their sales. Even though the place's pay had been shitty, I liked the desserts, so when Akers told me he was peckish—the word slipped out of his mouth like a seduction—I suggested my former employer. He said, "Sure," as he did for all my suggestions. He took my recommendation to try the S'more Sundae and gave it two thumbs up.

"I just thought I should tell you." He licked his spoon.

I'd come out to my friends just months before, telling them that I liked both guys and girls during my parents' Christmas party when I was bolstered by several glasses of eggnog. Everyone gathered me into a hug, their bodies a warm nest I didn't want to leave.

"You didn't have to say anything," I told him.

He stared at the red stalk of his spoon. "But I guess I'm kind of curious."

"About what?"

"That's the thing," he said, scooping out the last of his custard. "I'm not sure what I'm curious about. I don't know shit."

"Is that why you wanted to hang out?"

He shook his head. "No, you seem interesting. I wanted to get to know the guy who's giving me a run for valedictorian."

"Don't worry," I said. "I'm getting a B in Anatomy."

"I could make jokes."

"Yes," I said. "You could."

"But I'm not going to."

"Kind."

"Friends don't make those kinds of jokes," he said and smiled. When he did, I thought I heard the first whispers of laughter: a tremor of noise, explicably the tiny brook that bordered the custard stand's parking lot. I had no reason to hear it at the time, I told myself, and such feelings would get me nowhere. We left soon thereafter, and the only noise I could hear was the rumble of his truck's engine and the crooning voice of David Bowie on the radio.

• • • •

Akers had made it clear, the first time, that he just wanted to know what it was like to be with a guy.

"Literally," he said. "I just want to, you know, see it."

He'd asked me if that was cool. I said yes, trying to flatten my voice, to not give away that a part of me had wanted to see his body in full blast after being so close to the hinted biceps and the pudge of shoulder and pec hidden behind his t-shirts, the length and girth of thigh suggested by his bright canvas shorts. The first time, he'd produced a flask containing Johnny Walker pilfered from his parents' liquor shelf and demanded we take several shots before we shed any clothes. We each took three pulls before he produced a small bottle of Astroglide from his pocket and then stared at me, unsure what to do next. I'd taken my pants off first, thinking that this would give him ease. I was right. He laughed and unbuckled his shorts and said something about how it was like when he changed at the gym.

"But also nothing like that," he said as he pulled down his boxers, revealing a half hard-on and surprisingly well-manicured pubic hair.

That first time was fast. We both rushed, as if racing, and we didn't say anything. We kept our shirts on, our bodies turned slightly away from each other. I felt the liner of the truck dig into my hamstrings. He barely grunted when he came, and I tried not to look at him until we were both fully clothed again. The next time, two days later, he asked if I wanted to watch porn.

When I shrugged assent, he said, "Any preferences?"

"I'm pretty flexible," I said.

This made him laugh. "I guess you would be."

I blinked at him and his cheeks went red. He mumbled something I couldn't hear, then brought out his phone. He clicked away, and then I could hear moaning and slapping. I didn't really watch; I let him use it and instead drank from a Steel Reserve—following the Johnny Walker, he brought a fresh twelve-pack for us every time, even though we never came close to finishing them all—with my free hand.

After half a dozen of these sessions, he turned down the radio as he parked in front of my house.

"This isn't weird for you, is it?" he said.

"Not really, no," I said. "What about you?"

He shook his head. The night was clear, stars thrown across the sky. The porch light was on, as were the solar lights that lined the front walk. I could see slivers of freshly cut grass.

"It's cool. We're just having fun, you know?"

"I do." My mouth was tinny from one too many beers.

"Cool," he said, a word I never heard come from Akers' mouth. He nodded, and I nodded, and I let myself out.

The next time, the laughter started.

•   •   •   •

I asked my mother, over breakfast, when she first fell in love.

"Oh," she said, setting down her fork.

We were eating waffles because my father had given her a waffle maker for her birthday—along with a Tiffany bracelet she'd been hinting about—and her new thing was to experiment with the batter. Today's were stuffed with chocolate chips and drizzled with a home-made strawberry sauce; I'd already told her they were her best so far.

"Well," she said. "That's hard to say."

"But it shouldn't be, should it?"

She sighed. "That's true. It would be more fun if we had to figure it out for ourselves, wouldn't it?"

"Well?" I said.

"What's this about? You and that boy you've been hanging out with?"

I took a too-large bite of dough, the melted chocolate and hardening sauce coating my tongue. My mother squinted at me and puckered her lips as if to tell me she knew I was stalling. When I swallowed, I took a sip from my glass of milk and cleared my throat. "Maybe."

She reached across the table. "You should tell him how you feel."

"I know how he feels."

"So you've talked about it?"

I shook my head. "No."

She cocked her head. "Then how can you know for sure?"

I shrugged. I couldn't very well tell her what we'd been doing. As much as my parents and I shared things with one another, I certainly didn't want to tell her about my recent masturbatory behaviors. "He's my friend, that's all."

"And you don't want to lose that."

I nodded. "I'm afraid he'll hear it."

"That's true," she said. "That's certainly done it before."

"For you? Dad?"

"No," she said. "People I know."

"What did they do?"

"Well," she said, standing to clear our plates. "Most of them tell me they wish they'd been the one to say something. That the people they loved wished they'd heard it from them, not from the laughing."

I rubbed my eyes and lowered my head against the table.

"Oh stop," my mother said from the kitchen, yelling over the sink as she scrubbed at our plates. "Everything will be fine. Just tell him how you feel."

I shook my head, even though she couldn't see me.

The sink stopped its flow, and my mother appeared, drying her hands with a flower-printed towel. "One other thing."

"Yeah?"

"Has it occurred to you that you're wrong?"

"About what?"

"About the laughter."

"What about it?"

"That it might not be yours you're hearing. That maybe it's his."

•   •   •   •

I was thinking about what my mother said when I climbed into his truck. Akers said, "Hey," and shifted into drive and off we went. He was wearing a tank top, the veins in his arms pushed out against the skin like worms burrowing along the surface. He said he liked boxing because it built muscle and cut fat at the same time if you did it right. More than once he'd offered to take me to his gym—he got so many free visitors per month because he'd been going all of high school, he claimed—but I'd always sputtered out excuses not to. I was in decent shape myself, having run track and field, but at jv level, never forced to make serious physical commitment or push myself too hard. I hadn't ever earned a letter, and the coach let us sit out anything we didn't feel up for on a given day. But I'd liked the ache in my chest after sprinting, pushing my muscles and lungs as hard as I could. In the truck, "Angie" blaring on the speakers, I could feel a different pain lighting my sternum.

He drove to our usual spot. My heart was thrumming too fast, my throat dry, what little saliva was in my mouth tasting like something I might lick off a wet rock. Though it was only late afternoon, the sky was gray: on the horizon, thick clouds billowed, threatening rain. Only twenty minutes ago we'd been bathed in sunshine and hot wind. Akers rolled down the windows and cut the engine.

"I've been thinking," he said.

"It's summer," I said. "You're not supposed to have to do that."

He smiled, looking down at himself. His jawline was crystalline and sharp, of course, like something out of a cologne advertisement.

"What if we tried something new?"

"New?" The word croaked out dry as the chaff wavering before us.

What I had not told Akers was that the first time we touched ourselves together was the first time I'd done anything more than make out with a girl at a party. I'd played a few games of spin the bottle and locked lips with a Homecoming date or two, but that was it. Akers seemed to think that I was some kind of sex expert, that I was the one guiding him into a new zone to see if he wanted what was on offer. That was why, he said, he wondered if we might try blowjobs.

"Just this once," he said.

"This once?"

"Unless we like them," he said. "I guess we could do it again. We'd have to see, wouldn't we?"

"I guess so."

"So, what do you think?"

"We could. Try it out," I said.

He smiled.

"But I think it's gonna rain."

"Then I guess we'd better hurry, huh?"

He was already pulling off his tank top as he exited the truck. I tossed myself out the passenger door. The air had cooled and was chilly against my chest; I felt my nipples harden. By the time I was behind the truck, Akers was already kicking off his shoes and shimmying his shorts down past his knees. I moved more slowly. Over the whistle of the breeze, which was kicking the pampas grass sideways, I thought I heard the muffled cry of laughter.

Akers let down the tailgate, which squealed with rusted anger. He hauled himself up and then turned in his underwear and held out a hand. I took it; both our palms were sweaty, and he made a joke about this. From the cooler he kept in the back he fished out a pair of beers, which he opened before passing me one.

"For the nerves, right?" I said.

He drank. "You'd think we wouldn't have that problem any-more, huh?"

"You'd think so."

We stood there in the back of the truck for a long time. I looked toward the horizon; the clouds were gathering in a thick blanket, pushing the light away. Trees shimmied, their sound swishy: more noise to get in the way of laughter I both did and did not want to hear.

Akers finished his beer first, crumpling the can and tossing it to the side of the truck, where I knew he would pick it up later. He was that sort, unwilling to dump even the smallest bit of litter, whether it be a receipt or a strip of lint or looseleaf. He collected cigarette butts that he found on the curb outside his house on the weekends.

"So," he said.

I finished my beer, the aluminum flavor numbing the backs of my teeth and the hard width of my palate.

"So."

"How do we?"

I shrugged. "We probably need to take off our underwear."

He laughed. "Pretty silly that we did everything else but that."

"Yes," I said. "Silly."

And then, before I could say more, Akers had dropped himself to his knees and plugged his index fingers into the band of my underwear, sliding them down with a slow care. The proximity of his fingers to my crotch turned me on, and I could feel myself getting hard. He pulled them down all the way to my ankles, and then his hands were on me, pulling in tight, short strokes. He kissed my inner thighs, right then left, his lips moving up along the tender, ticklish muscle there.

"What about you?" I said, my voice breathless. He didn't say anything, and I wasn't sure if he could hear me.

Once he had put me in his mouth, I did not last long. But in that short duration the wind erupted, whistling through the truck's open windows. The storm came, fat drops that spattered my eyes and Akers' shoulders, pattering a percussive noise on the truck's roof. He kept going as if he didn't notice. I told him he needed to stop, that I was getting too close, but as he kept his grip on me with his hands and mouth, I heard it: deep, guttering laughter, hearty and thick. It consumed the wind and the rain and even the far-off thunder that shook the ground after lightning lit up the sky. Even when I groaned and Akers didn't take his mouth off me the laughter rang out, fresh and endless. Finally, he looked up at me, his lips pulled into a wide, working grin. He made a show of swallowing and then standing.

"What about you?" I said, squinting through the rain.

He shook his head. "Too wet," he yelled, as if we were in a movie. Then he leapt down from the truck and gathered his clothes and mine and gestured for me to follow him into the truck. As I expected, he bent down, back muscles stretching and sliding as he grabbed the empty beer can. He tossed it into the truck without looking. It clattered against my ankle.

I sat, naked and spent, in the truck, my skin squeaking against the leather. Akers rolled the windows up and turned the ignition. Chilly air spewed out of the vents and I shivered. The laughter was still there, still loud, but Akers acted as though he couldn't hear it. The radio spat out "Welcome to the Jungle."

"Well?" he said, his voice back to a normal volume.

I wanted to ask him if he could hear the laughter, if he cared at all that it was so loud, cratering around in the cab of the truck. All I could manage was, "Well what?"

"What did you think of that?"

I looked down at myself. My pubic hair was matted and tangled with spit and rain and come.

"It felt good," I said. "The surroundings could have used some improvement."

Akers smiled.

"What about you?" I said.

"It was different. Not how I'd thought it would taste."

"That's not what I meant," I said.

We both looked at his groin, where he was limp and small, as if his penis was cowed by what was happening. The laughter had subsided to a soft, consistent gurgle, like the sound of water at a rolling boil. Akers leaned toward the center console and turned up the radio. "I like this song," he said. "Willie Nelson."

"Oh." The song was slow, twangy guitars and a slow drumbeat: *You are always on my mind.*

"We should put our clothes on," Akers said.

I still hadn't touched him. While he'd been blowing me, the only thing I'd done was press one hand to the back of his head, not to force or direct him, but to make some kind of contact. I felt not just obligated to do so but had wanted to, to feel the tender back of his neck, the bumpy knitting of his parietal and occipital lobes, how the bone crushed up in a tiny mountain where they met. To feel the heat of his ears, the hard hinge of his jaw.

I didn't say any of that. Instead, I watched him wriggle around and pull on his shorts. He didn't bother with his underwear. I plucked up my clothing, which he'd bunched on the gear shift between us, and dressed.

"Everything okay?" he said when I had put my shirt back on. I was still shivering.

"Yeah," I said.

He bobbed his head. "Good. Yeah. Thanks."

"For what?"

"This," he said. "It helped, I think. You know?"

I didn't know, so I said nothing. We drove back to my house in silence, the truck filled with music. The DJ played a live version

of "Sweet Home Alabama," a concert crowd hooting and screaming during the intro and singing along during the chorus, when
Ronnie Van Zant dropped away and let them take the lead.

"I love this song," Akers said, reaching to turn up the volume. He sang along, his voice pitchy and breaking as usual. He
looked at me and slugged me in the shoulder, begging me to join
in. We were only blocks from my house, but I did. I could still
hear the laughter burbling beneath our shared voices. When we
reached my house, the song was still going, winding down with
the pounding of the piano. Although there were no more words
to sing, Akers started humming along, pounding his fingers on
the steering wheel like it was a baby grand.

And when it finally ended, Akers laughed. The sound came
from his belly, deep and rich and real. It matched the laughter
that had surrounded us at its highest, most feverish pitch, and he
stared at me as he giggled, so hard that tears came to his eyes. I
bit my cheek and opened my door, not asking what was so funny.
Still laughing, Akers waved goodbye. He may have said he'd
see me soon, but I wasn't sure, because I crossed my yard and
shut the door behind me, the sound of his voice and the laughter announcing love—mine, his, who knew—ringing in my ears
long after he was gone.

The Right Kind of Love, the Wrong Kind of Death

AFTER MY FATHER DIED, MY BOYFRIEND REGREW HIM in our fraternity house's backyard, behind the toolshed where we kept the lawnmower and inflatable waterslide we hauled out during freshman orientation week. He used, as a seed, my father's pocketknife, the only thing I'd taken with me after his funeral. I had bought it for him myself, a gift for his fortieth birthday. A few days before my father was ripe, my boyfriend hauled me outside. The sky blazed a bright tourmaline, the sun radiating warmth and invitation. I had been working on a Latin translation assignment and was annoyed by the interruption. When we reached the toolshed, I stopped and stared. I recognized my father, who was pinkish and rooted to the ground at the ankles, his slack legs slumped so his body leaned against the back of the shed. His eyes were pasted closed, his body smushy like he was made of putty that had melted. I recognized his forehead and the jut of his chin.

"He'll be ready tomorrow," my boyfriend said, rubbing my back.

I loved my father; I cried at his funeral. He was kind, if inaccessible, a high school English teacher who'd wanted to be a novelist but couldn't ever find the mental fortitude to string together enough words in the right fashion. He preferred reading to playing catch, and he would blink at me with owlish unknowing when I talked about baseball players or tennis matches. The first time they were introduced, my father gobbled up my boyfriend in a back-slapping hug and asked him what his favorite book was.

My boyfriend told me that he'd turned the clock back on my father, so that he would be a prime-of-life dad, a pre-cancer dad, the dad who had swum laps each morning at 6 a.m. in our in-ground pool even when the water was stinging cold and breath-sucking, the one who insisted that half of our dinner plates always be loaded with cruciferous vegetables, the dad whose genes I could thank for my lean, strong torso but also my fears about dying young.

I had trouble sleeping that night, my boyfriend a warm sack of heat next to me. His knees burrowed into the backs of my legs, and his right hand slid along my hip. I was facing the windows overlooking campus. The buildings were dark blurs that I stared at until my eyes drooped. Every time I came close to sleep, though, I would be rocketed by the image of my father firming to completion in the backyard. I wondered if his voice would be his real voice or the one, wheezing and enflamed, that had plagued him in the final weeks of his life. I trusted what my boyfriend had said about him, even if I didn't quite believe. Trust, belief: slivers of difference that I tried to swallow down as the night ticked by.

I turned off my alarm before the clock shrieked at me. Hazy morning light, washed-out Easter colors, seeped into my room. My boyfriend groaned and rolled toward the wall, burying his head under a pillow. When I stood, he sat up and blinked, shaking his head like a dog wriggling off water.

"Right," he said. He blinked at me. "I forgot where I was, for a second. Weird, huh?"

I nodded as I pulled on my shoes. I didn't bother with socks.

Outside, the grass was covered in a slick of dew. As we approached the shed, my stomach contorted. I took loud, shallow breaths, and my boyfriend grabbed my hand, kneading his thumb over the bones.

"Relax," he said. His black hair shimmered like the depths of the ocean in the sunlight, which bounced off his cheekbones like he was being photographed by a professional. "I know what I'm doing."

He had brought with him a bottle of water, a towel, and some clothes—his, not mine, because he was taller than me, like my father—which he had slung over his shoulder: a plain white t-shirt and a pair of black shorts. When we reached the shed, my boyfriend didn't so much as hesitate as he turned the corner to where my father was growing, so I didn't stop either.

I took in a sharp breath: what had been a pink lump that only vaguely resembled the shape of my dead dad the day before was now a perfect likeness. He was still slumped, and his eyes were closed, his body slippery with morning dew like the grass so that his skin—tan like it had been when he still played beach volleyball and went running without a shirt on—glistened like a cooked slab of beef. I stared at him, the familiar roll of his shoulders, the splatter of his hair. He was naked, and I couldn't help but look at his most intimate places, which I had only seen once in my life, when he failed to close his bedroom door when I was six and didn't yet understand the concept of privacy.

"How do we, you know, wake him up?" I said.

"We excavate."

"We what?"

My boyfriend pointed to the ground, where my father's legs were buried up to the ankles.

"It's like yanking out a root vegetable."

"I've never yanked out a root vegetable."

He rolled his eyes and, after handing me the towel and water and clothes, bent down in front of my father and started scooping dirt out of the way like a dog lazily digging a hole. I should have helped but I simply watched, first my boyfriend and the muscles of his back sliding and flexing beneath his t-shirt as he groped at the ground, then at my father who, as his feet slowly came unstuck from the earth, started to stand taller. His eyes rolled beneath their lids. As my boyfriend finished releasing his feet, my father's arms unfurled themselves from around his body. I felt like I was watching a flower spool out its blooms in high speed.

"The towel," my boyfriend said. He stood, wiping his hands. I held it out and he shook his head. "No, your dad."

I started cleaning my father's face. His lips were still stuck shut and I could hear him taking in raspy breaths through his nostrils; when I got close, I could see the gunk dribbling out of his nose. When the towel bashed against his forehead he leaned back and smacked into the fence separating our house from the property behind it.

"Careful," my boyfriend said and took over. He cleaned my father up and got him into the shorts and t-shirt. He rubbed my father's back as he helped him stand, my father's knees wobbly, his first steps on the grass like the unsure trots of a small child or a foal. He paused when my father paused, bent close to whisper encouragements in his ear. My father hobbled like he was geriatric, and I remembered his wasted body, destroyed by medicine and his own rebelling cells, the way his mouth, cracked and dry, gaped like a fish's as it yearned for water. His skin had been pulled tight, every vein a tunnel, every bone a mountain.

My boyfriend turned to look at me and raised an eyebrow in my direction to say, *Well?*

I caught up with them as he helped my father onto our back porch. When I took my father's right arm, I felt a jolt at how warm he was.

My boyfriend saw the look on my face and said, "Well, he has been outside."

We made our way to the back door, which I pushed open. When we guided my father inside, we stared up the steps.

"You up to this?" my boyfriend said.

I nodded. As we led my father upstairs, I felt my insides twist and tangle like sheets knotted by a heavy wind.

•   •   •   •

Everyone loved my father. In high school, he encouraged me to throw parties, and by the time I was sixteen, he was winking every time he mentioned that he'd bought several cases of beer on his last grocery run. As long as I didn't let anyone drive if they had drunk even a single drop of alcohol, he looked the other way.

"It's going to happen," he'd say to me when I asked why he didn't mind. "I just want it to happen safely."

My friends adored him; he always tried to stay holed up in his bedroom or the second-floor office of our house, but my friends would go slinking up the stairs, beers sweating in their hands, and cajole him to join us. He would always resist, though minimally, and while he never sat down while we played Circle of Death or Fuck the Dealer, he stood in the periphery and laughed at our bad jokes—sharing, periodically, his own awful bits of comedy that my friends, inexplicably, found hilarious—drinking slowly and carefully from his own single can of Budweiser, his arms crossed over his chest as he observed our goings-on. We often caught one another's eye, and he would usually give me a tiny wink, the slightest tip of his can, and then bark out some silly insult at one of my friends. In the morning, I would wake to the smell of bacon and maple syrup, and after eating gargantuan, greasy breakfasts that settled my stomach, he would help me clean up the messes my friends left behind.

I never knew my mother, who passed away when I was an infant, the misty details always out of reach. I asked questions periodically when I was young, and in response my father would tug photo albums from a bookshelf in the living room and sit with me, poring through Polaroids tinged orange and purple. She was beautiful, my mother, with long, dark ringlets that curtained her face, which was pointed and shiny.

"She wanted to be an artist," he said. He would clear his throat and add, "She was an artist."

She'd been a painter, but my father only had two of her pieces. One he kept in his bedroom, the last thing she finished, a Picasso-like visage of me as a baby, my eyes bright blue and shiny and both stuck to the right side of my head. The other was an abstraction, like a Jackson Pollock, sprays of yellow and green and blue. It hung over my bed.

"She never really knew what she wanted to be," he said. "That held her back and also made her great. Sometimes I wish I'd kept more of her work, but then other times even the two we have are too hard to look at."

By the time I was old enough to understand death, I also understood that asking about my mother hurt my father, and so I stopped. I didn't feel the achy void of loss that people seemed to expect when I told them my mother was dead. How do you grieve an absence whose presence you've never really known? When people fawn-eyed at me with sympathy and pity, I felt a hard hunger rush through me, not for my mother to be alive but for whoever was pumping out their vacuous condolences to vanish.

When my boyfriend and I first met as college freshmen who had chosen to join the same fraternity and I told him about my mother, he didn't look at me like I was drizzled in sorrow. He said, "That sucks. Wanna get drunk?"

"Because my mother died when I was a baby?" I said.

"No," he said. "Because it's Friday."

•　　•　　•　　•

My father came back to life fast. I worried that leaving him in my room while my boyfriend and I went to our classes would somehow damage him, that I'd return to find him curled up in a ball, aching for death. But when I came back after lunch, I found him performing jumping jacks on my throw rug, which he'd vacuumed. All my dirty clothes, which had a tendency to congregate around rather than in my laundry basket, had been picked up. My bed was made. He'd even tidied my desk, notebooks stacked neatly, pens in their coffee mug.

His face was shiny, but the sludge of rebirth had been replaced with a crown of sweat. He dropped to the floor to do a set of pushups.

My boyfriend came trudging to my bedroom door.

"Is this normal?" I said.

He gave my father a once-over and smiled. "Is it?"

"My father was tidy, but he never cleaned my bedroom, if that's what you mean."

"Well," my boyfriend said, laying his arm over my shoulders, heavy and hot like a boa constrictor, "this is his room now, too, isn't it?"

After my father died, I went home for a week, given dispensation by all my professors to skip out on quizzes and homework, to take tests late and turn in papers a week after they were due. Neither of my parents had siblings, and my grandparents had passed away when I was a child. My father had loads of friends, and they crowded into the house and fluttered about during the reception, handling the food and drinks and bereavement cards and flower arrangements, so many that my eyes started watering and I had to sneak out onto the back porch. One of my father's good friends was an attorney, and he found me after most people had slunk home and I'd had too much merlot to still see straight and to fully understand what he was saying, which was that he'd be happy to sort out the estate business, all the mountains of paperwork that appear out of nowhere when someone dies. I nodded and let him see himself out. My boyfriend stayed with me for two days, ostensibly to help me sort through some of my father's things, but all I could do was lie in my bed. That's where my boyfriend stayed, rubbing my shoulders and back, nudging his fingers against my hips. He tried, one time, to nuzzle at my throat, but when I didn't move, he understood it wasn't the time or place.

Place, I thought then and now while I watched my father move so he could do some sit-ups. Watching my father wending through my personal space made me feel dizzy. I looked at my boyfriend.

"What do we do with him?"

"Have you tried talking to him?"

I set my teeth. For some reason, it hadn't occurred to me that my father could speak; he'd been silent as we trudged him into the house, and I imagined it would take him days, weeks even, to master speech again, so I hadn't bothered.

"Hey, Dad," I said.

He was mid-crunch, and he held his position, back hovering at a forty-five-degree angle. He smiled and waved like a giddy child and then collapsed onto his back, massaging his abs with his hands.

A group of guys spent every Friday afternoon playing beer pong in our fraternity house foyer, and people would wander in and out, watching and drinking from their own cases of beer once their classes were over. My boyfriend thought maybe my father should come. We took him downstairs, where he received handshakes and hugs and slaps on the back from everyone who came through the house. When one of the guys standing at the table received a series of angry texts from his girlfriend, he invited my father to take his place.

"Is that a good idea?" I said.

"I don't see why not," my boyfriend said as my father, who'd been slouched in a folding chair near the action, stood. When he plucked up one of the ping pong balls, he looked at it, slick and white, like it was a foreign object. But then he squared his shoulders to the cups on the other side of the table, his weight on his back foot, and lunged just so like a basketball player shooting a free throw and sent the ball plunking with a light pillow of noise into the freshly poured beer at the top of his opponent's triangle. Everyone hooted in approval.

I woke on Saturday morning in my boyfriend's bed, sunlight beating through his window in hard, wide strips because he'd accidentally knocked down the Venetian blinds a few weeks ago when he was drunk. We'd left my father in my bed. He'd played three games of beer pong, winning them all, before shaking his head and backing away from the table, ignoring the desperate wishes of my friends. My boyfriend had gotten to him first, helping him back up the stairs while I trailed behind.

I yawned and stretched; all of my muscles were stiff, my joints like twisted bark. My foot slid against my boyfriend's leg and he groaned. I looked over at him and nearly shrieked.

My boyfriend was athletic, lithe and tan and smooth-skinned, his midsection bumpy with muscle, his arms striated. I liked to run my hands over them and feel what twitched beneath. But the sun streaking over his body revealed something gone sour and aged, his body wrinkled and laden with white fuzz like a peach left to rot. He blinked awake. My boyfriend's face was also fleshy and slack, wrinkles drooping along his eyelids and mouth; his throat was wattled, the skin bunched.

"What happened to you?" I said.

He groaned and sat up, breathing hard. "I was worried about this," he said.

"What is *this*?"

He let out a sigh and his body shuddered. A roll of skin and fat that hadn't been there doubled over his belly button. His pubic hair had gone gray and white and wiry. Something squelched in my stomach.

"The price I had to pay."

"Oh god," I said, understanding immediately. "This is insane. You shouldn't have done this."

"Why not?"

"Because I don't want you to be like this."

He patted my back twice. "Let's find your dad. Or maybe you could. I'm a bit stiff."

I found my father on my bedroom floor, stretched out in downward dog, using my throw rug as a yoga mat. He lifted his head at an unnatural angle, like something out of an exorcism movie, and raised one hand from the floor to wave at me. His body's contortion made me feel ill.

"Can you say something, please?" I said.

"Hi."

His voice was rich with honey and warmth, a deep shock. Familiar and exact.

I watched my father turn the downward dog pose into a handstand. His arms barely shook and his legs stayed straight. Then he dipped down, an inverted pushup focusing on his shoulders. Effortless.

"When did you learn to do that?" I said.

He let his body topple downward, feet landing with solid strength. He unfurled himself and smiled at me. "Just now."

My father's face was smooth and bright, like last night's beers had been slurps from the fountain of youth.

I left him to his stretching and a fresh set of air squats. In his room, my boyfriend was still in his bed, but sitting up, taking in deep breaths. I sat down on the bed.

"Why'd you do this?"

"You were wrecked."

I ground the heels of my palms against my eyes. "I was grieving."

He set a hand on my back. His fingers were leathery and cold. I sat up straight.

"It was horrible to see you that way."

"Well, it's horrible to see you like this."

"I had to get this way eventually."

"Not for, like, forty years."

He smiled at me. "Did you ever imagine you'd see me like this?"

"I don't know how to answer that."

"Answer it honestly."

"Sometimes, maybe. Yes. But not like this. You should have told me what it would cost."

"But then you wouldn't have done it. You wouldn't have let me."

We both knew this was true. I pictured my father, jocular and lithe, doing burpees or triceps dips on my bedroom floor.

"As much as I missed my father, I didn't miss him enough for this." I looked at my boyfriend, his frazzled, grayed temples, the wither of his arms, the new bulge to his stomach. His jaw was covered in a patchy fuzz, discolored like mange. "You look really bad."

My boyfriend laughed. "I know."

"Are you still you?"

He tapped his skull. "Still sharp up here." He waved at his body. "If not here."

I leaned my head against the wall and let out a long breath. "What do we do? How do we fix it?"

"You want me to fix it?"

I nodded.

"You're sure? Your dad."

"I know," I said. I couldn't decide if my heart was beating fast out of relief or fear or sorrow. "I know."

•   •   •   •

We waited until nightfall because some guys who lived off-campus were throwing a kegger and no one would be around the fraternity house. My boyfriend suggested my father and I have a meal alone, so we went to the one decent pizza place in town and built our own pie, ordering half a dozen of my father's favorite toppings: Canadian bacon, sausage, pepperoni, double green pepper, feta cheese. When the pizza arrived, the dough was barely able to keep the thing together, it was so belabored by meats and veggies. I watched him eat three slices until I took one for myself. His mouth was ringed with grease. He slurped from his soda, served in a gargantuan red cup.

I tried to smile at him.

"Don't be sad," he said through a mouthful of cheese. "We got so much extra time."

I leaned back and felt a cold wash on my neck.

He smiled. "I know that I can't stay. It's all right." He leaned forward and patted my hand. "This has been nice, hasn't it?"

He tried to pay the check when we were finished but I pointed out that my boyfriend had not resurrected his credit cards or any cash, so I forked over a wad of bills to a girl I knew vaguely from a few parties. She waved goodbye to us through the window as we walked back toward campus while she was wiping down our table.

We didn't say much until we arrived at the house. My boy-friend, as if pre-planned, was waiting on the back deck, his body slumped against the rail. He was breathing hard, like he'd run miles. His clothes barely fit him.

"He doesn't look so good," my father said. He tossed an arm over my shoulder and it was only when he made contact with my body that I realized I was shaking. My dad looked at me. "It's okay, you know."

We each took my boyfriend under one arm.

"Where are we going?" I said.

"You know," my father said, but he pointed to the shed anyway.

A crater of displaced dirt and grass was carved out where my father had sprouted from the ground. Still entangled, the three of us stared down at it in silence, as though we were paying our respects at a memorial. Then my father, with delicate ease, leaned my boyfriend's heft against me. He slid his feet out of the old pair of my sneakers he'd been wearing and peeled off a pair of my socks, tucking each into one of the shoes, which he placed together on the grass as though sliding them into a spot in a closet. Then he started removing his clothing—my boyfriend's clothing—and I winced at the sight of his naked back.

"Is this necessary?" I said.

"Yes," my father said.

"Yes," my boyfriend said.

"How come?" I said.

"It just is," they said at the same time.

I watched my father slide his feet into the earth, shocked at the ease and willingness with which he planted himself in the ground. Bent over, he packed the loose soil up around his ankles. My boyfriend squeezed his arm around my neck and I looked at him. His lips were dry and cracked. I could see how his eyes were asking for forgiveness. I pressed my hand against his side, which felt like a half-melted candle.

My father stood up straight, and I tried not to look at him.

"Now what?" I said.

He was holding his pocketknife by the blade, the red sheath pointed at me. I wasn't surprised that he'd had it this whole time.

"You take this," he said.

I did.

"And now you need to cut me."

"I what?"

He drew an invisible line across his throat.

"No. Are you kidding?"

He shook his head.

"This is wrong," I said. I looked at my boyfriend. This had, after all, been his idea. He'd dragged my father back to life without asking me if I wanted that, and it was thus his fault I was standing here, my father's knife in my hand, expected to drag it across his throat and spill his blood into the grass.

"You can't ask this of me," I said.

"Of course not," my boyfriend said, and held out his hand, palm up.

None of us spoke. My father stared at me. I stared at my boyfriend's palm. He looked down at my father's feet. We were a gruesome triangle.

I gave him the knife.

"I can't watch whatever is going to happen here," I said. I looked at my father. "I'm sorry."

"No apologies," he said.

We didn't say goodbye. I didn't tell him that I loved him. The words hung in the air, invisible and silent. Right before my father died, he'd sent me back to school, demanding that I not ruin my education on his behalf. He'd promised that he'd be around long enough for me to get in a final goodbye, but that didn't turn out to be true; his doctor called, told me that I should get on the road as soon as possible, but the three-hour drive to St. Louis turned out to be too long. I'd thought, immediately after, that getting to speak to him one last time would have made everything okay, his death filing itself away into the history of things that had happened to me. That if I'd had one last moment to speak what I felt, everything would have been fine. And now I felt stupid and queasy and angry and incapable of doing anything except turning my back on him and my boyfriend and walking across the grass and the porch and through the door and up the stairs and down the hall and into my bedroom, where I waited. I took a deep breath. The air was tinged with the smell of my father, wisps of his sweat still in the air. When I lay down on my bed, I could feel him there, the weight of his body on the mattress. But I could also smell my boyfriend's skin, the tart of his underarms, an aroma of cool, wet rocks.

I heard footsteps approaching, could feel a body hovering in the doorway. My eyes were closed, and I wasn't quite ready to open them up. I pictured what might have happened in the yard, and for the briefest moment I wasn't sure who I hoped had killed whom. My heart yearned in conflicting directions, and everything in my stomach was blended and confused. Like a boat on choppy waters, I bucked and swayed until I finally opened my eyes and welcomed the future in.

Spin the Dial

A MONTH BEFORE HIS SIXTEENTH BIRTHDAY, NATHAN sat down at the breakfast table and told his parents he'd decided to give up his left hand. His mother's coffee mug landed so hard that hot liquid poured over her knuckles, skinning the flesh a bright, sour red. His father cleared his throat and frowned over his newspaper. Jenny, twelve, went wide-eyed but kept munching on her toast, craning her neck forward like a spectator at a football game wanting to get a better look at the carnage on the field.

"Why would you give up your whole hand?" his mother said, finally.

Nathan, who sat before an empty place setting—he hadn't bothered with pouring a bowl of Wheaties or a glass of OJ and now regretted having nothing to fill his mouth with to avoid offering an explanation—shrugged.

"What about concert band?" his mother said.

"I can skip a year. Take a study hall instead. That way I can get a job and don't have to worry about missing out on finishing my homework."

His father lowered the sports section. "And what job would you get with only one hand?"

"There are lots of things I could do."

"Like what?"

"I don't know. What do people who have actually lost their hands do? You're saying they're all unemployed?"

His father cleared his throat. "First of all, you will actually lose your hand. Just because it will reappear doesn't mean it won't really be gone. And second of all, those people have had lots of time to figure out how to function with only one. You won't have that luxury."

His mother had started sponging up the spilled coffee, her napkin going soggy fast. The fingers of her burnt hand were limp, as though she'd killed them. Giving up, she crumpled the napkin into a ball and threw it into the mug, where it floated like a buoy. "What about one of your toes?"

"Ryan Hoover's older brother accidentally cut off one of his toes while he was mowing the lawn in sandals last summer," Nathan said.

"Gross," Jenny said. "Stupid."

"It screwed up his balance. He had to go to physical therapy just to walk." Nathan stared at his mother and father. "He still limps."

"Just think about it some more," his father said.

"I have thought about it. I've decided." He looked from his mother to his father. "You just have to agree. You know what happens if you don't."

This made his mother sit up straight. "This isn't something to joke about, Nathan."

"I'm not joking." He held up his hands, elbows propped on the table, and flexed the fingers of his left hand. "I've decided. Now you need to."

•   •   •   •

Because he was young for his grade, most of Nathan's friends had already turned sixteen and made their choices. Tony gave up his right ear, and Nathan had joined the others in gathering around to see the blank space on the side of his face, a weird sheen of flesh below his hairline where the knot and flap of his ear belonged. Devon had stupidly chosen his left ribcage, thinking that he could just wear a protective steel plate that his metalworker father built for him to safeguard his lungs and spleen and heart. What no one in his family had considered was how his left pectoral muscle would collapse, his abdominals going weak. Calvin, Nathan's lab partner in sophomore biology, had given up one of his kidneys, which proved inauspicious when his sister was diagnosed with lupus and her body attacked hers. He was a perfect match and she went on dialysis, his family hoping she could hold out until his seventeenth birthday in November.

The worst, though, was Eli, who played soccer and played it well. No one but Nathan knew how much Eli hated the sport, the practice, the pressure, the expectations. He told his parents he wanted to give up his right ankle and they said, "Absolutely not." His father, apparently, threw a wineglass, splashing merlot against a wall full of family photos, staining the most recent portrait. Eli wouldn't budge. Neither would his parents. On his sixteenth birthday, he woke up and his entire left leg was gone. He'd yelled for his mom and dad, who came rushing into the room to see Eli, splayed on his bed, the left leg of his boxer shorts a flag of deflated fabric. His mother screamed like something out of a horror movie. Eli had, apparently, smiled.

He came to school on crutches. People stared and whispered. Nathan had felt his heart heave.

"Don't," Eli said. "I'll be fine." He leaned against Nathan's locker and waved one of the crutches around. "I'm a natural at these. I broke my ankle in seventh grade."

Nathan had nodded. Sometimes, Eli's body tilted against his for balance and support, his fist pressed against Nathan's sternum, a knuckle pinching at his chest. Eli always smiled and apologized, but the pain didn't bother Nathan; it was a focused, acute hurt, overcome by the pleasant wave blossoming across his entire body.

•　　　•　　　•　　　•

The drive to summer band camp was silent. Nathan kept flexing his hand and looking at his father, who kept his head straight forward. The soft case containing his flute sat on Nathan's lap, which he strummed with his fingers.

"I'm not trying to be difficult," Nathan said as they pulled into his high school's parking lot.

"I know that." His dad was the girls' volleyball coach, and while Nathan worked through the work of Irving Berlin, he would be drilling back sets and slide attacks with the varsity team.

Nathan gripped the flute case hard. "I just want to try something else. Maybe running or something."

"Have you ever heard of spinning the dial?"

"No."

They were idling in front of the main entrance. Once Nathan got out, his father would drive around to the far side of the building.

"It's a volleyball thing. If your team loses a set and you don't like the matchups across the net, you give yourself and your opponents a different look by starting in a different rotation." He perched the fingers of his right hand in his left palm and twisted. "Spinning the dial."

Nathan nodded. "I guess I want to spin the dial."

"I'll talk to your mom."

"Thanks."

Nathan was hit by a hard ball of heat when he stepped out of the car. He saw the tuba player and two trumpeters marching inside, their backs already crowded with sweat. On the athletic field, the soccer team's summer practice was underway, the grass split between them and the football players, who were crashing into blocking dummies. Normally, Nathan would look through the hard sun to find Eli, but he knew he wasn't there. Someone up ahead called his name and he turned from the field. When he glanced at the parking lot, his father was already gone.

• • • •

Boys dared one another to give up their dicks. They would squawk and laugh, hitting each other in the shoulders no matter how many times someone made the joke. Girls sometimes gave up one or both of their breasts, filling their bras with tissue or crumpled paper to keep the shape and avoid ridicule. Teachers told them about their own choices. Parents were brought in to discuss the decision, how a balance between the child's wishes and the practicality of losing something was necessary. Some kids wanted to do deeply stupid things, giving up parts that they couldn't see: the pancreas or liver or diaphragm, their uneducated brains not aware of the essential need to keep those. Others went the easy route, jettisoning their hair or wisdom teeth or a single fingernail, which would result in minimal return on investment. Willingness to make sacrifices, after all, was a desirable trait on college and job applications. Being able to explain why you'd opt to give up only your appendix or tonsils when so many other people had to excise those parts anyway wouldn't get you very far.

Nathan's father had given up his voice, which had been challenging but had taught him the value of precise language. His mother had given up one of her eyes, which on the surface had perhaps seemed like a lazy, easy sacrifice because her prescription glasses were already thick and heavy, but when her left eye returned on her seventeenth birthday it brought along with it perfect vision, in both eyes, an immediate reward that lasted into early middle age; she liked to boast, sometimes, that her optometrist called her his easiest patient, all of her tests coming back perfect, her retinas and the scans of her optic nerve the cleanest he'd ever seen.

"It happens sometimes," she'd told him. "Things come back better than they leave."

Nathan tried pointing this out at dinner when he broached the subject again. "Imagine how well I'll play when it comes back."

"But you play well now," his mother said. "And you don't know for sure you'll be better."

"I certainly didn't become some superstar singer," his father said. He didn't mention what had passed between them in the car: that Nathan wanted to do something else. He didn't hate playing the flute; far from it. The artistry made his teeth vibrate. When he mastered trick passages like the ones he overcame when memorizing and perfecting *Andalouse* for the individual district solo competition—earning, for all that work, a one, sending him to state, where he scored a two, an "Excellent" and a red ribbon— he felt a warm spread of joy and confidence. But he'd spent years laughing away the blowjob jokes and homophobia, always willed his face not to go hot at the truth simmering beneath the insinuations and insults. Nathan always wondered if people would be nicer, would withhold their queer-bashing, if they knew that what they said bore kernels of truth.

His father cleared his throat. "Why don't we think about it some more. We have time."

Nathan curled his fists under the table but said nothing. He nodded. His mother nodded. Jenny, watching, nodded. Heads bobbed everywhere. Nathan felt a swell of dizziness that he knew, really, was anger, a subfloor of irritation that had sat in his stomach for as long as he could remember.

●   ●   ●   ●

Eli flopped back on Nathan's bed, hands braided behind his head. "I don't know. Your hand?"

"Need I remind you that you wanted to dump your ankle? You?"

Nathan was sitting at his writing desk. During the school year, they spent hours this way, Eli splayed on Nathan's bedspread, propped up by a pair of shams, Nathan hunched over his desk, scribbling answers to math problems that Eli solved, often without needing to see them written down. Nathan wondered if he was the only one who knew this side of Eli, the numbers genius that he possessed. He wondered if other people knew he wanted to go to somewhere like MIT or Tulane instead of one of the soccer powerhouses.

You just never knew who knew what.

Eli smacked the small sliver of twin mattress next to him and Nathan plopped down. Eli's breath was citrusy from the orange-flavored gum he chewed perpetually, a habit he'd developed when he was only twelve and popped a stick in his mouth right before a soccer game in which he scored three goals in the first half. Ever since, he was incessantly gnashing, his jaw hard, teeth surely on their way to rot.

They had only known each other since freshman year, when they were assigned the same homeroom and neighboring lockers. Eli, outgoing, had said hi on the second day of school as they both tried to wrap their heads around which books to stuff into their bags. Their class schedules had no overlaps except that first, brief block of time when everyone was still too sleepy to listen to the morning announcements, but Eli developed a daily habit of greeting Nathan at its start and, when they managed to meet at the end of the day, he would ask Nathan how he was doing. They'd become friends quickly, stitched together with a tightness that was stronger than Nathan's longer friendships with Devon and Tony. And then came the party, at the close of sophomore year, held at a soccer player's house, a turreted brick in a fancy neighborhood in which Nathan had never set foot. Despite his lack of a leg, Eli drove, and they stood aloof, Eli greeted by fellow athletes while Nathan was summarily ignored. After just one beer, Nathan felt groggy and loose, and in the low, dim light, he felt his body sway and tingle. Eli, saying nothing, swayed with him even though he was totally sober, and it was like they were dancing. Nothing else happened that night, and Eli had not mentioned it again. But he started allowing for physical proximity, a closeness Nathan wasn't permitted with his other friends. Sometimes, they lay so near one another that Nathan's right leg pushed into the territory where Eli's left belonged. It felt odd to see, and more than once Nathan had glanced down and thought he was staring at an optical illusion, that if he looked long enough and from the correct angle Eli's leg would reappear, though of course it never did. It wouldn't be there again until February.

"Have you been working out?" Eli said.

"I've done a few pushups, I guess."

"It's nice. I can tell." Eli poked at Nathan's hand. "But you won't be able to do them without that."

Nathan groaned. "Not you too."

"No," Eli said, reaching out and grabbing Nathan's hand. "You should do what you think is right for you." His thumb dug across the back of Nathan's hand, pulling the skin across the veins and metacarpals. "Your parents aren't happy."

"Of course they're not." Nathan twisted and patted at the empty space where Eli's leg should have been. "But I think you've served as a cautionary tale."

Eli smiled. Nathan liked what that did to his forehead, the little crinkles of flesh that emerged from the smoothness of his face. "Anything to help."

• • • •

Nathan's mother was lying on the living room sofa, a magazine about gardening propped against her stomach. He sat down in the chair opposite her and watched her skim an article. He could see a photograph of a pair of gardening shears. For the last few years his mother had been building up an impressive backyard garden, one of those raised box beds. Tomato vines had flourished under her watch, along with spinach and various peppers. She wanted to invest in some fruit trees but hadn't decided what kind.

"It's almost time," he said finally.

She sighed and shut the magazine. "I know, Nathan."

"What did your parents say? When you told them you wanted to give up an eye?"

His mother sat up. She was wearing a pair of capris that showed off her calves. She jogged from time to time, and her legs had retained their musculature. He knew she'd been an athlete in college, but he could never remember what she played.

"They weren't happy, but they went along."

"I don't want to be like Eli."

"I know." She slapped the magazine onto the coffee table. She sighed, her body slumping as she exhaled. "You know we'll do whatever you want."

"That's not what I mean."

His mother frowned.

"I mean," he said, lifting his hands, "I like playing the flute. But it's not all I want to do."

"What else do you want to do, then?"

"I don't know. I've spent so much time with it." He swallowed, willing his voice not to crack. "I just want to know what else I might like. Experiment a little bit."

"It's just, a year is a long time to lose. What if you don't play as well after?"

Nathan cocked his head and gave his mother a long look. "Did you lose something special by giving up one of your eyes?"

Normally, she laughed off questions like Nathan's by making jokes about her balance and how she was sure that her brain was lopsided now because only one half of it had received visual stimulus for a year, even though Nathan knew that wasn't how the optic nerve and occipital lobe worked. Her job now had to do with numbers, a record-keeping and bill-dispensing job at a local auto body shop that paid well because she was good both at haggling with insurance companies and at getting clients to pay their own bills on time. She could research parts suppliers for the best deals without skimping on quality. As far as Nathan knew, these skills had little to do with her restored, improved vision, but how could he know for sure?

His mother sighed and took a long breath. "I played field hockey."

"I guess that would require good hand–eye coordination."

"I also shot guns."

"What? Like, you hunted?"

She shook her head. "Targets. I was good. I knew how to steady myself, breathe deep and clean."

"What happened?"

"I lost it."

"You couldn't do it anymore after?"

"I didn't want to." She looked around the room, eyes landing on bits of décor: family photos, a ceramic vase Nathan's father had bought for his mother during a trip to North Carolina, the wicker baskets full of plush blankets they never used for whatever reason, paperback originals stacked on a side table, unread. "After not shooting for a year, I thought I'd be desperate to get back to it. But then the idea of it made me feel, I don't know."

"Ill?"

"I wouldn't go that far. Just, I wasn't interested. In shooting or in field hockey."

"You think you made a mistake?"

"I think I didn't have a backup plan." She leaned over the table and pressed a hand to his knee. Her knuckles had healed from the burns from spilling her coffee, but Nathan thought he could see the ghostly outline in her smooth, peach skin. "I just don't want you losing more than your hand unless that's what you want. I want you to know what you're giving up."

"I've thought about it a lot. Maybe I'll—" Nathan thought for a moment. "Maybe I'll play soccer."

His mother smiled, finally, and removed her hand. She sat back, arms folded over her chest. "Soccer, huh?"

"Or something else."

"I think you might like soccer."

"I think I might, too."

●　　　●　　　●　　　●

Nathan wasn't sure how long Jenny had been standing in his doorway. He'd been lying on his bed, staring at the ceiling, letting his hands creep into the hem of his athletic shorts without thinking about it.

"Jesus," he said, pulling his hand onto his chest when he saw her. "What are you doing?"

Jenny was licking a popsicle, her mouth ringed grape, as though she'd forgotten how to properly eat. "What'd you do to Mom?"

"What are you talking about?"

Jenny rolled her eyes. "She's in her room crying."

Nathan sat up. "What?"

"Are you deaf?"

"Why's she crying?"

"Ugh. Would I be asking you if I knew?"

Nathan felt something curl in his stomach. He shoved past his sister, who followed him down the hall. He stopped in front of his parents' closed bedroom door and listened, imagining— hoping—that Jenny was wrong or making shit up. But he heard it, the soft lullaby noise of his mother's sobs. He thought he should tap on the door and ask her what was wrong, but he stayed still.

"Aren't you going to do something?" Jenny whispered.

Nathan fluttered a hand as if to shoo her away, but she stayed put, crunching on the last of her popsicle and waving the stained stick toward him like it was a magic wand.

"I think she just needs some alone time," Nathan whispered, moving away from the door. He gestured for Jenny to lead the way back down the hall. At first she didn't move, but then she rolled her eyes again and stomped off. Nathan followed her downstairs.

His phone vibrated: a text from Eli, asking if Nathan wanted to go to the pool. Eli's parents always bought summer passes, and they didn't expire for another three weeks. Despite his missing leg, Eli loved going, even if he just lay on one of the plastic chaise lounges with its rubber stripes, body splayed out so people could see his missing leg. Nathan replied *sure*, even though as soon as he sent the message, he felt a hard jab in his gut. Even though his body was blooming thanks to the hundred pushups he put himself through each morning, lactic tightness stinging through his chest, Nathan still felt like a string bean, sticky and concave and pale.

Nathan stopped to listen at his mother's door before changing into his swimsuit. She had stopped sobbing. His phone was warm in his hand. Eli was waiting.

He knocked on his mother's bedroom door and tried the knob, which turned freely in his hand.

His parents' room, which he hadn't stepped foot inside for a long time, was a large suite, with a walk-in closet and giant bathroom with both a tub and shower stall and double vanity, everything white and pristine. The room had a bay window that looked out over the backyard and two other windows, one on each side, that let in heaps of natural light. But Nathan's mother had pulled all the blinds shut, unfurled the sashes. She'd closed the bathroom door. The room felt like a mausoleum.

She was lying on the bed, dead center, staring at the ceiling, a pillow clutched to her chest like a stuffed animal.

"Mom?" Nathan said.

"Hi," she said. Though she was no longer crying, her voice was mucky with tears.

"Is everything okay?"

"Oh," she said. "It will be."

"When?"

She laughed. "Good question."

"I don't have to give up my hand."

His mother sat up, her back resting against the headboard. She released the pillow and slapped the bed. When he sat down, his mother launched herself forward and wrapped him in a hug. He let her hold him for a long moment, then touched her hands where they were knotted at his chest like a gargantuan medallion.

"I just want you to be happy, you know."

"I know that, Mom."

"I thought I always knew what made you happy." She released him and leaned away. "But I guess I'm realizing we can't always know what makes other people happy. There's so much we don't know about one another."

"I guess, yeah."

They said no more. Nathan watched his mother, the puffiness of her eyes taking on new complexion. They shimmered but not with sadness or nostalgia or regret. She was looking straight at him, her fingers twisting a clump of the cotton sheet beneath her.

"You're getting so old," she said finally. "I don't think I was ready for that to happen."

Nathan's phone vibrated.

His mother smiled. "You have somewhere to be. Of course."

"I don't have to go."

"Of course you do."

"It's not a big deal."

"That's the thing," she said. "Sometimes things seem small but they're bigger than they look."

She shooed him away.

In his room, Nathan scrambled to change into his swimsuit, a pair of white shorts with blue swirls along the front. He ignored Jenny's yelled exhortations wondering where he was going when he trundled down the stairs and pulled open the front door. Eli had texted, saying he was nearly there and would be outside in just a few minutes. Nathan hadn't asked whether Eli had invited Devon or Tony or anyone else to come, and when Eli's car—a clunking, coughing Camry that Nathan was pretty sure would fall apart if it moved any faster than forty miles an hour or was caught out in a heavy rainstorm—pulled up, Nathan saw that Eli was alone. Nathan took a hard, careful breath. He clenched his fists and looked down at his tight fingers, the knuckles going a bright pink. As he crossed his yard, he made a promise to himself: he would, before his hand was gone, tell Eli how he felt. That, if he was going to lose one thing, he would gain something else. It might be joy; it might be sorrow. He might cry tears like his mother had, but at least he would know.

He opened the passenger door. Eli's car smelled like suntan lotion and a locker room, heady coconut and sour-sweet sweat that the dangling evergreen air freshener bobbing against the rearview mirror couldn't send packing, even when Eli kept the windows rolled all the way down.

"Hi," Nathan said as he tossed himself in the passenger seat, crushing an empty paper soda cup from McDonald's under his feet.

"Sorry about the mess," Eli said as he put the car in gear.

"No worries."

Nathan tried not to look over at Eli as he drove, one elbow sticking out the open window. He was wearing a loose tank top, the seam along Eli's side long and dangling, exposing the shark gill shape of his serratus muscles and the lines of his obliques. His swim trunks, bright blue, wheedled up his right thigh, showing off his glowing golden hairs and the sinews of his quads. The left sleeve was an empty space that held its own strange allure.

"Any progress?" Eli said. He was smiling at Nathan, his teeth a brilliant match for Nathan's shorts.

"Some," Nathan said.

"That's good. Every little bit, you know?"

"Yeah," Nathan said. The sun was high in the sky, the air streaking in through the windows hot and heavy. Nathan felt warm. He felt sure. He pressed his fingernails into the soft flesh of his palm and looked at Eli. "Every bit."

Churchgoing

WHEN CHAD CALLED, I ANSWERED, BECAUSE WE agreed to try to remain friends. I admit that I almost swiped the call away when I saw who it was from, but I'd made a promise to myself to start keeping my promises to other people, so I picked up the phone.

"Can you come over?" he said by way of greeting. This was not new. I couldn't remember the last time Chad had said hi, either via the phone or in person. Even his text messages had always cut right to the quick, instructive and commanding rather than inquisitive or driven by any desire to simply communicate for the sake of it.

"Why?" I said.

"I found something."

At first, I thought he meant something on his body, like a lump in his nut sack or a lesion on his chest, and I felt a horrible chill wash over me. I was thrown into a future where I was forced to take care of him while he whittled down to pencil-thin and gray-skinned—we both knew Chad didn't really have any close friends, ergo the need to cling to me even though we were no longer together—or, worse, where I, too, was battered by horrible disease and dying, my hair gone, my musculature atrophied, my blood poisoned and my breathing labored. I nearly chucked the phone down to run to the bathroom to vomit, but then he added, quickly, "In my yard."

"You what?" I said.
"I can't decide if it's freaky—"
"Or what?" I said.
"Or a sign."

•   •   •   •

Every Sunday morning, in lieu of brunch or late-morning sex, Chad and I would go to church. We always arrived late and left early, slipping in during the first reading (we only hit Catholic churches) and sneaking away before the Eucharistic Prayer because it was so long and kneeling made me uncomfortable. We didn't really dress up, donning jeans and solid-color t-shirts, maybe the occasional polo. Neither of us did much fixing of our hair, letting it lie tangled or floppy atop our heads, scraped to a scrawl against our foreheads. Chad had been raised Catholic, but he'd stopped going to church midway through his first year of college, when he joined a fraternity and spent his Sunday mornings trying to squash hangovers instead of contemplating the state of the Trinity. I had given up much sooner, at the start of high school, when my parents, in order to save money, opted to send me to the local public school rather than shell out tuition at the pricey private high school that most of my grade school mates would attend. I was angry at this choice, not because I was looking forward to taking theology classes or being required to attend mass every Thursday or wear a uniform, but because I would be severed from my closest trio of friends, my only real friends, and so I told my parents that if a religious education was not in the cards for me, neither was going to church. They looked at one another and shrugged and said that was fine. I gaped at them, but I didn't back down that Sunday, refusing to get out of bed. My mother made only one attempt to haul me up, then let me sleep. I heard the garage door growl up and down and I watched from my window as they drove off without me for the first, but hardly the last, time.

The trips Chad and I took to churches weren't some reinvigoration of either of our spiritual lives; a Great Awakening this was not. We'd gotten drunk one night early in our relationship and talked about the absurdities of a Catholic Mass, all the sitting and standing and kneeling, the ritualized responding. When our Catholic friends got married, the first question we'd always ask ourselves was whether the ceremony would be accompanied by a full Mass. We talked about how, despite our years out of practice, the words came flying back like we'd been going to church non-stop, some deep-tissue muscle memory shooting the right phrases out of our mouths.

"We should go to church tomorrow," Chad said, slurping on wine. I'd opened a bottle of Beaujolais. "Just for fun."

"Okay," I said, and even though both of us were looped, we kept our word the next day. My head was throbbing—we'd opened a second bottle and then had beers—but we made it all the way until the end of the homily before we snuck out. Chad drove us to our favorite taco place for an early lunch, where, in my pinched, hungover state, I ate three corn tortillas stuffed with carnitas and drank a margarita that eased the throbbing in my face. Chad talked all the way through our meal about his memories of going to church as a kid, his face lit up and joyous as he remembered his First Communion and the time he and one of his friends snuck out of Mass the morning after a sleepover and walked laps around the church before being caught by his friend's dad and yelled at, even though the dad was smiling the whole time.

"Sounds like you miss it," I said.

"Oh no," Chad said, shaking his head with screwball vehemence. But I could see that he was lying, even if he didn't realize it himself.

•　　　•　　　•　　　•

I barely knocked before Chad threw open the front door. He lived in a subdivision where almost all of the houses were architecturally identical, the door facing the driveway rather than the street, the concrete front porch lined with a trio of floor-to-ceiling windows with thick blinds that Chad was always leaving open, even at night, so anyone driving by could see him moving around, framed by the lamps he kept on either end of the living room.

He was still striking in his beauty, which I'd managed to forget in the weeks since we'd broken up. I had a knack for this, my brain letting people's features go fuzzy with time apart. The blackness of his hair had faded to a grayer, mutable color in my mind, the sharpness of his cheekbones blunted. I had managed to remember the cut of his jaw, the bone prominent where it jutted from his neck.

Chad wrung his hands as if unsure how to invite me in. My recollection of this quirk had not gone to seed: for all his bulk and confidence, he had a way of wilting at moments of transition or invitation. When we'd first gone out, I had seen quite clearly at the end of the night how badly he wanted to, at the very least, kiss me, if not do more. But his eyes kept wheeling about as we sat in his car in front of my apartment building, his hands drumming the console between our seats. I finally leaned over and planted my lips on his and I felt him relax beneath the pressure of my mouth as he set one of his hands on my shoulder and the other on my side.

"What did you need to show me?" I said, trying to keep my voice friendly, as though we were frat brothers meeting up for an afternoon barbecue.

"Right," he said. "Come with me."

We walked through his house, which was small and boxy, the living room and kitchen separated by the stairs leading to the

basement, bedrooms tucked down a pair of incredibly short hallways. Chad flung open the sliding door that led onto a covered
patio, the house's best feature, which he'd filled with wicker furniture that was dusted with leaves and cobwebs and a hammock
that we had, one time, had very awkward and difficult sex on. We
turned right, around the privacy fence that kept prying eyes away,
and marched into his yard, where a single huge oak tree sprawled
over the scroll of grass. I stopped. He'd been digging; the backyard looked like—I couldn't decide—either an archaeological dig
or the start of a mass grave. I raised an eyebrow.

"I decided I wanted to try one of those raised gardens. The
home kind."

"Uh huh," I said. Chad had never demonstrated any interest
in outdoorsy, hands-in-the-soil sorts of activities when we'd
been together. Once, when I suggested a hike, he said he had an
extreme fear of getting bitten by ticks and dying of Lyme disease.

He marched toward the area he'd dug up. The yard looked
like a room where a strip of the carpet has been yanked out, the
clay-colored dirt the subfloor. When he stopped, I looked down.

"What the hell is that?" I said.

In the middle of the dug-out area was a deeper hole, and inside
the hole was a Bible.

"It's what I found."

"Why's there a Bible buried in your yard?"

"I don't know. But that's not all."

"It's not?"

"No. There's more."

●   ●   ●   ●

Chad kept a list of churches. He printed out a map of our area, a
little white-flight suburb outside of St. Louis, and affixed it to a
bulletin board. Then he popped thumbtacks through the locations

of all the Catholic churches he could find, scribbling their names on little pink Post-its. When we went to one, he would write the date of our attendance beneath it. Every Sunday after we came back to his house we went into his guest bedroom, where he'd hung the bulletin board, and I watched him jot the date down. He'd then pick our next destination and spend the next few days wandering through the church's website, finding out the name of its parish priest and reading PDFs of old bulletins.

"So I know what we're going to experience when we're there."

He shared with me the details he thought significant enough, and we would wager with one another about what kind of church it would be. Would the music be uptight, formal, old-school organ and single singer? Or would there be drums and saxophones, young people singing along with the hymns? Would the homilies be gentle and contemporary or brimstone, steeped in tradition? We even tried to guess if the pastor would have a decent singing voice. I always said no. Chad always said yes.

•   •   •   •

Chad picked up a shovel he'd left in the grass and started digging next to the unearthed Bible. I stared down at its black cover, bent in the center where the hard spade had smashed against it as he dug. The leather was cracked and dull, lacking the shine I associated with holy books. Dirt smeared the embossed lettering, the K in *King James* fully obscured by ruddy soil. The gold edges of the pages were slashed and grody. It was the saddest Bible I'd ever seen.

As Chad worked, he slowly unearthed another, identical Bible.

"How many are there?"

"I don't know. But over there," he said, pointing to the corner of the area he'd dug out, "I found a rosary."

"What's next?" I said. "A baptismal font? A crucifix?"

He slammed the hard edge of the shovel into the grass so it bit and stuck, then leaned against it like an old man propping himself up with a walking stick. His forehead was slick with sweat after only a few minutes of effort. I remembered that: though he was in excellent physical shape, could run or swim for long periods, was twisty and fast on a basketball court, rounded the bases in softball games with efficient speed, he was a sweater, his back going gunky and his hair wet at the first efforts his body made.

"Do you think this isn't real?" he said.

"It feels like a bad practical joke, if I'm being honest."

"And why would I have done this?" he said.

I raised an eyebrow. "I didn't say you did it."

"Well, who else do you think would have done it?"

"No idea."

"And why would I?"

I shrugged. "Attention?"

He let out a loose bark of laughter, and I chuckled too. He continued to smile, and I smiled back at him, wondering if I should kiss him. Wondering if I'd messed up by letting this man loose. Wondering if I'd ruined a good thing.

"Thirsty?" he said.

"Sure."

Chad left the shovel behind. I followed him inside, but as we walked I turned to look back at the garden, and wondered what, exactly, was growing there.

●   ●   ●   ●

I broke up with Chad after one of our trips to church. We'd been sloughing down sangria the night before, sitting on a patio illuminated by strings of fat Christmas lights. The next morning I barely remembered getting home. My head felt thin and thick at the same time, and my jaw ached. Chad leapt out of bed when he realized we were going to be late, and I groaned and rolled away from the sun pouring through his bedroom window when he tossed the curtains open, burying myself under his sheets, which smelled clean and fresh. He was good about those kinds of things, household chores that were signs of adulthood—like changing your furnace filters and paying your property taxes—that I was always forgetting.

"Can't we just skip this week?" I said when he threw my jeans at me.

"It's the Lord's Day!" he said.

I eyed him, not sure if he was joking. I sure hoped so, but I wasn't positive. For weeks, I'd been watching him out of the corner of my eye when we slipped into churches. At first, I'd been giggly and goofy about the whole thing, and so had he. But then he shushed me and pressed for us to get there earlier and earlier. He hadn't yet advocated for us to stick around for an entire Mass, but I could feel the words forming in his head. A solemnity began gathering itself around him like a corona, an invisible halo like the ones formed around Jesus and Mary in the stained glass or pewter slabs that depicted the Stations of the Cross.

I grunted and rolled away from him, sandwiching my head between a pair of pillows, and mumbled something about feeling like I might throw up. Chad didn't listen. He tugged away the sheets, then cuffed my ankle with his fingers and started pulling me from the bed. My headache was already worse, my mouth dry and sticky at the same time, and I felt a throbbing ache in my knees.

"Stop," I said. I didn't yell, and maybe that was a good thing, because he might have thought I was playing around, feigning anger, which would have only made me madder. He stood up straight and blinked at me.

"Seriously?" he said.

"Seriously."

He went slack, his arms droopy ropes. His chest rose and fell, and he frowned.

"But we always go."

"But we don't have to go. We're not religious."

His jaw tightened and loosened. I could practically see his tongue moving around in his mouth as he tried to decide which words to let loose. And that was the moment when I realized that this wasn't just a fluffy, silly thing for him. It was serious. Chad went to church on Sundays because he actually wanted to.

So I got out of bed. I muddled through putting on clothing, trying to ignore the throb in my temples. I downed too much ibuprofen and wore sunglasses. Chad drove, and he smiled and kept looking at me, but neither of us spoke. I knew, when we arrived at the church, that it would be the last time I'd go with him, there or anywhere.

•   •   •   •

We drank bottled waters, standing on opposite sides of his kitchen island. Chad was still sweating, gloms of perspiration caught at his temples and hovering over his lip. He was breathing hard, but this, I thought, was for show, though I had no idea what he could be trying to show me. We didn't say much. I kept screwing the cap back on my bottle and then almost immediately unscrewing it so I could take another sip.

Finally, I said, "So what do you think that's about out there?" Then I added, "If it's not some practical joke?"

He shrugged and drank. His Adam's apple bobbed as the water sluiced down. I remembered how I liked to run my tongue over that gritty arrowhead, a spot that was always a bit rougher than the rest of his throat because he was weird about shaving there, never quite able to get the skin as smooth with his razor out of some weird fear that he would hurt himself if he wasn't overly cautious. I didn't mind the sandpaper texture; that spot, somehow, had a sweet, wondrous taste to it. I took another gulp of my water.

"Maybe there used to be a church here." He gazed out the sliding doors to his backyard, but the privacy fence cut off his view.

We stared at one another for a long moment. Well, I stared at Chad, and he stared outside. We both knew where each of us was really looking.

•   •   •   •

The conversation always comes up eventually, even if the tilt and flow to it is slow and scrambled. It took a long time for either of us to broach the subject of how we'd come out to our parents. When I finally asked Chad, we had just left church and had decided to take a long drive to nowhere. Neither of us was hungover for once—we'd stayed in the night before—and the sky was crispy blue, like a splash of buttery paint filming the sky. The drive was Chad's idea; I didn't really care for the notion of "a drive," which seemed antiquated and anti-environment, but I said, "Sure, why not?"

We were fifteen minutes out of town, stumping along some hilly backroads. Chad had all the windows of his sedan open and the radio on, but I couldn't make out many of the words. He churned open his sunroof, too, and I felt like I was standing in a wind tunnel. He didn't seem particularly thrown off by the silence; I watched his hands on the steering wheel, lazily hooked at four and eight, fingers unfurling to thump along to the beat of music I couldn't hear. Chad was smiling, and when I glanced at him at the right angle I could see the pinched joy in his eyes, snuffed behind his sunglasses.

It seemed like as good a time as any, so I asked: "What did your parents say when you told them you liked guys?"

He tilted his head toward me as if he couldn't hear, so I said it again, shouting this time. I had one hand out the window to feel the stream of air in my fingers. I balled them into a fist and bobbed my arm like a fishing lure.

The car slowed; we'd been going about sixty on a hilly country road, my stomach flopping up and down as we coasted and ground upward. At first, I'd wanted to tell him to slow down, but my body had grown accustomed to the car's lurch, the grind of the engine, the threat of being pulled over for motoring well over the speed limit, and now, as we seized with slowness, I felt my guts punch uncomfortably, like I was falling.

I thought Chad was going to stop, but we kept moseying, now a good ten miles per hour beneath the legal limit. He drummed his fingers on the wheel, which he held with only one hand at lower speed.

"I don't know that I ever really told them," he said eventually. "I just told them about a boyfriend like I was talking about a girlfriend." He shrugged. "They went with it. Didn't ask questions."

"Really?"

"Yeah." His eyebrows arched over his sunglasses and he tilted his head toward me while keeping his eyes on the road. "What about you?"

I told him how I'd come out right before college, the week before I moved out of my parents' house, a delay I'd chosen so that if they kicked me out I would only be homeless for a little while.

"You really thought they'd do that?" Chad said.

I hadn't really thought that, but one could never know. My parents were friends with a lesbian couple who came over for dinner sometimes, drinking dry red wines by the bottle and playing Scrabble, my parents going red-cheeked from too much of the pricey merlot and getting their asses kicked at wordplay. I didn't play, but they let me sit and watch while each team set down their tiles and added up their scores. I watched the women lean into one another, laughing and slapping each other's shoulders with delight. I was entranced by their hands sliding against one another, their faces pressed close, and I could feel my own cheeks going flush and had to tell myself not to stare.

My parents were in my bedroom with me, helping me untack posters that I wanted to take off to school, blow-ups of my favorite movies: *Goodfellas*, *The Sting*, *Saving Private Ryan*. I had just finished rolling up a still from *Trainspotting* and decided it was time to tell them. I don't know what made that moment the right one. Perhaps it was the fact that the scene was so normal and everyday, my father standing on a squat stepladder so he could wrench out thumbtacks wedged into the wall, my mother sitting on the bed untangling her heap of rubber bands and whistling to music only she could hear, her sandaled foot bobbing up and down.

"I think I like boys," I said, holding up the poster like a combat staff with which I could strike either of them if they decided to attack me.

My mother stopped whistling, a rubber band dangling from her fingertips. My father twisted around, hands still pressed against the wall, careful not to wrinkle the poster of *Dumb and Dumber* he was working on. They blinked at me.

"I mean," I said, "I still like girls. But I think I also like boys."

My mother looked at my father. She'd been sitting facing away from him, so she had to turn. She didn't try to be inconspicuous, which I appreciated. He glanced down at her, then turned back to the poster.

"Give me just a second to finish this," he said. "I don't want to drop anything."

While my father finished working, my mother stood and dropped the rubber band on the top of the heap. I was still clinging onto the poster and didn't think to move it out of the way before she gobbled me up in a hug. I smelled her almond body lotion and her tropical-fruit shampoo. When I tried to let go she let out a little peepy noise like she was a squeaky toy and I was the dog biting down on her, so I didn't move, and neither did she, until my father clambered down from the stepladder and, cupping the thumbtacks carefully in his palm and draping the *Dumb and Dumber* poster on the bed, joined us in our embrace.

"It's like something out of *The Brady Bunch*," Chad said.

"Except there were just the three of us. And we never had a maid."

"You know what I mean."

I shrugged. "I guess I do."

"So we both turned out okay," Chad said. He started driving faster again, the engine purring with effort.

I remembered how, despite that hearty embrace, my parents stopped asking about girlfriends after that, as though my romantic life was akin to drug abuse or extreme weight gain, a thing acknowledged and hovering but never discussed. I brought a girl home for midterm break that first semester, and I kept catching my parents side-eyeing one another like they weren't sure what to do or think. I never addressed it, and then the next time I brought someone back from college I brought a boy, the first boy I did more than kiss, and they stumbled through introductions and two awkward days of meals and lounging around before I decided it was time to leave.

"I guess we did," I said to Chad as we bumped over a high hill and I felt my stomach dip and drop and rise again.

•   •   •   •

It would have made sense if something happened at Chad's house: if, as I was leaving, he cuffed a hand around my arm and pulled me to him, or if I reached over the kitchen island and stroked his cheek, or if as I was backing out of the driveway he came bursting through his front door, yelling for me to stop so he could tell me that he didn't want me to go.

But none of that happened.

What happened was I told him, again, how weird the mystery of the Bibles was. Then I said I should go, and he didn't slow or stop me leaving. I never asked why he wanted me to see them. I drove around for a while, something in my chest unsettled, like a rib had broken loose and was floating around my thorax. Eventually I went back to my apartment. I lay down on my couch and turned on a tennis tournament, letting the whack of the ball drill me into a light nap.

I did tell Chad to call me if he found anything else, but he didn't. I kept expecting some strange coincidence, where I'd be watching the news and he would appear, subject of a local story about his discovery of the Bibles. But no, nothing. I dreamt a few nights after the call that he found new things: a chalice, a marble altar at the foot of the tree, tangled beneath its roots. These nighttime hallucinations were vivid and hard. I let days, weeks, pass, and tried to let his face fade.

• • • •

A week after our first churchgoing, Chad and I both woke early on Sunday morning, the noise of songbirds outside my apartment pulling us both from sleep. We didn't say anything to one another, but I pressed myself against his back and inhaled the bready scent of his unwashed skin. I let my hands linger along his side, where the muscles shifted and stretched as he breathed. For a long time neither of us acknowledged that the other was awake aside from the shared wriggle of our toes. The night before had been calm and quiet; we stayed in and watched a trio of bad horror movies on Netflix and slow-sipped gin and tonics and only had two apiece, so I knew that we were both clear-eyed and headache free that morning.

Eventually Chad took in a deep breath, nasal and flush, and said, "Wanna go to church again?"

I snorted, thinking he was joking, so I played along. "Sure," I said. "I'm feeling holy and spirited today." I rolled away from him and let out a yawn. I stretched my arms up toward the ceiling, letting the bedspread slide down both our torsos. Chad tossed himself out and found his underwear.

"I'll have to go in last night's clothes," he said. I wouldn't recognize, until much later, that the regret in his voice was real.

"Then I'll do that too," I said. "Wrinkled fabrics be damned!"

We took our time getting ready; he kept a spare toothbrush in my bathroom, and we jostled for counterspace, elbowing one another and trying not to choke on our froth as we laughed. When we were both finished he kissed me before we put on our shoes.

"Let's try a different one," Chad said.

"A different what?"

"Church," he said, and that was how our pattern of finding a new place each week was born.

On that drive, twelve minutes, I didn't really watch him. I wasn't worried yet about the roots of his faith regrowing through his body, a faith we hadn't spent much time talking about aside from our shared distaste for most of the old-fashioned Catholic dogma, particularly the parts that condemned us to hell for our attraction to one another.

"You know," he said as we got out of his car and walked toward the church, a looming gray monster with stained-glass windows along its sides and a pair of spires that appeared to be shish-kabobbing the plump clouds hanging low in the sky, "we could do this every week. Different church each time."

"Why?" I said.

He shrugged and held the door open for me. The vestibule was cool, the air conditioning a hearty blast. I rubbed my forearms and took a bulletin from a pile on a small table by the door. We both skipped the holy water. A hymn was in full blast as we slipped into a row at the rear.

"It could be our thing," Chad whispered, opening his bulletin and giving it an intense read, as if he knew the people mentioned therein. I watched his fingers flutter over the names of those being prayed over this week, as though they were jotted down in braille and he was blind.

I sat back and pretended to listen to the first reading. Though I'd woken up fresh, I was suddenly tired. Maybe I was feeling, deep down, the first aches that Chad's renewal of faith would cause me. Maybe the pew was simply uncomfortable, compressing my lower back. Either way, I felt my body pulsing, letting out little blips whose message, like that of the priest at the altar, was lost on me.

What You Have Always Wanted

NO ONE CARED THAT JACK AND JAMES DUNKIRK WERE married, or that every Halloween Jack painted his body tan and James' silver with black dots drawn over his nipples and belly button and along every point and seam, Jack a sleek Cowardly Lion and James the Tin Man, their lean musculatures on display every time they opened the door and dumped full-sized Snickers bars into our kids' plastic pumpkins. We didn't care that during Pride Month they could be seen climbing into their hybrid car in the morning wearing leather harnesses like they were donning suspenders, their shaved legs exposed in bright-colored shorts that cinched around their quads like handcuffs. When we saw them at the public pool, we envied their pectoral muscles and the cut of their hips, and all of us would have probably sacrificed our first-born sons to have James Dunkirk's shoulders. We did find their, not one or two but three, rainbow flags a bit gaudy.

But the real problem was the ducks.

Jack Dunkirk was a sous-chef at *Moos,* this expensive gastro-pub in the reinvigorated downtown district, surrounded by wine bars and Bikram yoga studios. Prices were whole numbers and the descriptions of dishes were as curt as could be, lists of ingredients but nothing about how they were prepared. Some of us went and were taxed by the pulsing, wordless music and the strange black lights that glowed beneath the tables and revealed every stain and dusting on our pleated pants and every run in our wives' pantyhose. They did not serve PBR or Anheuser-Busch or Jack Daniels and when we tried to order wines, the options were overwhelming: a sea of reds and rosés and blancs that made our eyeballs hurt. *Moos* was all about farm-to-table cooking, which made us imagine live cows being slaughtered in the kitchen, dragged in directly from a pasture attached to the restaurant. Maybe they kept goats in the industrial fridge for extracting cheeses, strewing the non-skid floor with feed for chickens and lambs soon to be chopped up for masalas and Kievs. When we paid the bill, we mentioned that we knew Jack, who came out to greet us, shaking our hands. His sleeves were rolled up, and his forearms twitched, splattered with fancy sauce. He hoped we liked the granita, and we nodded like we knew what he was talking about.

The Dunkirks' backyard was a booming garden, vines of Brandywine tomatoes climbing a trellis, blackberry bushes lining their fences, rows of beans and haricots verts and bok choy and radishes bursting from raised beds. These we had no problem with. We oohed and aahed at the magical way vegetables and fruits manifested throughout their property—they were blessed with an apple tree that dropped Red Delicious down into the grass like rainfall—and more than once we stared as we sweated through mowing our lawns. Our children asked if we could plant our own fruit trees, our wives tsking that they'd love to have their own basil and mint. They dreamed and wished and we ignored them as best we could, even when our children whined about wanting to plant cherry trees after they learned about George Washington, pointing to the Dunkirk yard when we said no, we couldn't do that. We pretended not to hear the train engine chug of their *why, why, why?*

Jack Dunkirk decided he wanted to make his own duck confit. And if the Dunkirks could grow their own kohlrabi and pepperoncini, why not living creatures? One day we saw Jack and James kneeling in their backyard near their hammock strung between two Eastern Redbuds. We'd seen them out there before, lazing and reading, often pulling off all but their underwear as they wobbled back and forth, their bodies somehow fitting together like obnoxious, perfect puzzle pieces. They were both bent to the ground, hard at work with shovels. When we asked them later, they explained they were digging out a small pond.

"For what?" we said, sipping the fancy, microbrewed Kolsches they offered us.

"Well," Jack said, looking at James with sly eyes, as though they were flirting with one another, "we're going to raise ducks."

"And koi," James said. "But mostly ducks."

They took us into their guest room and showed us the incubator.

"Eggs," James said. "We're waiting for them to hatch."

"Is this a thing?" we said. When they nodded, chests puffed with pride, we said, "What about the mother? Don't they need a mother to sit on them so they hatch?"

"That's what the lamp is for," Jack said, tapping the curved metal of its shade. We imagined the heat stinging at his fingers.

"What are they for? Why would you raise ducks?"

That was when Jack explained. We tried to hide our horror by drinking our beers. We could not imagine raising a thing from a fuzzy little ball of yellow, like a smeary, unfolding sun, into a quacking creature whose head would get whacked off and body butchered into parts for searing and serving. We looked at Jack's hands, his fingers curled around his beer, eyes shiny with possibility.

"How will they eat? How will they grow?"

"We googled it," James said. "It'll take a while, but it's an adventure. Like going to Venice."

None of us had been to Venice. We'd taken our kids to Branson a few times, getting photographed at Silver Dollar City. A few had gone to Disney, or maybe the Great Wolf Lodge.

We nodded and let the Dunkirks lead us back into the kitchen, where we were already picturing the slaughter, the dead ducks' heads laid out on their marble-topped island, blood from severed necks staining their cutting board. We imagined feathers seething through the air, getting stuck in the air vents and clogging the sink drain, as if some sexy pillow fight had gone down but none of the scantily clad girls were anywhere to be found.

At home we hopped onto our desktop computers and did our homework. We were horrified. Backyard poultry could give us or our kids salmonella or E. coli or bird flu. The ducks' poop could carry Campylobacteriosis, which could strike our babies and aging parents with Guillain-Barré syndrome. The ducks might even spread West Nile virus thanks to the mosquitos that buzzed through our Missouri climes.

This, we decided, would not do. We washed our hands vigorously after reading all these things. We wiped down our doorknobs and our computer keyboards. When we brushed our teeth, we held our toothbrushes gingerly, between two fingers, convinced little swarms of germs were crawling up and digging into our gumlines. When we went to bed, we told our wives about the Dunkirks' plans, and they clucked. They glared at us over their reading glasses, legs tented to hold onto their magazines

and novels, and they told us we were overreacting. They said it
was neat, what the Dunkirks were doing.

"Neat?" we said.

"They just do whatever they want," we said.

"They don't think about other people."

Jack and James filled their little pond, then dropped several
large goldfish into the water from sealed bags they'd brought
home from an artisanal pet shop. We wondered why they
couldn't just adopt a mutt from the shelter like the rest of us
and eat frozen chicken strips and toasted ravioli and double
cheeseburgers.

They brought us over when the ducklings hatched, and we
stood over the brooding box, looking at the smooth, slimy bodies. They waddled around in an old aquarium the Dunkirks had
wiped out and filled with wood shavings. The lamp shone with
hot, harsh light on the side. Starter crumbs were scattered around
the ducks' tiny feet.

"Aren't they supposed to be fluffy?" we said. "And yellow?"

"They'll grow," James Dunkirk said.

"And what's with the eggs?" Two cracked-open chicken eggs
sat in the corner, yolks swimming in the center like brains.

"It's for the runts," Jack explained. He pointed to two tiny
ducklings that teetered, smaller and slower than the others. "They
need the nutrients."

"And what is that?" We pointed to the paint roller tray that
took up the left half of the box.

"It's their swimming pool," James said. "So they can swim."

Eight ducklings made it to the pond outside; one somehow
drowned itself in the makeshift pool and one of the runts died
in its sleep. James said Jack was distraught about it. When we
pointed out that they were all going to die anyway, James scowled
at us and said, "So are you and your kids, but that doesn't mean
you wouldn't cry if they died young, too, does it?"

We felt punched in the gut, the nose, the groin. We took deep breaths. We thought of our children, how they were growing too fast, shooting past us in athleticism and grace and their understanding of technology, and for a moment we felt the urge to rush home and squeeze them tight and demand they stay young. James apologized and offered us beers, which we drank and clinked together.

The ducklings were born in March, when dew and frost still pebbled and slicked our grass and patios. The Dunkirks' fruits and veggies were dormant, bushes turned brambly and thin. After nine weeks inside they brought the ducks out to the pond in ceremonial fashion, two at a time, a ball of feathers in each of the Dunkirks' hands. The sun shone down like the slick yolk of the eggs they had fed the runts, the weather tumid. Flowers were reaching up in awakened bloom.

The ducks were loud. They squawked from early morning until the afternoon. James Dunkirk, who taught at the local liberal arts college in the communication department and took his summers off, spent whole days outside with them, swaying back and forth in the hammock, body roasting to a nutty color. He read books and looked over their spines toward the ducks as they bobbed and waggled in their pond. If they started to stray toward any of the vegetables he would stand up and rush toward them, darting around the little tubes of gray-white poop they left everywhere, and grab the ducks up, redirecting them toward their water supply. We watched him sometimes sway out of the hammock and squat down by the pond. The ducks would waggle up to him, wriggling their bodies so sprays plumed off their feathers. They would sniff at his hands like cats or dogs, and sometimes he would pick one of them up and cradle it between his beefy arms, the stark gray of its plumage matching the stenciled tattoos that drizzled his forearms and left shoulder. We pretended that he'd spent time in the slammer, earning the smudgy, artsy-fartsy shapes because of the men he'd beaten, or killed, or raped, even though we knew he wasn't the sort to do any of those things.

At first, we liked the sounds the ducks made. We felt in tune with nature. We could picture ourselves on the East Coast, standing in Central Park or along Manhattan Beach. We stood on our back decks with steaming coffee mugs in our hands and listened to the quack-quack noises before shuffling back inside to read our newspapers and eat our oat cereals that promised good heart health. We tried to ignore the fact that the ducks would soon be food. Our kids tugged at our shirtsleeves and begged to be allowed over to pet the ducks, feed them from their hands. We shook our heads no, staring toward the Dunkirk yard and feeling tingles of angry jealousy. We batted our kids away and told them to stop pouting.

But then the ducks got louder. Their quacks started to sound like broken car horns or comically screwy bike bells. It was like when you hear a car alarm start up a block or two away and you imagine the absurd, useless sound crooning for hours and hours and you're suddenly ready to just knock off the owner, because who sets their car alarm anymore, don't people know they aren't deterrents and that instead of everyone pouring out of whatever building is close to a car whose horn is going nuts and its lights are blinkering like something having a seizure everyone nearby just bitches and moans and wonders how long it will take for the blaring to stop, and if it doesn't stop soon will we have to call the cops to make it stop and what kind of asshole sets one of those things off anyway, what are you doing, touching someone's car like that, even though we all know it could be just about any-thing: a twig, a squirrel, a heavy wind, a bicyclist barely nudging the bumper with a tire or handlebar, whatever. Hell, it could be a duck, its bill rapping on the wheel well.

Despite the bloom of berries and flowers, the Dunkirks' yard started to smell, a rich manure odor we associated with farms and Nebraska. We didn't like it. We waited for Jack to take the ducks by the throat and chop them into edible pieces, but all summer the ducks waddled about while James cared for them, flinging food through the grass and bringing the squawking creatures inside their garage every evening so they could sleep in the makeshift henhouse the Dunkirks had erected, so large it forced them to park in the driveway.

When we asked when they'd be turned into confit, Jack finally admitted: "I think James is too attached."

"You're going to keep them?" we said. "As pets?"

"I think so," Jack said. He shook his head. "I knew this would happen."

The idea that we would hear the quacking of those ducks for years—one of us looked it up and said they could live anywhere from five to ten years—just about drove us to madness. Our wives rolled their eyes at our chagrin and told us to feed our dogs and go buy milk. They told us to stop being dramatic, that the ducks were a nice flavorful addition to the neighborhood. We sputtered out angry raspberries of noise and filled rocks glasses with bourbon and sulked in our studies or basements, turning up the volume on baseball games and late-night talk shows to prove how annoyed we were.

The Dunkirks had a reputation for running, often in the early morning or at dusk, when the heat was in its least pressing form. They would canter out of their garage, already warmed up from stretches they performed by their little duck pond. Some of us watched them get started, their shirtless bodies mean jokes, James with his monster shoulders gathering our jealousy in tight knots that bivouacked in our paunches, which felt even slouchier and droopier in comparison to the tight, serrated squares of muscle twitching on their stomachs. They left the ducks to wander the yard, convinced that now that they were older they couldn't hurt themselves. During these three-mile bursts the Dunkirks would be gone for at least twenty-five minutes, more if neither of them had gorged on summer shandies or vodka martinis the night before.

So we decided to snatch a duck.

Grabbing the duck took some work. We first had to scramble through the latched gate in the side yard, careful not to nick ourselves on the overgrown brambles of one of the rosebushes lining the fence, which the Dunkirks had let get out of control, their gnarled thorns reaching out at us like the teeth of mutant guard dogs. After that, we had to wend our way past their gardens, where the tomatoes had shot up thanks to the damp air and ample sun; their smell, we worried, would tar us, later signal to the Dunkirks exactly what we'd done. We slipped past the sprouting beans and other stalks of green we couldn't identify by name. The ducks, whose attention we'd caught, stared at us, suddenly silent. They peered our way with their glossy marble eyes, and we could see the suspicion in their webbed feet. One of them honked at us and hopped into the little pond, and then the others followed.

We darted at them. Soon we were dashing through the grass, circling the little pond like morons. The ducks, smartly, dove into the underbrush surrounding their little paradise, putting most of them immediately out of reach. But one was slower, maybe stupid. We managed to get our fingers around him, even though his feathers were slick. He honked and howled and tried to beat his wings but we came together and held him fast, each of us laying hands on him.

"Now what?" we said to one another.

We would have looked like a cartoon to anyone who was watching. We slithered in a single mass of limbs, the duck quacking and squalling so loud we were briefly convinced the Dunkirks would hear the noise wherever they were on their run and come sprinting back, catching us in the act. But we managed to escape the labyrinth of their yard, even relatching the gate so they wouldn't know what we'd done. We slid next door, keeping the duck still while the garage door lowered.

We stared down at the duck. It fluffed itself up and padded around, dipping its beak toward an oil slick on the epoxy floor. We left it there, turning away and into the kitchen. Our kids and wives were out doing summer things, swimming at the public pool, working pathetic little jobs at the sno-cone stand, playing meaningless games of pick-up sand volleyball. We stood around drinking beers, ignoring the duck's noises, trying to figure out what to do next. None of us were sure. We hadn't thought that far. Would we set the duck free? Would we dispose of it? Maybe we could take it to the pond on the far side of the neighborhood. There were other ducks there, right? We could introduce a foreign duck into a new environment with no problem, yeah? Or maybe, we could make our own duck confit.

What we knew we wanted to do was watch the Dunkirks realize their duck was missing. We slipped outside, arranged ourselves around a frosted-glass patio table so we could all take glances into their yard, and waited. We thought, were sure, that they'd be back soon, but for whatever reason, on this day, they opted to run longer, or farther, or whatever. We grew antsy. We worried: were they hurt? Lost? Was one of them dead? We listened for the sound of ambulance sirens, the low honk of a fire engine charging through traffic, the woozy din of a police cruiser. All we heard was the chuff of the larches and maples in our yards as they were shaken by the breeze.

Finally, after what felt like an ice age, the Dunkirks appeared. We saw their bodies flash between the houses one street over, so we sat up straighter in anticipation. We waited. After a typical run, Jack and James would march into their backyard, bodies heaving, arms shimmery with sweat, and they would greet the ducks like we would our children after long days at work. The mallards would pad up toward them in recognition, and one of the Dunkirks—usually James—would dash into the garage and grab their bag of feed, returning to sprinkle it on the grass and near the pond.

None of the ducks materialized. They had scrabbled away from us when we snatched up their friend, but we assumed they would come back, magnetized to the familiar water of their little pond. But as we watched the Dunkirks, we could tell something was wrong. James was turning in frantic circles like a dog, his sweaty head spraying perspiration as though he was a sprinkler. Jack started making a strange clicking sound with his mouth, bending down and snapping his fingers. We couldn't hear or see any of the ducks. Our backs stiffened. Our cheeks filled with coppery worry. Our stomachs coiled, corkscrewed through with fear. We drank beers in an attempt to settle our nerves.

The Dunkirks saw us. We gave them little hand waves, cocked our beer bottles toward them.

"Have you seen our ducks?" Jack yelled.

We shook our heads no. He yelled louder.

"They're missing. The ducks are gone."

We frowned in real, true confusion. They couldn't be gone. We'd just been in their yard. We'd seen them scatter into the bushes. Some of those bushes bordered our yards, and the ducks weren't there. Our fences were strong and smart enough to keep the ducks out.

"Huh," we said to one another, low and grunting so the Dunkirks, still in a tizzy, couldn't hear us. "I wonder where they are."

The Dunkirks started calling out absurd names: Batali, Ray, Guarnaschelli. We realized they'd named them after famous TV chefs.

"That's sick," we said, "considering what they were going to do to them." In that quick finger-snap of time, our sympathy vanished.

James looked as though he might cry, the sweat drying on his face giving him a sickly, shiny pallor.

"It's okay," we told them. "Surely they'll come back."

The Dunkirks, trembling with awful worry, trudged inside their house to shower. We stared at one another and then rushed to the garage where we'd stored the one, wondering if it, too, might have vanished. But it was there, sitting with an unsettling calm on a bag of to-be-recycled Diet Coke cans. It quacked and stretched its wings, stumbling as it tried to march off the heap of crushed metal. We spent some time getting it in our clutches; it hid behind an old Igloo cooler and then waddled behind the charging station for a DeWalt battery, but we eventually got it, though it let out such a ruckus in our hands that we were sure the Dunkirks would hear it. But again, no, they did not.

"What do we do with it?" we said to one another. "Should we give it back?"

We could not give it back without admitting what we'd done.

"What if we say it wandered over here while they were in the shower?"

We decided that would have to work, so we slipped into their backyard and dumped the duck in its pond. It waffled and kicked in the water to get purchase, then began quacking up a fresh storm, fluffing its feathers like a cat whose tail has gone large in a moment of distress. Its black eyes seemed to follow us as we scrambled back out of the Dunkirk yard, all of us breathing hard, our hearts strumming, sure they would catch us as we dashed away.

They did not see us. But they did come back outside immediately after they were cleaned up, hair combed and gelled, fresh t-shirts tight and monochromatic. James had shaved, even, a day-old scruff whisked away so his chiseled chin could gather the sun. We waved when they appeared on their back patio and waited for them to see the duck. When they did, their faces lit up as though they'd been told they won the lottery or a trip to the Bahamas. They dashed to the duck pond and squatted down in identical postures, hands on their knees. They muttered words we couldn't make out, but we could hear their joy. James Dunkirk bent lower, one knee in the grass, and snapped his finger toward the duck. He said something to Jack, who dashed into the garage and reappeared with a bag full of food. Slowly, they coaxed the duck from the pond and James cradled it in that fatherly way we'd seen so many times.

And then, like some kind of miracle, the other ducks started squawking in a tinny chorus, appearing from all corners of the Dunkirk yard. Jack actually squealed. We held our fresh beers near our mouths, unable to swallow. From the underbrush they emerged almost as one. We looked at each other, wondering how this could be.

The Dunkirks did not care. The Dunkirks rushed toward their ducks, who seemed nonplussed by the stomping gallop of their feet and the joyous noises erupting from their throats. Jack managed to pull one of them to his chest with one hand, and with the other he dumped half of the duck feed onto the ground, allowing the rest of them to swarm over and take it into their beaks.

We looked at one another. The Dunkirks saw us and gestured with wild gladness. Even from so far away, we could see the joy in their eyes. This was something new. This was something we had not felt in so very long. We forgot the horrible, scratching noise of the ducks' quacking. We forgot the smell of their scat. Instead, we thought of our wives at their book clubs drinking Zinfandel and our kids at their summer camps and their jobs doling out French fries or cleaning up movie theatre popcorn. We thought of how they came home and dismissed us, passing down hallways and up staircases and into bedrooms and bathrooms where they locked themselves away, reappearing only when we beckoned them for dinner, where we served them our clumpy pasta and sad, bland chicken breasts.

The Dunkirks yelled out to us, curling their hands in gestures of invitation.

"We're celebrating," Jack said.

"We're so glad they're okay," James said.

They continued beaming. We felt little holes in our chests, as if we'd been shot through with bottle rockets. But we went.

They told us to take our empty beer bottles inside and trade them for fresh drinks, local unfiltered wheats. Jack said to swirl the bottles in a circular motion. James said we should cut ourselves lemon wedges and spray the acid in like dropping limes into Coronas. When we stared at them, Jack said, "Really. Go. Our hands are full."

They would not drop the ducks. They would not come inside with us. We were assaulted by the cleanliness, the balsa wood, the pots hanging above the kitchen island, twinkling and clean. We did as were told. We thought, for a moment, about fucking with them some more. Maybe we would draw on their fancy shirts with permanent marker or hide one of their Adidas sandals behind the stove. Leave their wine fridge open or uncork one of their expensive reds. But we could hear their cooing laughter, their happiness. So instead we took our drinks, looked at one another, and wondered how long we could hate the Dunkirks, these men imparting such love on their ducks. We peered through the kitchen window and watched them while we drank. They were hugging the ducks, mumbling baby-talk words as the ducks lay impassive against their chests. We felt worry. We felt confusion. Hatred, but also joy, both for the Dunkirks and for their ducks, their fucking ducks: ducks they'd meant to eat, slathering butchered thighs and legs in fat and butter, ducks that were, suddenly and forever, recipients of the kind of affection that spreads and beams and means you finally have what you have always wanted.

When You Sink Your Teeth In

THEY AGREED THAT SHANE WOULD GET THE PROCE-
dure because Andy worked from home, in their basement, while
Shane's corner office walls were carved out of glass, and even though
the fruits and vegetables wouldn't see any direct light thanks to his
bespoke suits, the filtered vitamin D sheening his face was as good
a thing as any to tip the scales. Andy, in a show of support, also
fasted for twenty-four hours before the appointment, tricking his
stomach into a semblance of fullness by drinking glass after glass
of water. His urine was clear as a mountain stream, and he had
to get out of bed twice to pee. He slid away as quietly as possible,
but Shane still grunted and turned over when Andy pushed back
under the covers. Andy's stomach churned, and he thought about
sneaking back out to the kitchen for a snack but hated himself for
even thinking about a minor deception. Shane had told him not to
bother with the fast, that it was stupid to punish himself like that,
but Andy had told him they were in this together, always, to which
Shane said, "All right," but then rolled his eyes.

The hospital smelled like aerosol lemon spray. Andy and Shane were directed to the third floor, where Andy was made to wait in a room filled with other stoic men and women, their heads bent toward the television in the corner or the cell phones in their laps. No one spoke, and the air was filled with the low hush of far-off hospital sounds, doctors' mumbling voices, codes being called out over intercoms, swinging doors swishing. The procedure wouldn't take long, they had been told. Minimally invasive. Shane wouldn't have to stay overnight, but he would be groggy. After several hours spent staring at the tiled floor, Andy was roused by a nurse in pink scrubs and told to come with her. She still wore her surgical cap and face mask, and for a moment Andy was jolted with fear, but as they walked to the recovery room she said everything had gone just fine.

"Now," she said, "he's still out of it, so we'll need you to choose a starter seed."

"Oh."

"Normally we take care of that pre-op, but somehow it didn't happen. Sorry about that."

"It's not a problem?"

She shook her head. "Nope. It's just, you'll need to pick for him."

Andy was to choose between a cherry tomato, a clementine, and a blueberry. He picked the tomato because he thought the nurse stared at it, sitting on a tray like a dessert on offer, the longest. She nodded when he made his choice, then waved for him to follow her. She parked him in Shane's room, where he was still out of it, eyes shut, nose stuffed with a cannula, a thin sheet pulled up to the top of his chest. Andy wandered over to the side of the bed and looked down at Shane. He didn't dare touch his bare right arm, where his hairs were shiny under the halogen lights. Shane's lips were wet with saliva, a tiny sliver of drool like a rolling tear dribbling from the edge of his mouth. For a second, Andy thought Shane might be in a coma. His stomach flopped and he felt his breathing go shallow. Then the nurse returned with the tray, a single yellowed seed sitting atop a clean, white cloth. He filed the image away, and a day later he would sketch it using a set of new Derwent charcoal pencils.

"Would you like to do the honors?" the nurse said.

"Me?"

She blinked at him.

"Okay. But I don't know what to do."

"You just take this," she said, pointing to the seed, "and put it in his mouth."

"That's it?"

"He'll swallow it, don't worry."

The seed, smaller than a sequin, was a hard nub between Andy's fingers when he pinched it, careful not to let it squirt out onto the floor. The nurse said nothing, watching as he turned to Shane. Andy felt an unsettling queasiness as he approached his husband's mouth, as though Shane were playing dead and, like a monster in a horror movie, would gnash and snarl and chomp down on Andy's fingers as he came closer. But he didn't so much as stir.

Shane's lips parted with no resistance. The edges of his teeth felt soft. Like a priest laying a host on a congregant's tongue, Andy set the seed on the bed of Shane's mouth, then retracted his fingers, the tips wet with Shane's spit. He wanted to wipe them off, but he couldn't bring himself to do so in the presence of the nurse, who had surely found herself mucked in all sorts of bodily fluids—blood, feces, urine, tubs of sweat and seminal fluid and vaginal discharge—so he let his arm fall to his side.

"Now what?" he said.

"Now we wait for him to wake up and for the growth to begin," the nurse said with affected excitement. Then, before Andy could ask any more questions, she turned and left the room. She didn't say whether he could stay or had to go, and at that moment, he wasn't sure which he wanted to do either.

• • • •

The tomato grew just fine, appearing as a bulbous lump just below Shane's left pectoral. The location was innocuous enough, though it required careful maneuvering during sex, and Andy had to take up the big spoon position when they slept, which neither of them particularly enjoyed; Shane liked to cup himself around Andy, his knees knit into the backs of Andy's legs, and Andy loved falling asleep with his back to the warmth of Shane's body. They tried facing apart, but this led to unintended battles for the sheets.

They were both happy when the skin split, Shane assuring Andy that this caused no pain. The tomato appeared, shiny as a ruby, round and plump and yearning to be plucked into someone's mouth. Andy wanted Shane to do the honors, but Shane shook his head and demanded they cut it in half and share it.

"Okay," Andy said. He fumbled with a knife, juices squirting over his thumb and index finger as he cut. It reminded him of the feeling of jamming the seed into Shane's mouth, which they had never talked about except for when Shane woke up and Andy told him that he'd made the choice on his behalf. Shane, still groggy, had nodded and mumbled that Andy had made the right decision.

The tomato smelled of that loamy sweetness and hint of bitter. Andy swallowed fast, but Shane took his time. Andy pictured the pulpy rind stuck in Shane's molars, the juice slathered across his taste buds. Andy made sure to save a few of the seeds that spilled onto the cutting board.

"Well?" he said when Shane finally swallowed.

"Tastes like a tomato."

"Isn't that the point?"

Shane strummed his fingers on the kitchen island, tapping at the butcher block. "I don't know. I just thought it would taste different, you know?"

Andy didn't know what to say, so he lifted Shane's shirt and felt at the spot where the tomato had burst out of him. The skin there was already smoothed over, the only thing Andy could feel the heat of Shane's flesh and the bumpy ridge of hidden rib. He pressed his hand flat and felt the rise and fall of Shane's breathing. He leaned in and Shane embraced him.

"Thanks for doing this for us," Andy said.

Shane let out a breath that cascaded over Andy's ears. He smelled of tomato, of soil, of sunshine, of pungent green vines.

"It doesn't hurt, by the way."

"I'm glad," Andy said, ashamed for not having wondered or worried about that. "So what now?"

Shane held Andy by the shoulders. "Now, we load me up. We see what I can do."

●　　●　　●　　●

Shane could do a lot. Over the next few months, Andy found himself plucking grapes from Shane's thighs, asparagus and cabbage from his shoulders, artichokes and mung beans from his shins. The tops of his feet produced boysenberries and tindas, lemons and nectarines. Passion fruit bulged at his stomach, watercress rippled along his forearms. Lemongrass, arugula, and muskmelon dimpled his chest. At the follow-up with the doctor, Shane's body was praised for its ability to deliver.

"Everything ripe and edible?" the doctor said.

"Yes," Shane and Andy said at once.

"Good. Even a watermelon. Usually we suggest waiting for that."

"Sorry," Shane said. "I guess I'm ambitious."

The doctor nodded, scribbled something in Shane's chart and closed the folder. He had zaps of silver at his temples. "Well, everything looks fine. We'll want to do one last check-in at the half-year mark, but I can't see anything going wrong if it hasn't already."

"Knock on wood," Andy said, though there was only plaster and laminate nearby.

Once each week, Shane would pose for Andy, who would turn his sketchbook to a new page or uncap his gesso and paints and stretch a canvas. Shane would sit on a stool, shirtless, the recessed basement lighting gleaming off his round shoulders and high cheekbones. He willingly perched for however long it took for Andy to grab the angles he wanted, to capture the new hills and ridges of Shane's body. Andy spent most of his time as a free-lance graphic and web designer, having accepted long ago that his dream of being a full-time gallery artist wasn't going to come true. Most of what he produced sat along one wall of the basement next to his discarded easels and enlargers and hardboard panels. Until Shane's procedure, he'd not completed a drawing or painting in a long time, but now, the sight of fruits and vegetables rupturing up through human skin gave him something new to press onto canvas and paper.

The one thing Andy missed was being wrapped up in Shane's warm weight. Shane preferred to grow things on the front of his body, he said, because he liked to be able to feel and trace and see.

"Yes," Andy's mother said when he called to speak to her. "That's pretty much how it goes."

Andy's father had been the one to get the procedure. It hadn't come into practice until well after Andy had left for college, so he had not borne witness to how it had changed things between his parents. When he was a kid they were egalitarian, each taking turns making dinner or reading to Andy before bed, splitting laundry duties and dishwashing and even the mowing of the lawn. They both worked, his father an accountant and his mother a coder for a small tech support company who took outsourced jobs from community colleges and small businesses that needed help with network infrastructure. Neither had given up their job when Andy was born; his grandmother had stayed with him during the day until he was eligible for pre-kindergarten.

But their dynamic shifted when his father underwent the procedure. His mother took care of most of the housework, citing the need for his dad to avoid ramming laundry baskets against nascent snow peas or cantaloupes.

"Does it bother you?" Andy said.

"No," his mother said. "It's how relationships work. They change, you adjust. You discuss and agree."

"What if you don't agree?"

"Is everything okay, Andy?"

"Yes. I'm just thinking ahead."

"I would think ahead positively, for starters."

"Okay."

"Talk to him about whatever's bothering you."

"Nothing's bothering me."

"Andy."

He didn't tell his mother that sex had become complicated, that although Andy had always preferred slow, careful, and tender to rough and hard and quick, he and Shane now had to navigate delicate blooms of squash and zucchini, fuzzy newborn kiwis and mandarin oranges. Often, Andy was tempted to press his weight against one of those blossoming fruits. They didn't hurt, Shane said. They weren't tender or delicate enough that a touch would rock pain through his body, but Andy was sure such declarations were either a test or posturing. Sex became a game of acrobatics and careful body arrangement, especially when something was on the verge of slipping out of Shane's body; they didn't want to sully the sheets with fruit or vegetable juice. Unless his kneecaps or tibia were involved in a new growth—rare for the former, as this inhibited his movement, but one time a pomegranate decided that was where it would build its hard shell, right against Shane's left patella, which left him immobile for four days—sex was most navigable with Shane on all fours, Andy behind him. But Andy hated this position, its animality, the debasing feeling that ran up and down him when he couldn't see Shane's face. The planes of Shane's back were pleasant enough to look at, muscles built from two decades in the pool as a breaststroker, a habit he didn't give up even when he landed his job in a tax attorney's office where he regularly put in sixty-hour work weeks. The pool was his haven even when he was growing their cucumbers and red onions, which took on a mineral bite from the chlorinated water. As Andy thrusted, he kept his body close to Shane's, but he had a hard time holding him with tender urgency, always concerned his fingers would slam into a growing radicchio bulb or plantain. When he came, he was always worried about Shane's own pleasures, but these were always waved off, Shane carefully leaning away and flipping onto his back, breathing hard so his ribs expanded, abs stretched, whatever was growing across his body going taut. Andy would move to go down on him but Shane would, more often than not, shake his head, smile, and whisper out a breathy, "That's okay. I'm good." But then he would slip into the bathroom and stay there for a long time, the shower pounding in the stall, and Andy pictured him masturbating. His stomach would burn with worry and doubt, but they never spoke of it, Andy's fear sliding between them like something rotting on the vine.

•   •   •   •

No one could explain what had happened. One day, tubers came out of the ground rotten and slimy. Kohlrabi and yuca and jicama lost their snap and color. Runner beans and luffa and summer squash fell to the ground tiny and ungrown, dotting tilled soil like rabbit feces. Fruiting trees dropped their wares early, branches turning to gnarled, angry arms with barren fingers. Banana peels split, drooping their inner fruit like dead bodies. Cherries withered into tiny, dried-up testicular bunches.

All other plant life was fine; in fact, it flourished. Grass grew with inchoate speed, bamboo shoots threatened to become skyscrapers. Evergreens were flush and hydrangeas bloomed to the size of basketballs. Tulips were like goblets, phlox out-of-control hair. In the Everglades, orchids shot out of the swampy muck like obelisks. Cypress in Louisiana bayous cast shadows the length of buildings. The lawns of Wimbledon had to be mowed twice as often. Weeping willows brushed the ground with their blooming branches. Wisteria popped. Bougainvillea swallowed windows; sweet potato vines trawled like Rapunzel's tresses. Everywhere, amaryllis and azaleas and hollyhocks and asters bloomed for even the worst gardeners.

Climate scientists cited pollution. Geologists wondered about tectonic shifts. Apiologists screeched about the declining honeybee population. Plant biologists and pomologists blinked during interviews and shook their heads, unsure. Evolutionary science offered nothing. Philosophers spouted bullshit that no one listened to. Sociologists were fascinated. Conservative Christians blamed gay people, adding to the hurricanes and dust storms and earthquakes and monsoons and tornadoes that queers had apparently brought to bear on the planet.

"Good god," Shane said, turning off the television while one evangelist spewed his drivel. "Fuck CNN for letting that guy on camera."

Shane and Andy had freshly moved in together when it happened. Shane, in his little time off, liked to grow his own Roma tomatoes and spinach, and he'd watched them wilt while the angelonias and speedwells the previous owner had planted along the side of the house rose up like armor to protect the vinyl siding.

"They just want the ratings. Talk is talk. What do they say about no bad PR?"

"Let me tell you," Shane said, rubbing his temples, "that saying is not true."

And then the procedure, which had at first been bad-mouthed as absurd, crackpot bull-honkey, science-fiction masturbatory fantasy. The kind of thing you'd see on *Futurama* or *Rick and Morty* or *Mystery Science Theater 3000* or some quack *Doctor Who* episode. A ridiculous attempt at nutritional salvation, a hail Mary for mimosas and edible arrangements and chocolate-covered strawberries. It would kill people, skeptics claimed. It would save us, believers responded. An anatomist went on Fox News to explain how it would work, but his diagrams were squished and illegible on screen next to his bulbous head, his jowly mouth. Online, conspiracy theorists claimed the procedure was just another way for the government to track you, to inject you with poisons, to turn you into a mindless slave, to make you addicted to drugs, to convince you higher taxes were okay, to lower your inhibitions, to make you vote for the incumbent. But when the first subject responded with no problems, growing a stalk of celery along his sternum that cracked free like his skin was a door being opened, people volunteered themselves in mass numbers, desperate for their fruit smoothies and Caesar salads and dals and margherita pizzas and avocado toast and acai infusions and blackberry pies and blueberry pies and pumpkin pies and Key lime pies and bananas fosters and roasted red peppers and sauerkraut and pickle relish and plain old Red Delicious apples. It became so popular that households were limited to one procedure per, and the bounty blossomed, the country and the world flush with fruit and vegetables to the point that food was shipped overseas and those who had been starving saw their bone density and muscle tone rise while diseases like kwashiorkor, marasmus, anemia, heart attacks, strokes, stunting, diabetes, and scurvy all but vanished.

"It's a miracle," some pontificated.

"It's the earth taking care of us."

"It's got to be aliens."

"It's God."

"Yahweh."

"Allah."

"Jehovah."

"Shiva."

Shane started searching the internet for strange fruits and vegetables they could grow, ordering seed packets of rambutan, durian, horned melon and Romanesco broccoli and mangosteen, ackee, jackfruit. They blossomed out of his body, juicy and wet and ready to be eaten. Every week Andy drew a new sketch.

Then one night, in the midst of sex, Shane said, "Bite me."

"What?"

Shane turned onto his back, careful not to put too much pressure on his left oblique, where a brambly curl of samphire was growing. He pointed toward a bulb of garlic about to break through just above his navel.

"Bite me. Bite it."

Andy cleared his throat. "That seems unsanitary. Unsafe."

Shane shook his head. "I read about it online."

"Where? When?"

"There are forums."

"Forums?"

"You know. For people who've had the procedure. There's a whole community."

"Oh."

Shane was in the middle of tax season, and the usual signs of his exhausting workdays were etched all over him: baggy eyes, pale cheeks, frazzled hair, fingers drizzled in paper cuts. Andy could imagine Shane's hunched posture from hours spent at his desk squinting at audits, lawsuit filings, business sales, wills, tax court reports, requests for delays in back tax payments, stacks of paper and piles of emails.

"Come on," Shane said. He pinched at the bulb of garlic with his index finger and thumb, as if it was a pimple he was about to pop. "Please. I've read about it. People say it feels good."

"I don't know if I can."

Shane grabbed Andy's elbow. "Can you just try?"

Andy knew what was unsaid in this request: can you just try because look at what I've done for us? Because look at how hard I work? Because look at how tired I am? Because look at how many times I've let my skin open up? Because look at how often I let you fuck me and not the other way around? Because look at how my body keeps us both fed?

So Andy bit.

He leaned down and opened his mouth, setting his teeth around the lumpy growth. He bit down, the smallest bit of pressure, but his teeth went right into Shane's skin as if his flesh was the warm surface of a ripe peach. His incisors cut through the epidermis and his tongue met the papery outer layer of the garlic bulb. He expected his mouth to fill with blood, but just as when anything else came out of Shane's body, there was no weeping bodily fluid, no quiver of pain. Instead, his hand went to the back of his head as if Andy was giving Shane a blow job, and he sunk his teeth in further. Shane let out a moan of pleasure.

"Oh my god," Shane said. "More."

So Andy extended his jaw like a snake swallowing its dinner. He tugged at the garlic bulb, which gave up its place against Shane's sinewed abs with little resistance. Andy held the bulb in his mouth, the garlic's taste filling his nose. He resisted the urge to cough and sneeze.

"Chew it, please. Please."

The bulb felt like a cue ball in Andy's mouth, a jawbreaker whose outer layer was melting in an unpleasant way, the thin tissue going wet and slimy. Shane was staring at him, his grip on Andy's wrist hard and yearning. So Andy maneuvered the garlic, wilting and bitter on his tongue, so that he could chew, his rear molars cutting through to the raw cloves, which felt like hard plastic as he bit down.

When he let out a little coughing noise, Shane tugged on his arm. "Again." He said it over and over until the garlic bulb was a mushy mess in Andy's mouth, his eyes watering at the overpowering taste. He swallowed and Shane nodded and when Andy was finished he showed Shane his empty mouth, stuck out his tongue. Shane kissed him, tugging him down so their bodies were close, all regard and concern for the things still growing seemingly cast off. Andy could feel Shane's erection press between them, but Andy had gone totally soft. He was sweating, his stomach churning, his breath dragon-fire and discomfort. Shane didn't seem to notice and, as usual, slipped away after they kissed and spent thirty minutes in the bathroom.

Shane made this request on three subsequent nights. He grabbed Andy's wrist and whispered, "Bite me," like he was offering a seduction or a secret. Andy would take whatever fruit or vegetable was on offer—wasabi peas, honeydew, ramps—between his teeth, feeling Shane's skin release the earthy rough or citrusy sweet into his mouth, and then he would chew and chew, feeling Shane's arousal in the form of goosebumps, shuddered breath, digging heels, squeezing fingers. Sometimes, when Shane was gone at work, Andy searched for the forums and websites he'd mentioned. Andy discovered a world of food fetish, videos and fan fictions, stills and clips that left Andy's bowels heavy and his stomach fluttering. He went clammy, shaky, sweaty, scared, angry, still, hot, cold, anxious, disillusioned, disappointed, discombobulated. He lay on the couch, his eyes throbbing, neck stiff, back aching, hands tremulous, elbows popping, knees pulsing, ankles swelling, toes curling, fingers fluttering.

"What if we run out?" he said one night when Shane wanted him to bite away a pepperoncino.

"We won't. There's always more." Shane pointed to bulges on his body: raspberries, rutabaga, a head of romaine.

"I feel selfish is all. Wasting food."

Shane blinked. "We're not wasting it. This is good for us."

"Okay."

In the middle of the night Andy woke, his mouth filled with the bitter aftermath of a spray of raw kale. Despite how hard he'd brushed his teeth and flossed and swished a capful of alcohol-burning mouthwash, he could still taste the greenery, its sallow crunch, how it had smelled of Shane's perspiration, its ribs caulked with the ghost of coppery blood. Andy looked Shane over, his skin bright and milky in the moonlight seeping through the window. His lumps appeared to pulse with alien life. Andy touched them—cranberry, Brussels sprouts, radish—and imagined plucking them out right then and there, emptying Shane and dumping the crop into the trash, seeds and skin and nutrients all discharged to compost and landfill.

Instead he wandered the house, empty and ticking in the dark. He filled a glass with water at the kitchen sink and stared into the dark of their backyard where the flowers and grass were climbing with their insatiable vigor.

He went outside.

The air was dewy with chill, the grass slick between his toes. The yard was home to a single large oak tree that Andy had been long convinced was dying; a smear of its leaves were brittle orange and from its trunk ruptured a long crack where the bark should have been uniform and smooth. He'd not said a word to Shane, nor had he bothered calling an arborist, even though the tree was tall and if it were to fall it would surely crash into their kitchen, destroying the oven and sink and hand-carved cabinetry. Andy sat down with his back scratched up against the trunk. He could feel bark flaking against his bare skin. He wriggled, relishing the feeling as the hardness bristled across his spine. He dug his toes into the dry dirt and grass. Beneath his calves he could feel the tree's roots, which had risen closer to the surface thanks to the previous winter's cold. Andy shut his eyes. He could see himself painting a self-portrait, his legs curled into knotted tree roots, the ends beckoning like cadaverous fingers.

Time became a spiraling nothing: it might have been just past midnight, or deep in the ink-black of three a.m., or maybe closer to five, when dawn would start bleeding up against the horizon, the telephone cables, the houses' pitched roofs, the puncturing steeple of a nearby church. The tree's rough surface bit into the back of his head, which Andy rocked back and forth so the notches pushed and bumped against the base of his skull. He felt tiny bugs dot at his face, attracted by the heat of his cheeks, and he resisted the urge to slap them away. They dribbled against his lips, forked up his nose, tickled at his ears. His entire body was subsuming to the world around him. He wished for some kind of envelopment, for something that would take him in and make him part of itself.

It wasn't jealousy. He decided this when he finally stood up, no longer able to stand the itch crawling across his skin. Andy did not wish he had been the one to undergo the procedure. His mother had said the same more than once. She laughed every time he mentioned it, assuring him that she was glad she didn't have to worry about squashing a nascent parsnip or Barbary fig. That the idea of eating something that had come from her own body felt too much like auto-cannibalism. That she could rationalize the fruits and vegetables she sliced and sautéed and juiced and diced and pureed and squeezed and peeled and blanched and fried and boiled and baked and pickled and flambéed. They weren't her, so they weren't something to fear.

So what was it, he wondered as he slid in through the back door. He drank another glass of water but could still taste the kale. He opened the refrigerator and tried milk, swishing and gargling and letting it coat his teeth and taste buds and palate and gums. Still the taste sat there, unwelcome. Shane had just shed a fresh pair of apricots, so Andy bit into one of them but stopped because the skin reminded him too much of his husband's flesh. Andy stared down at it, a squishy, pulpy streak left behind where he'd ripped the sinews and fibers apart. Maybe that was it: when he bit into Shane, his body was quick to sew itself up, all markers of Andy gone, his skin a clean, blank canvas. All that was left behind was the taste in Andy's mouth.

Andy returned the apricot to its bowl, its smooth, untrammeled side facing outward. As he slipped into bed, Shane stirred and reached out to him, catching Andy's wrist with sensational accuracy.

"You okay?" Shane said.

"Yes," Andy said. "Sure."

Shane gave him a loose hug. He sighed, his breath mucky like a wet cave. Then, as he always did, he turned away, his body a wall. Andy stared at its smooth surface, the vine of Shane's spine, the planes of his shoulder blades, the stirrup width of his rear deltoids, the knot of his coccyx. Nothing grew or pulsed. Andy reached out a hand but then stopped himself. As always, he turned onto his side and, tugging up the top sheet, pushed himself close.

Sing With Me at the Edge of Paradise

MITCHELL LEANS AGAINST ME, HIS EAR SQUASHING on my shoulder. We're sitting at the edge of a cliff, looking down into the Garden of Eden. We're alone, which is surprising, considering just how many people have been trucking it to St. Louis to gawk at the Tree of Life and to eat the forbidden fruit of the Tree of Knowledge. Most people, I guess, decide to hire out a guide to lead them down the winding trail into the Garden itself while we are content here, far away, Mitchell drinking canned kombucha while I slurp from my water bottle.

He starts humming, a medley of his favorite Tina Turner songs, starting with "Proud Mary" and shifting to "The Best" when he gets to the part where the metronome takes a hard uptick. Then it's "River Deep, Mountain High" and "What's Love Got to Do With It." I can feel the vibration of his vocal cords in my neck, and I wrap my arm around him to feel it in my bones. He doesn't object when my fingers press against his jaw; in fact, he starts humming louder, eventually setting down his can and screaming out, the words echoing across the highest treetops. He lets out a warbling "Oooooo," then turns and buries his mouth against my neck, making me tweak and squirm away, but not so very far because I like the feel of his lips, slick and sticky, against my skin. I let him nibble there, and when I turn my head he kisses me straight on the mouth, his vinegary spit slipping onto my tongue.

We don't leave until the sun is going down, turning the foliage of Eden into a bright emerald shimmer. Most of the tours stop when darkness slips in because the trails are treacherous with tree roots and brambles. My blood tingles between my ears, which are hot as if they've been ironed. When we tumble into Mitchell's car he kisses me again, pushes his hand against my sternum. I feel the impression of his fingers long after he's let me go and turned on the engine. He clicks off the stereo before any music can stream out.

"I need to tell you something," he says.

"What?"

Mitchell leans back, flicks a strand of hair out of his face; it's grown long and wild, beachy. He opens and closes his mouth.

"I'm leaving, Charlie."

"What do you mean?"

He turns to look at me square. Somehow, I've never noticed that his nose points slightly to the left.

"I'm going to California." He says something about a friend's cousin who has an in at a recording studio, some low-level producer who will give him a chance. I don't hear the details. Something warm seeps into my chest, like blood is pooling in my lungs.

"Oh," I say.

He puts the car in reverse and backs away from the cliff. Eden slips out of view. Mitchell rolls down the windows and lets hard wind whistle in as we barrel down I-70, brake lights flashing like rubies on one side of the highway, headlights like pearls on the other.

•   •   •   •

I am unable to sleep after Mitchell drops me off at my apartment, so I turn on the television to the news. It seems another Eden has been found, this time in Palermo, Italy.

The St. Louis Eden is not the only Eden. They've been popping up for the last six weeks, in dipping valleys and forests around the world. St. Louis is the only American location so far, but intrepid explorers are scouring Tongass National Forest, Pisgah, the White Mountains. Sects of hikers are convinced there must be one somewhere in the Grand Canyon or tucked away along the Appalachian Trail. As each Eden is discovered—in Jakarta, Algiers, Sarajevo, Nagoya—more people flock not only to these new slabs of paradise but into the wild, hoping to be the ones to uncover yet another Garden, another Tree of Knowledge, a Tree of Life. Biblical scholars have gone on PBS and Fox and pointed out the problem of claiming these places as Gardens of Eden: "Genesis," one spectacled, tweeded academic said, "is very specific about the flow of the waters that wind through the Garden, that they must flow to particular places." But most people don't care. It doesn't matter that the little creeks in the St. Louis Garden can't possibly dump into the Tigris or Euphrates or Gihon. Such details don't keep pilgrims away.

This new Garden has been found in Monte Del Gallo Park, right near the Tyrrhenian Sea. On TV, a wind-blasted reporter with salt-and-pepper hair stands near the edge of the Garden, the sharp blue water at his back looking like a painting. Despite the fact that the story of discovery has just broken, there is already visible activity in the Garden; the people scrumming through look like ants, blurred and bitty.

When the first Garden was discovered, I asked Mitchell, "What do you think it all means?"

He sighed and smiled. We were at the cliff but didn't know yet what we were looking at. "Oh, Charlie. I don't know. It's a beautiful mystery."

"So it has a solution? All mysteries have one."

He looked at me for a long, silent moment, then looked out at the trees. "Maybe," he said. "But is it so important to always understand the logic of the world?"

I wanted to say, "Yes, of course," but instead I set my teeth, which were starting to chatter. The evening had gone chilly, but Mitchell made no move to leave, so neither did I.

•   •   •   •

Mitchell comes by in the morning before work; when he isn't playing shit-paying gigs, he loads up as often as he can on double shifts at Zapps, a wings place that offers deep discounts on beer from two to four every afternoon. He works straight through from eleven to nine, but he doesn't complain. He's genial and fast and doesn't forget sides of ranch dressing, so he rakes in generous tips and manages to eat mid-shift, washing his hands so many times that his fingers dry and crack. He hums to himself as he runs food or fills drink orders and the other servers demand he serenade them while they do side work, refilling sugar caddies and plopping scoops of sour cream into tiny plastic containers.

"When did you cut your hair?" I say.

"Hi," he says. "I had it done this morning."

Where he before had thick swoops that flew back from his forehead at a diagonal, he now has short bristles. When he stands in the light of my living room window he glows. I tell him he looks angelic. He smiles. I wonder if he's told his manager yet that he's leaving.

"Come to the restaurant tonight," he says, tickling a hand against my left arm.

"Why?"

"I want to take you somewhere after I'm done working."

"Where?"

"It's a surprise," he says. But then he leans in close, grinning. "But I'll give you a clue."

"Okay," I whisper back.

I can smell his Pert shampoo and the crisp, oceanic scent of his deodorant. He drapes his arms over me like he's a heavy cape I'd never take off. "Think of paradise."

•   •   •   •

I walk into Zapps, which is low-lit and smells like cigars even though smoking in restaurants has been a no-no for years. There's no hostess but the sign next to the abandoned podium says to wait to be seated, so I stand there with my hands in my pockets. To my right is the bar, a long L-shape behind which a bartender is pouring beers from a tap for a trio of guys my age, each hunched over and gnawing on a chicken wing. Their heads are cocked toward the massive flat screen television airing a baseball game. This is the one kind of place, I imagine, where the news is never on. A reprieve, of sorts, from talk of Eden.

Mitchell appears around the corner; with his new, short hair it takes me a moment to recognize him. He stops and smiles, then waves for me to follow him. I snake around the bar, which is buffeted by a trio of booths and then some pub tables after the turn. Mitchell leads me through a pair of glass double doors into a private dining room that is unoccupied except for another server and a tub of silverware with a stack of napkins next to it.

"I have to finish rolling these," he says, "and then we're off." He sits down across from the other server, a good-looking redhead with muscular arms. "This is Doug."

"Hi," Doug says. He waves one hand at me. He's wearing a yellow Livestrong bracelet.

"You want help?" I say, slipping into the seat next to Mitchell. I squeeze his thigh under the table and he smiles.

"English majors know how to roll silverware?" Mitchell jokes.

"Not only that," I say, "but I can explain its symbolism until you die of boredom."

We develop a steady, quiet rhythm, and the silverware disappears quickly. As we roll the last of it, Mitchell hums his ubiquitous Tina Turner medley. Then he whistles. Doug smiles and bobs his head, asks, "Who is that?"

Mitchell tells him.

"I don't know her music," Doug says.

Mitchell shakes his head.

When the silverware is all wrapped, towered in a square of cinched-up napkins kept closed by plastic tabs with *Zapps!* printed on them in black letters, Mitchell vanishes for a few minutes into the kitchen. When he comes back he's already got his apron off, a folded loop of fabric in his hand.

"Ready?" he says.

"Always."

Mitchell drives. As we hit I-70, he rolls down the windows and the sharp cool of night comes streaming in. I put one of my hands against the back of Mitchell's head and feel at the bristle of his hair. It tickles my fingers and he leans back against my touch, which sends a throttle down my arm. I want to bring up his departure, the doomsday clock counting down the days until he is gone, but any words I might say turn sticky and tarry in my throat.

"So what's the surprise?" I say when he swoops off the interstate. We're at the exit for Eden.

"You'll see," he says, even though we both know what he's up to.

Mitchell takes our regular route. Hard, silver light from the moon hanging fat in the cloudless sky illuminates the trees and the slashes of lane markers on the frontage road. When we turn onto a rural route with clipped shoulders of gravel and dust the path grows dimmer. As usual, there are no other cars around as we pull into a small, barren splash of ground and Mitchell throws the car in park. He squeals open the moon roof before cutting the engine.

"Do you know what day it is?"

Of course I do. Two years ago, the summer after we graduated from college, he dragged me to a party where, it turned out, we knew no one. We left before either of us had so much as a pull from the keg of shitty beer or any of the sterilizing Jell-O shots mounded in a messy kitchen filled with gyrating bodies. We drove here, to this spot, a hidden cliff off the interstate that overlooked a wooded area that had not yet become a Garden of Eden. Mitchell turned off the engine, just like now, and started humming. When he was finished, I asked him why he liked Tina Turner so much.

"She's unabashedly her. I wish I could be that way."

And then, as we sat in the silence of late May, I leaned over, ignoring that my seat belt was trying to choke me, and I kissed him. He smelled like sourdough bread and ranch dressing even though he hadn't worked that day.

When I leaned away from him, Mitchell stared out the windshield. For a second I worried I had done the wrong thing. But then he said, "Thank you."

"For what?" I said.

"For doing that. I wasn't sure I could." He held out his hand, resting his knuckles against the gear shift. I laid mine in his.

"You're welcome." Then we stared out at the treetops flickering in the moonlight. For nearly two years that's all they were, trees and brush that served as a backdrop when Mitchell drove me out here during my breaks from graduate school. We spent two gap-filled years kissing and collapsing into one another, gearshift be damned, and now I am here for good and he is leaving.

Mitchell leans across the seat to kiss me. He presses his thumb up behind my left ear, his fingers tracing the swoop of my zygomatic bone.

"I'm still glad you did that," he says, his lips close, his hand hot. He still smells like bread and dressing. He waves his free hand out toward Eden. "That's not a miracle." He taps at my chest. "This," he says, "is the real miracle."

Then he pops open the driver side door and gestures for me to follow him out of the car. He lifts open the trunk and extracts a log of canvas fabric.

"What's this?"

"Think of it as an anniversary gift," he says.

The log is a tent. From the trunk, Mitchell also extracts a pair of sleeping bags and a red Coleman LED lantern that he turns on with a twist of its base; the car, the supplies, the entire dusty outcrop where we're hidden away is lit up like a movie set.

"Powerful," I say. "But what are we doing?"

"Camping out near paradise."

"But why?" I say. "It's hot."

"It'll give us a leg up."

"On what?"

"Our hike tomorrow."

"We're hiking?"

"We're going down there," he says, pointing.

"Why?"

"Why not?" The entire time we've been talking, Mitchell has been unfurling the tent and manhandling thick, wiry poles. He pauses, one in each hand like a pair of nunchakus.

"I prefer looking down at things," I say, even though it's not right or true. I don't even know what it means.

"Well," Mitchell says, "why don't we try being in them?"

I have no real way to contend with this, so I help him erect the tent. Then we unfurl a pair of swishy sleeping bags that provide no back support. The ground is hard, pebbly, uneven beneath us when we squirrel into them, but at least the tent fabric keeps the mosquitos out. I expect Mitchell to curl toward me, to make our two sleeping bags into one, for his warm breath and slick mouth to find mine, for his hands to wander, for the stiff, hard parts of his body to meet me and turn the unfriendly environment into one of comfort and bliss, but he lies on his back and breathes softly, eyes closed. He falls fast asleep with the lantern still blazing, and I have to wrestle my way out of my sleeping bag to turn it off.

•   •   •   •

I fall into something like sleep shortly before Mitchell jerks to life without so much as an alarm. When he does, he leans over me and gives my throat a gentle peck. I don't bother pretending to be asleep, but when I try to pull him toward me he moves away, saying we need to get going. Before I can object, he's starting the tent's deconstruction, so I scramble out. The morning—a discombobulating combination of gray and pink, like smoke warbling through a field of azaleas—is filled with hot mist, a low-hanging sheet that blurs the Garden of Eden below. I'm sweaty almost immediately. In a bit of a miracle, I can hear no other human traces besides our own footfalls and Mitchell's whistling.

"Ready?" he says when we've loaded up the car and ourselves, trading out the tent for a pair of backpacks Mitchell produces from the trunk, handing me one. Its weight is like a sandbag.

I want to tell him I am not ready. That my stomach has curled into itself like I've been swatted with a virus. That I like perching on the edge of paradise with him, listening to him hum and sing.

That the fact that he wants to go into the Garden of Eden looms like a bad omen. That I am sweating and queasy and the idea of the granola bar he holds out to me going into my body makes my nausea worse.

Instead I tell him to lead the way.

We march through scutch grass and scrub. At first, I think Mitchell is just going to send us charging through underbrush until we punch our way into Eden, but after a few minutes we are tossed onto a walking path that has been tread by legions of pilgrims. Trash bludgeons its edges: candy bar wrappers, fast food containers, crumpled soda cans. Mitchell says nothing of these earthly scars.

I can immediately tell when we've entered. The flora is green with summer bounty, but as soon as we cross some invisible line the plants and trees kick it up a notch. Everything is as verdant as in a high-def film. Fronds the size of my legs fan from huge trees. Animals that don't belong in the same biomes—rhesus monkeys, blue monarchs, even a pair of jackals—rush through the knotted trees and bounce from branch to branch and flutter across leaves. The predators blink and stare and at first I'm hit with a cold shock of fear, but then they simply watch, heads cocked and eyes blinking at us through heavy blankets of bougainvillea and Spanish moss.

The sun shimmers as it climbs into the sky. All I can hear is the scrabble of animal claws, the shuffle of Mitchell's booted feet, and my own heavy breathing. The Garden smells like fresh rainfall, and there are no signs of animal scat or carcasses anywhere. I wonder how the carnivores survive if they are not eviscerating prey, but I chalk this up to the miracle of paradise.

Mitchell seems to know where he's going. There isn't a set path: once we've entered the Garden, we aren't so much on a trail as we are wandering through a series of pleasant grottoes, bulbous grassy spaces where the trees bevel out and leave room for standing and sitting, as though Eden has carved out little private picnic cubbies. But Mitchell doesn't stop as we traipse through these. He doesn't pause to observe the macaws or the panthers, isn't distracted by the sight of a giraffe stuffed into a small plain or a lion stalking amongst the brush. Even the flash of a skunk darting past us doesn't hitch his gait.

"Where are we going?" I ask after we've been in the Garden for ten minutes. From our usual bird's-eye view Eden looks small, traversable in mere minutes, but Mitchell has taken some kind of circuitous path; I feel as if we've backtracked and looped, wandering through a hedge maze.

"We're almost there."

"But where is there?"

"Just trust me, Charlie."

"You know I do."

"Then let's go."

His voice is brusque, filled with an impatience I do not recognize. I wish he would whistle, or hum, or sing. Anything to tether me to him. But all I hear is the shuffle of our feet through the grass, which is short and even. I wonder if paradise has its own landscaping company, or if even the St. Augustine knows not to get tangly and unkempt. Everything knows its place.

• • • •

When he stops, I recognize the Tree of Knowledge, with its thick-ribbed greenery and heavy fruit. I know where we are, now, within this maze; from our usual spot on the cliff the baldness of this one space is obvious, the thick hairline of trees opening up for this sprouting deciduous giant. The Tree of Life is somewhere nearby too, its tantalizing gifts of youth humming.

"So," I say. "Here we are."

"Come on," Mitchell says.

I'm not surprised that the tree is lush and full of fresh fruit, that no matter how many grubby hands pluck its wares each day it is always bountiful and giving. Each Eden's Tree of Knowledge is different; ours is weighted with peaches. Mitchell marches right up to its trunk. I expect to see a serpent slithering around, or for something to happen as we get close. Maybe I should feel a deep tremor of holy reverence. But I'm simply out of breath from our long haul through the Garden. Mitchell looks pristine, glimmering with morning light and effervescence.

He plucks a peach from the Tree and takes a bite. He is messy with his teeth; juice sprays down his chin. He's staring at me as he chews. When he swallows, he takes another bite, his face glossy with sticky sweetness, and although the thought of licking all that pulp and liquid from his mouth makes the back of my head tingle, I am queasy.

After another bite, Mitchell clears his throat, bobbing his head as if a song is playing that only he can hear.

"I needed information," he says.

"What?"

"Knowledge." He half-turns toward the Tree. Juice oozes onto his fingers. "I needed to know what to do."

"About you leaving?" I say. Finally, the words are there, out, spat. I feel like I've hocked up a wad of gum, old and wizened and hard.

"Yes. About that."

"I need to sit down," I say, but I don't move.

"No, you don't," he says.

"Did you get your answer?"

"I think so."

"That was quick."

He nods at the peach. "It's good fruit." He holds it out to me so I can see the long, narrow trenches where his teeth have scraped through. "Do you want to know anything?"

I shake my head. The idea of food sounds repulsive.

Mitchell shrugs and looks at the peach, then tosses it over his shoulder like it is nothing. It lands somewhere at the base of the Tree. I imagine it rotting, pulling Mitchell's DNA into the soil where the roots will grab it up. He will enter every peach anyone ever plucks from the Tree of Knowledge, a little bit of him moving through visitors from far and wide. I imagine his singing and humming vibrating in their cells, their bones, their muscles aching to belt out Tina Turner.

"Are you going to tell me what you found out?"

"Charlie," Mitchell says. He takes my hand.

He bends down as if stretching his lower back, but then suddenly he's on one knee.

"What is this?"

Mitchell smiles. The sun catches in the prickles of his hair. He reaches into a side pocket of his backpack with his free hand, the fingers that are holding mine tightening but never gripping me painfully; he knows how to treat my bones. He rummages, blindly, and never stops smiling. Mitchell has this way of turning up his mouth just enough that you know he's full of joy. I'm surprised he isn't singing.

"Here we are," he says, and produces a small felt box.

"Mitchell," I say.

"Here's the thing." He holds the box tight in his fist. "What I needed to know was whether I should ask you."

My mouth is gummy like it's full of jam. I open and close my lips, feel spit caked there.

"I needed to know if I should ask you to come with me. When I leave."

"You weren't sure?"

"No," he says, shaking his head. His hair flashes in the light. I can see the precious tenderness of his scalp. "That's not it. I just couldn't bear the idea that I might ask and you might say no."

He pops open the box. There's a small onyx band nestled inside. It gleams dark and hard, smooth and reflective.

While Mitchell blinks at me, I feel like something's rattling up my intestines. I try to hold it in. I picture myself leaving everything I know behind. I've never been to California. I picture bright beaches and sunshine. I picture shirtless people strolling down wide boulevards, the sounds of weights clanking around outdoor gyms in Venice and Santa Monica. Then my mind slips into a darker future, where Mitchell is soaked into the music industry, dragged down into a world of cocaine and Quaaludes, tequila shots and absinthe, discotheques and raves and bars that I can't afford to dress nicely enough for. I hear the horrible silence of him no longer singing to me.

Mitchell's hand clenches the box tighter, his knuckles going white. Sun gleams down.

"Mitchell," I say.

He starts to stand. "It's okay, Charlie, if your answer is no."

"Of course it isn't." I bray out the words, spittle flying from my teeth. Mitchell must have known I would say yes, thanks to the fruit. And of course I'm saying yes.

"Really?"

"But you can't stop singing to me, okay?"

He grins. With no warmup he starts, his voice syrupy and thick:

In your heart I see the start of every night and every day
In your eyes I get lost, I get washed away.

When Mitchell stands, he grabs hold of me, tight. He's still holding the box, and I haven't touched the ring, but I don't care, because he keeps singing, and though his voice is muffled against my throat, I can feel the vibration of his body. It travels up and down and out, sinking into the grass and threading its way through paradise.

•   •   •   •

The drive to my apartment is quiet; Mitchell keeps the windows rolled up and the air conditioning high, the cold blasting the sweat on my face into a hard, chilly shell. His eyes go to the ring, which is hard and heavy on my left hand. I've never worn jewelry of any kind, and I fiddle with it, twist the ring around, my fingers needing motion and distraction. I'm trying to picture life on the West Coast. I'm trying to picture myself emptying my tiny apartment, boxes scattered on the floor like blocky landmines. I run through the phone calls I'll need to make, to my landlord, the electric company, my internet provider. I try to picture Mitchell and me standing in my tiny kitchen, choosing which drinking glasses and plates we'll need and which we won't, whether we'll move my bed or his. I try to see myself finding work, cobbling together a gaggle of adjunct gigs to get by while Mitchell is meeting famous DJs and auto-tuned pop stars, spending spectacular nights in high-rises and forgetting about our sojourns to the Garden of Eden. I'm trying to tell myself that it would be okay for us to find another thatch of trees to look at.

We park in front of my building, and Mitchell asks if I want him to come inside. I say yes, even though I want to be alone. As soon as we step through the door, he kisses me, his hand on the back of my head. He is celebratory, and why shouldn't he be? Our legs get tangled up as he marches us toward the bedroom, where my mattress seems suddenly lumpy and expendable. Everything around me feels unnecessary.

"Charlie?" he says when he's lying atop me. The wideness of his eyes makes it clear he's only now seeing that something is wrong. "What is it?" His voice is at my chin.

"Nothing," I say. "I'm tired. Long day." Something cold crawls down my throat.

"Okay," Mitchell says, but I can hear the doubt in his voice.

"Do you think we'll ever come back here?"

That makes him smile.

"When we're there, will we come back here?" I say again. "Maybe once in a while, to look at Eden?"

"What if we discover another one? Tacoma, Palo Alto. There's got to be one somewhere out there."

"I like ours." I can smell the sour buildup of sweat from the day. It clings to him like film.

"Well, what if we make our own?"

"How would that work?"

"It wouldn't be hard. *As long you're near me—*"

"I know the line."

Mitchell's breath is close, hot. "I know you do."

"Okay."

"Okay?"

I nod. I'm not sure what I'm agreeing to.

When I slip into sleep, Mitchell heavy and close like a small moon, I dream of Eden. I'm standing on the edge of our familiar outcrop, the nose of Mitchell's car scalding at the backs of my knees. It's nudging me forward even though there's nowhere to go. And so I tumble into thin air, dropping toward the treetops like a rocket. But then when I spread my arms I slow down, as though my flesh has become a parachute, and I land softly on the canopy of leaves and branches. I can walk across them like Jesus on the surface of water. But I'm directionless. I've no idea how to find my way. When I look up and behind me, all I can see is the sharp sun. But I can hear Mitchell, humming and then singing, the words familiar. And even though I'm not sure how to get to him, I hope that he will somehow lead me home.

Acknowl-
edgments

I OWE DEEPEST GRATITUDE TO ALL MY WRITING teachers, past and present, starting first with Michael Kelley and Dominic D'Urso, who convinced me while I was in high school that I could do this. Then, in college, I was inspired, driven, and guided by Joe Benevento, Robin Becker, Monica Barron, and, of course, Priscilla Riggle, who shaped both my undergraduate senior seminar project and my master's thesis.

My deep gratitude to Daniel Smith, my dissertation director, and to Joe Andriano, who read my stories with such kindness. And to Marthe Reed, who is much missed.

I am grateful to my friends and colleagues, who have championed my work, especially the English gang: Jayme, Jeff, Annie, Shannon, Corey, Christy, Cathy, Lindsay, Bryonie, Rachel, Michelle, Aaron, Heather, Michael, and David. Especial thanks to Jacqueline Gray and Karen Jones.

To all my friends from Truman State University and the University of Louisiana at Lafayette, for being who you are.

Massive thanks to Katie Cortese for selecting this manuscript; you've truly changed my life. Travis, for all your work and wonderful communication, and to the entire Texas Tech University

Press family. To Leslie Jill Patterson for bringing me into the *Iron Horse* family in the first place. And an especial thanks to Hubbard Savage, editor extraordinaire, who helped me tighten these pages into the best version they could be. What great insights and suggestions you provided; anyone would be lucky to have your eyes on their work.

I am fortunate to have a family that has always supported my work, even if my sister thinks I don't have a real job. To my mom, especially: isn't this a better shout-out than at eighth grade graduation?

I am also grateful to the editors of the following journals that put these stories into the world first:

- "Give Us Your Pity, Give Us Your Love" in *Iron Horse Literary Review*
- "Melt With You" in *Phantom Drift*
- "The Water Is Coming, the Water Is Here" in *Sou'wester*
- "Shearing" in *Portland Review*
- "We All Yearn for Defenestration" in *Litbreak*
- "Where We Go After" in *Liquid Imagination*
- "There Won't Be Questions" in *Fantasy & Science Fiction*
- "How I Know You're Here" in *The Emerson Review*
- "Close the Door on This Laughing Heart" in *Passages North*
- "The Right Kind of Love, the Wrong Kind of Death" in *Penumbric*
- "Spin the Dial" in *The Hoosier Review*
- "Churchgoing" in *Adirondack Review*
- "Sing With Me at the Edge of Paradise" in *Subnivean*

Joe Baumann is the author of three forthcoming short story collections: *The Plagues*, *Hot Lips*, and *Where Can I Take You When There's Nowhere to Go*. His fiction and essays have appeared in *Phantom Drift*, *Passages North*, *Third Coast*, *Iron Horse Literary Review*, and others, and his debut YA novel, *I Know You're Out There Somewhere*, is available from Deep Hearts YA.

Photo credit: Lindsay Brand